KNIGHT MOVES

Book Two

Julie Moffett

Published by True Airspeed Press
ISBN: 978-1-941787-28-1

Cover art by Earthly Charms
Formatting by Author E.M.S.

Praise for Julie Moffett's White Knights
Book #1 in the White Knights Series

"This book is Hogwarts for geeks. It is the perfect blend of YA, computer geeks, and spies! ... I am so thrilled to be sharing this book with you...because I loved it! Like—stop a stranger on the street and don't stop talking about this book until they run away screaming, thinking you've escaped from the psych ward! Crazy good!" ~ **Ginger Mom and the Kindle Quest Blog**

"Love this new YA spinoff series from the Lexi Carmichael series by Julie Moffett. Same great pace, excitement, mysteries to solve, hacks to make, character growth, and an ending that makes me excited for the next book! Geek girls rock!" ~ **Amazon Reader**

"I loved the whole entire concept of the book... This book was completely intriguing and it was just so AHHHHH, it was amazing. The book I believe targets all people of all ages." ~ **The HufflepuffNerdette**

"Absolutely loved it—great first book in a new series. This Y. A. series has already made my keeper list. Can't wait for the second book!" ~ **Amazon Reader**

"As a child, I love mystery books; Nancy Drew, Hardy Boys, the Five Find-Outers by Enid Blyton and etc. So now, even when I've grown up, mystery books has been a soft spot for me. YA + Spy mystery is my weakness...I was surprised by how much I enjoyed this book. I am even looking forward to the next book. I think readers who love Ally Carter's Gallagher Girls series would enjoy this book." ~ **Erucchii's Books and Recs**

Praise for Julie Moffett's
Lexi Carmichael Mystery Series

"The Lexi Carmichael mystery series runs a riveting gamut from hilarious to deadly, and the perfectly paced action in between will have you hanging onto Lexi's every word and breathless for her next geeked-out adventure." ~ **USA Today**

"I absolutely, positively loved this book...I found the humor terrific. I couldn't find a single thing I didn't like about this book except it ended." ~ **Night Owl Reviews**

"Wow, wow, and wow! I don't know how Julie Moffett does it but every book is better than the last and all of them are awesome. I may have 6 authors in my top five now!" ~ **Goodreads Reader**

"Absolutely loved this book! I love the concept of a geek girl getting involved in all kinds of intrigue and, of course, all the men she gets to meet." ~ **Book Babe**

"This book can be described in one word. AMAZING! I was intrigued from the beginning to the end. There are so many twists and turns and unexpected agendas that you do not know who's on the good side or who's on the bad side." ~ **Once Upon a Twilight**

"Lexi Carmichael has to be the most lovable character I have come across. She is 100 percent geek and has zero street smarts, but she tries to think outside the box while putting herself in dangerous places without knowing how she got there. The author keeps you guessing who might be a double agent and who might want to harm Lexi." ~ **Goodreads Reader**

Books by Julie Moffett

White Knights Mystery/Spy Series

White Knights (Book 1)*
Knight Moves (Book 2)*
One-Knight Stand (coming Fall 2019)*

The Lexi Carmichael Mystery Series

No One Lives Twice (Book 1)*
No One to Trust (Book 2)*
No Money Down (Book 2.5-novella)
No Place Like Rome (Book 3)
No Biz Like Showbiz (Book 4)
No Test for the Wicked (Book 5)*
No Woman Left Behind (Book 6)*
No Room for Error (Book 7)*
No Strings Attached (Book 8)*
No Living Soul (Book 9)*
No Regrets (Book 10)*
No Stone Unturned (Book 11)
No Questions Asked (Book 12) January 2020

*Print versions (available or coming soon)
All Lexi Carmichael titles are available in audiobook,
and several on CDs.

DEDICATION

To my youngest son, Lucas.
Mommy lion will always have your back.

ACKNOWLEDGMENTS

I am beyond grateful for the guidance of my brother, Brad, for his excellent brainstorming sessions and brilliant suggestions; my mother, Donna, and sister, Sandy, for all their continued support and editorial assistance; my dad for his unflagging enthusiasm and support for my geek girls; my niece, Katy, who totally rocked the ideas; my wonderful cover artist, Su at Earthly Charms; my excellent copy editor, Sara Brady; the fantastic formatter Amy Atwell; and last, but in no way least, my extraordinary editor Alissa Davis who challenges me to write a better book every time. I couldn't have done it without any of you! Thank you so much! oxo

KNIGHT
MOVES

CHAPTER ONE

Angel Sinclair

It's not like I woke up on a Monday morning expecting to become a spy, but that's exactly what happened.

It's not the kind of thing a normal, almost sixteen-year-old girl expects to happen on a regular school day in early October. I guess that's the problem. I'm not exactly normal. My name is Angel Sinclair, and I'm a senior at the Excalibur Academy for the Technologically Gifted and Talented in Washington, DC. I'm younger than most seniors because I skipped a grade. I stand five feet three, have red hair, freckles, and blue eyes, and I'm definitely not the kind of person who leaps to mind when you think of the charm of James Bond, the physical prowess of Jason Bourne, or the wit of Mata Hari. I'm just an ordinary geek girl, hacker, and outsider. To put it bluntly, I like people about as much as I like Microsoft patches, which isn't much.

However, my life as a loner drastically changed a few weeks ago when two of my friends—Frankie Chang and Wally Harris—helped me save our vice principal and bring down a hacker using technology and old-fashioned teamwork. I wasn't sure what was more momentous—that I'd made friends or that I'd caught the eye of the NSA with my hacking prowess. I was still trying to decide if those were good things or bad things.

Regardless, Wally, Frankie, and I decided we were going to be kind of like a Scooby gang, solving mysteries and calling ourselves the White Knights. Frankie even made us a cool logo with a white chess piece. Unfortunately, no other mysteries had yet presented themselves, but we were hopeful.

After a week of random students stopping me in the hallway to ask me questions about how we'd saved the vice principal, things were slowly getting back to normal at Excalibur. Wally—one of the smartest guys I knew and an ace hacker—had basked in his fifteen minutes of fame at the school before most people went back to ignoring him. I returned to my usual invisible self almost immediately, which I should have expected, but it was depressing anyway. Frankie, on the other hand, continued to chat and make friends with everyone she met like they were her long-lost soul mates. I've never met anyone nicer, but sometimes her faith in people scares me.

Today, as the bell rang on a gloriously sunny afternoon, I streamed out of the school with the other students. Students bumped into me as I was carried along by the crowd to the bus. I saw Ms. Swanson, the headmistress, standing next to a man wearing jeans, a leather jacket, and dark sunglasses. He leaned casually against the bus, his arms crossed against his chest. I knew immediately who he was.

Slash.

That's not his real name, obviously. He works for the NSA and is probably a real spy, thus the code name. I was so surprised to see him, I stopped in midstep and nearly got trampled by the other students. The headmistress spotted me and motioned for me to come over, so I gulped and tried to act cool as I detached myself from the herd and turned their way.

"There you are, Angel," the headmistress greeted me. "There's someone here who wants to talk to you."

Slash's mouth curved into a smile. "Hello, Angel."

Slash was the most talented hacker I'd ever met, outside of my mentor and idol, Lexi Carmichael, a female tech head who was shattering ceilings left and right. She also happened to be Slash's significant other.

"Hey, Slash," I said. "What brings you to high school on a Monday afternoon? Is everything okay with Lexi?"

"Lexi's fine. I'm here to speak with you." He pushed off the bus. His eyes remained hidden behind the sunglasses, so I couldn't gauge how serious, or not, this visit was supposed to be. "The headmistress cleared this, if you're up to it. It's official government business."

"Oh." I looked between Ms. Swanson and Slash, my breath hitching in my throat. "Sure, I'm fine with it, of course."

Still, my heart beat a little faster. For a moment, I wondered if he had news about my father, who'd vanished when I was eighteen months old. I'd recently discovered Dad might have been a spy. Not at the CIA—where most spies are born—but at the NSA. I don't know for certain if my father was a secret agent or not, but I'd recently confirmed there was a good chance he was still alive and somehow connected to the NSA. Since Slash worked at the NSA, he might know or, at the very least, could find out. But I'd learned the world of espionage was devious and dangerous while trying to find out what had happened to my father. I wasn't ready to trust anyone, even Slash, until I had more information.

"So, what's up?" I'd been going for a nonchalant tone, but my voice sounded apprehensive instead.

Slash slipped off his sunglasses and hooked them onto the front of his shirt. His eyes were serious. "You got a few minutes to chat privately?"

CHAPTER TWO

Angel Sinclair

did, but my anxiety skyrocketed. I had no idea what the US government could possibly want with me, unless it involved my past hacking. I swallowed my nervousness and looked around the busy parking lot. "You want to talk about it here?"

"How about the park?" Slash dipped his dark head to the right. "It's quieter and just a short walk from here."

I nodded, so we parted ways with the headmistress. As we began to walk, I shoved my hands in the pockets of my hoodie. The air was cool but not cold, and the sun warmed my head and shoulders. Thankfully, my backpack was light, with just math and physics books.

As we cleared the parking lot, I noticed a brown sedan moving slowly down the street. There was something familiar about the car, although oddly, the driver didn't appear to have his eyes on the road, but on us. Why would he be watching us?

Now I remembered where I'd seen the car before. Right on my street at home when I was walking the dog. I'm sure it was the same car, because I'm naturally observant and it had been driving slowly past me. Now the same car just appeared at my school out of the blue? What were the odds of that?

Before I could mention it to Slash, the car sped off. For now, I held my tongue and focused on what he had come to talk to me about.

After we made it to the sidewalk, Slash spoke again. "Angel, I'm here to personally invite you to enroll in a specialized institution, a school, sponsored by the US government. Its existence is classified, so before I go any further, I must have your assurance that you will not provide details of this conversation to anyone unless cleared specifically by me."

I stopped in my tracks, confused. "A specialized school? What does that mean?"

He put a light hand under my elbow, moving me along the sidewalk again. "I'm about to tell you, *if* I have your assurance that this conversation will remain confidential."

I didn't have to ask him how he would hold me to my assurance. He was the NSA, after all. A part of me felt a tiny flicker of concern, but curiosity and interest roared to life in my brain.

"Of course, I give you my assurance." My voice held a little catch of excitement. "Tell me more."

We stopped under a large oak that cast long shadows. Slash stood in the shade watching the street while I faced him, staying in the sun and enjoying the warmth.

"The school is called the Underage Training Operative Program, or UTOP," he said. "It's a joint program funded by the CIA, NSA, and DIA."

"What's the DIA?" I asked.

"The Defense Intelligence Agency."

"Oh. What kind of school is sponsored by three government intelligence agencies?"

"A very sensitive one. It's a normal school in many ways. Students are required to take regular coursework in math, science, English, history, and foreign languages. It does, however, have an additional, and significant, curriculum that won't be discussed at this point."

That only piqued my interest further. "Does it include classes in computer science and cybersecurity?"

"Of course. The best in the country. I assure you, Angel, the curriculum is quite advanced. The student body is made up of American citizens aged sixteen to twenty-one from all over the US and corresponding territories—all of whom are carefully vetted and who must meet specific intelligence and skill parameters."

"Such as?"

"In your case, we are, naturally, interested in your hacking skills, both offensive and defensive. But that's not all. Your innovation and creativity intrigue us, as well as your IQ scores, which are high across the board. You show unique promise."

I didn't have to ask him how he knew my IQ scores. But I had a lot of questions. "You said UTOP. The word *operative* was in there. Are we talking about a spy school?"

He lifted his hands. "Some people might call it that. I like to think of it as a specialized training academy. Because of the sensitive nature of the material that will be covered, students must live on campus in dormitories. It's essentially four years of a specialized college, courtesy of Uncle Sam."

That certainly sweetened the deal, but the cautious part of me wanted to know more. "So, what's the catch?"

"The catch is a commitment of at least four years of work in whichever intelligence agency we decide to place you with after graduation."

"Wait. You place us? We don't get a say where we work?"

"You can express a preference, but ultimately, the

decision is made by a committee, based on a number of factors, including jobs where we may have a shortage of skills. But make no mistake. UTOP trains operatives. If selected to the program, that would be your primary function."

It was a lot for me to take in. My thoughts were jumping around so much, it made me dizzy. "Does this have anything to do with me, Frankie, and Wally taking down Omar Haider?" Haider was the Iraqi hacker who had been targeting US veterans. The three of us had managed to track him down and deliver him to the NSA. Not as quite so neatly as that implied, but that was another story.

Slash nodded. "All of you caught the attention of certain individuals at the NSA and CIA."

"Wow, that is so cool." Suddenly, my mouth caught up with my brain. "Wait. Are Wally and Frankie invited, too?"

"They are."

"No way!" I almost pumped my fist in excitement, but stopped myself, figuring it probably wasn't something a suave operative would do. "That's great."

Slash seemed amused by my reaction. I wondered if he knew how thrilled I was that my only two friends in the world had a chance to do this with me. "Okay, so theoretically, let's say I want to go to this school, college, training academy, or whatever you want to call it. I just tell my mom and sister I'm going to a spy school, pack up, leave Excalibur, and move into a dorm to begin a new life?"

"Not exactly." He glanced around as if making sure we couldn't be overheard. "You tell your mother and sister you have been selected as the recipient of a special government scholarship to attend an exclusive four-year university program with a focus in science and technology and a guaranteed job when you exit."

"Oh. What about finishing this year of high school? And I'm not sixteen for another couple of weeks."

"I know. You're close enough to meet the age deadline, and I'm confident you're more than capable, intellectually, to handle the academics at UTOP."

He'd placed an emphasis on *intellectually*, which made me wonder what other parts he might worry about me being able to handle. Still, I couldn't deny it was an amazing offer. I'd planned on going to Georgetown University. I was already taking college classes online there and had applied for a full-ride scholarship. I had a good shot at it, but it wasn't guaranteed. Neither was a job after graduation.

Technically, I *wanted* to work for the government after graduation. While I would certainly make more money in the private sector, the government is where I would see the real action. This school, UTOP, would guarantee me a job in intelligence and provide me with specialized training for exactly what I wanted to do...at no cost to myself or my family. It seemed like a win-win situation, although with the government, I knew better. There was always a price to pay, perhaps one I couldn't see at this point.

Still, I was intrigued. I regarded Slash thoughtfully, foreseeing a potential problem. "My mom has to sign off on it?"

"Of course. You're under eighteen, so it's up to you to convince her. Keep in mind, she will not know it's called UTOP. It's referred to as the George Washington National Training Academy in the official paperwork."

"Where's the campus located?"

"About a two-hour drive from here in central Virginia." He didn't offer any further details, and I realized that was all I was going to get for now. At the very least, it meant my mom could visit occasionally. I knew that would be important to her.

"There's something else you need to know, Angel. It's not as simple as being invited to UTOP and being automatically accepted. You have to pass the trials…or go home."

My bubble of excitement abruptly deflated. "Trials? What kind of trials?"

He nudged me forward, so we started walking again. "The government selects students who have important skills we need in the operative field. Those students who pass must show certain physical, psychological, and emotional skills to continue their training. I'll be honest with you, we invite a very small and select number of students to try out for UTOP. You'll undergo a series of trials for four weeks, most of which are highly challenging on different levels. Unfortunately, only a few of those selected to try out are able to make it through all the trials successfully."

"Wait. Are you saying I could flunk out because I can't do a pull-up?"

Slash chuckled. "I assure you, no one is flunked for not being able to do a pull-up. Scores are cumulative and derived from multiple sources. There are physical challenges, yes, but this is not a fitness test. It's testing your specific capabilities and skills in numerous areas in the field. But it's also testing the way your mind works, how you process information, and how you handle yourself in stressful and dangerous situations. Also, you don't flunk. It's just determined that you don't have the necessary skills required for an operative. It certainly doesn't mean you can't ever work for the government or an intelligence agency. In fact, most students who don't make it through the trials are given special handlers across the agencies. They go on to secure degrees at regular universities and come back to us later. In fact, the last time I looked, ninety-six percent of students who went through the UTOP trials and didn't make it still returned to work with one of the agencies. That's an extraordinarily high percentage."

"But not as an operative."

"No." He paused for a beat. "Not as an operative."

I stopped, crossed my arms against my chest, and studied him intently. "You actually think I have a shot? Me? A geeky girl with the upper-body strength of an infant?"

Slash's expression softened a bit as if he were remembering something. It occurred to me he might be thinking of Lexi, and maybe she'd once felt the way I did. "This isn't boot camp, Angel. Regardless, I won't lie to you. It will be challenging and test you to your limits. All your limits. But, yes, I think you have what it takes to make it as an operative or I wouldn't have recommended you."

That knocked me back for a second. "You *personally* recommended me?"

"I did."

So many thoughts ran through my head, most of them screaming in excitement that one of the world's best wizards behind the keyboard thought I had what it took to be a spy. "And, if I don't pass, I just come back to Excalibur?"

"Yes, at the four-week point. They will tell you then whether you made it or not. If you don't make it, you simply tell your mother it didn't work out. You cannot, however, tell her the details of the trials. That must remain classified."

"They can tell in four weeks whether I'm spy material or not?"

"They can. Sometimes even sooner."

I blew out a breath. "Wow. This is a lot to think about."

"Yes, it is." He slid a hand into his leather jacket and pulled out a manila envelope. "Here is the information and the registration packet for you and your mother to review. You have one week to let me know your decision. After that, the slot goes to someone else."

I swallowed hard. "Am I able to talk to Wally and Frankie about this?"

"You may, but you must be in a secure location before you discuss anything about it, and nothing can be exchanged electronically. We'll know. Do you understand what I'm saying?"

Oh, I knew what he meant, all right. The NSA would be watching me. Then it occurred to me that maybe they already were. Perhaps the brown sedan was from the agency, and all of this cloak-and-dagger stuff was part of the deal. It was odd, but I figured that was likely the life of a spy.

A mystery inside a puzzle.

I looked over his shoulder at the rest of the park. Some guy was throwing a Frisbee to his dog, while the young mother had given up on the ducks and was pushing her stroller toward the far side of the pond. It seemed so normal—just an average day in America. People going on about their lives, not having a clue that a short, freckled, redheaded teenager was being recruited by the US government to be a spy.

"I understand, Slash," I said. And I did.

I had one week to make the decision of my life.

CHAPTER THREE

Angel Sinclair

Slash dropped me off at our apartment complex since I'd missed the bus. I clutched the manila envelope in my hand so tightly I crushed one corner. To my surprise, my older sister, Gwen, was sitting at the dining room table working on a laptop when I walked into the apartment. Her presence was surprising because she usually spent most of her free time with her boyfriend, who lived in Jessup, Maryland. She didn't typically drop in on Mom and me during the week unless something was up.

Our little dog, Mr. Toodles, leaped from her lap and rushed to greet me, yapping excitedly. I bent down and petted him as he licked my hand, then I scooped him up with one arm and walked over to my sister.

"Hey, Gwen, what are you doing here?" I asked.

She glanced up from her laptop. "I needed to pick up some papers from Mom, so I swung by. Thought I'd stick around to have dinner with you guys, unless you have plans for tonight."

I shrugged out of my backpack, dropping it on the

couch, and put the manila envelope on the table. "Like my social calendar is ever full."

She smiled. She has the same color red hair and blue eyes like I do, but she's better with people. In school, she was popular, funny, and had a lot of friends—the polar opposite of me. While I do have two friends, it's a recent development and something I'm still getting used to.

I deposited Mr. Toodles on the couch and slid into a chair at the table across from Gwen. Taking a deep breath, I pulled the manila envelope toward me and opened it.

I scanned through the documents. There were several registration and information forms and one small brochure for the academy. The brochure for the GW Training Academy showed pictures of colonial-style buildings, trees, the inside of a dormitory, and a nice gym. There was no address, phone number, or mention of UTOP anywhere. I guess by accepting the nomination, I'd start down that slippery path of not exactly lying to the people around me, but not necessarily providing all the information at hand, either.

The life of a spy.

"What's that?" Gwen pointed at the papers now spread across the table.

"I've been invited to attend a special school, a college/training academy for students interested in working for the government."

"What?" That got Gwen's attention. She pushed her laptop aside and put her elbows on the table, her full attention on me. "Are you kidding? After you graduate?"

"Actually, starting now. They think I'm ready. It's a free ride for four years with a four-year commitment to work for the government after that. Then it's a clean slate. I can either continue to work for the government or leave for the private sector."

Her eyes widened. "Four years of school for free and a guaranteed job? And you've been accepted?"

"Well, not exactly. They have to see how I do at first. If I do well, I'm in. If not, I return to Excalibur."

"When did you apply for this? I thought you wanted to go to Georgetown."

"I do. I did. I mean, I didn't exactly apply for this. Slash nominated me after that thing with the Iraqi hacker."

She sat back in her chair, watching me. "So, the government is recruiting you."

"You could put it like that."

"Is it going to be dangerous?"

I hadn't thought about that part. I guess it was possible. It was a spy school, after all, so what did I know? Still, I didn't want to raise the danger factor, because Mom would never let me go. I shrugged it off. "It's college, Gwen, not Afghanistan."

"Hmmm..." She wasn't buying my nonchalance. "Where exactly is this academy located?"

"Virginia. I bet you can come and visit sometime."

"So, you're seriously considering it?"

"Of course I'm seriously considering it. My endgame has always been to work for the government. That's where the action is."

"That's where the *danger* is."

I pursed my lips at her. "Don't pull the big-sister card. You're overreacting. I'm going to work behind a computer."

"Yes, and look what just happened with that hacker guy. You could have gotten hurt."

"That was...not the norm." I pushed the brochure over to her. "See for yourself. It's totally tame. There are dorms, cafeterias, a gym, and classrooms. It probably has extracurricular activities, too. And, just so you know, I won't be alone. Wally and Frankie are invited, too."

15

"Really?" She looked up from the brochure, surprise on her face.

"Really. So, I'll even know people there. It should be fine. Trust me, if there were danger, Wally would be out. He's afraid to clip his toenails. Besides, I'll know after four weeks if I'm in. If it doesn't work out, I'll come back to Excalibur and hope the scholarship to Georgetown works out."

She resumed looking over the brochure. "There's not much information here." She passed it back to me. "But since Slash is involved, I feel better about it. He really nominated you for this academy?"

It was still hard for me to believe—like somehow I'd hit the jackpot. "He did. Me, Wally, and Frankie. He thinks we have what it takes to succeed there."

"Does this mean your mind is made up?"

I considered. Weird, but I'd already made my decision by the time Slash handed me the manila envelope. "Yes. I want to give it a shot."

She still looked doubtful. "You won't be disappointed if it doesn't work out?"

"Of course I'll be disappointed. But I'm not going to fail. If Slash thinks I can do this, I can."

I tried not to feel insulted that she looked so doubtful. "Okay, let's just hope Mom feels the same way."

CHAPTER FOUR

Candace Kim

Director of the NSA National Security Operations Center (NSOC)
NSA Headquarters, Fort Meade, Maryland

Crypto-Secure Phone

> From: Director of The National Security Operations Center (NSOC), National Security Agency (NSA)
> To: Deputy Director of the Operations Division (DDIR), NSA
> Classification: Top Secret, No Foreign
> 0248 GMT
>
> Message Follows:
>
> Please advise as to the status of the negotiations with the Hidden Avenger. Do we know his endgame or have any proof of the authenticity of his claims? This has director-level attention.
>
> End of Message

Candace Kim, director of the National Security Operations Center (NSOC) at the NSA, pressed the send button on her phone and leaned back in her desk chair as the text shot into encrypted cyberspace. She would have preferred to call the deputy director of the Operations Division, Jim Avers, from her office phone, but the day had slipped away because of too many meetings and a couple of unexpected fires she'd been compelled to put out. Now she was forced to use an encrypted cell to contact him, as he was no longer in the office. It wasn't an ideal situation, but she didn't want to wait a minute longer for an update.

No other recent issue had triggered her curiosity as much as the avatar called Hidden Avenger. Over the years he had thwarted the NSA's back door into the RSA encryption but advised companies and agencies about dozens of unknown security holes. Was he a good guy or bad?

Fourteen years ago, when she'd been a midlevel agent at the NSA, the agency had been able to spy on just about anyone in the world outside the US territory, where they were legally allowed to operate. Using a hidden back door built into the RSA encryption program—the program used by most of the world to transmit secure data—the NSA could open whatever encrypted messages they wanted from *anyone*, anywhere. Then along came a secretive self-proclaimed do-gooder calling himself the Hidden Avenger, who, without warning, had slammed the door shut with a patch he called ShadowCrypt. The NSA and FBI had spent fourteen years and employed dozens of their best hackers, researchers, and cybersecurity experts trying to track him down and had gotten exactly nowhere.

Now he'd resurfaced, and Candace wasn't sure if he was a potential asset for the agency or someone playing them for fools. Either way, his furtive communications had landed on her desk, and sorting out the differences had become her problem.

At this point, the Hidden Avenger was offering them critical information to prevent a major terrorist attack, and access to the new back door he'd created in ShadowCrypt. Since nearly all the criminal and terrorist groups worldwide used that encryption, the ability to monitor their communications could return the NSA to its glory days before the patch. If she handled this right and brought him in with his new back door, she'd get a lot of credit right at the time when the political leadership would be looking for outstanding candidates to replace the director when he retired.

It was hard to tell if the timing on all of this was chance or purposeful. Was it coincidence the Avenger had abruptly surfaced just as the director of the NSA had internally announced to a small group of high-ranking staff he was retiring next year? She hated the active positioning of some of her peers that had followed, while they tried to establish themselves as his logical replacement. She wouldn't stoop that low. But if her job performance merited the recognition, *and* if the country were safer because she'd help bring down a terrorist group, well, then she wasn't above becoming the first woman director.

Her phone suddenly dinged, and she picked it up. Pressing her finger to the button, she typed in her password, scanning Jim's reply.

Crypto-Secure Phone

> From: Deputy Director of the Operations Division
> (DDIR), NSA
> To: Director of the National Security Operations
> Center (NSOC)
> Classification: Top Secret, No Foreign
> 0254 GMT
>
> Message Follows:
>
> I stopped by your office earlier today, but you
> weren't there. The Hidden Avenger will not
> offer us anything more until we can assure him
> immunity and safety for his family. Where do
> we stand on the request to the Justice
> Department?
>
> End of Message

Candace had expected the answer. The Hidden Avenger was as cautious as he was clever. He was going to keep a low profile until he received assurances they could deliver, and he wouldn't be tricked into exposing himself until he received what he wanted. Technically, he was holding all the leverage right now, but that depended on him remaining anonymous. She was both puzzled and intrigued by reports that the Avenger was actually one of their own, a former NSA agent named Ethan Sinclair who'd vanished fourteen years ago without a trace.

There was important information on his departure and disappearance that she was missing and needed to know. His personnel records indicated he was a superior performer with no known personnel issues. What would cause him to quit or vanish? What was he afraid of that would lead him to abandon a family that he loved dearly, by all accounts? Why was he asking for federal protection for himself and his family, as well as immunity from prosecution for any real or accidental crimes? What else was he hiding?

None of the Avenger's requests were simple, but, at this point, he was holding all the cards. And he wouldn't play unless the NSA could deliver on what he wanted.

Well-honed intuition told her the Avenger was running from something, or *someone*, at the NSA. She was also certain the director of research at the NSA and Sinclair's former boss, Isaac Remington, knew a lot more than he was sharing. Was he hiding something that would enhance his chances to bring in the Avenger himself, so he could showcase his resourcefulness and became the next director? Or did he know something else—something more sinister that could implicate someone within the agency?

Remington would bear watching either way. From this moment on, she'd have to be extremely careful with whom she shared her concerns. Right now, she trusted Jim Avers implicitly and would rely on him for assistance.

> We can't move forward fully yet because the Justice Department needs to understand why he needs immunity. What potential prosecution is he attempting to avoid? It's one thing if he wants immunity for the ShadowCrypt patch. It's entirely another if he's stealing credit card numbers or hacking into commercial firms. If he has engaged in the latter, the Justice Department could not provide immunity from civil suits for the damages. They can deal in federal charges only.

She sent the reply, then went to the small refrigerator in her office, removing a bottle of water and taking a drink. She was supposed to go to the gym to prepare for a duathlon—mountain biking and running—but she was leaning toward a quiet night in front of the television instead. She tried to remember if there were any shows on tonight that she liked when her phone dinged again.

> Understood. Will go back to the Avenger and see if I can narrow things down a little. Don't forget he wants to meet with the director. It's part of his request.

Candace stared at the text. Wasn't it strange that the Hidden Avenger would insist on a private meeting with General Norton? What could possibly be the purpose? It was not widely known within the NSA that he intended to retire soon, nor was the information public yet. In her mind, that meant the Hidden Avenger had inside connections at the NSA or was a former employee, further strengthening the case that Ethan Sinclair might indeed be the man they were looking for. But what had happened to make him go rogue?

> I spoke with the director yesterday, and he's agreed to the meeting. General Norton is intrigued by the possibility the Avenger is one of our own. We've also been monitoring the terrorist group the Avenger gave us information on and have confirmed heightened chatter. But without the encryption-breaking back door, we can't follow what they are saying. Still, the FBI has identified and is tracking the individuals, anyone communicating with them, and identified associates. The reports appear to confirm the Avenger's information.

Jim answered almost immediately.

> Avenger is using code names for the next time
> and method of communication with us and will
> send instructions within two days providing the
> connection details. He says we'll know the
> communication is from him because it will
> include the word "Ahab."

Ahab? Candace frowned at the screen. What was the purpose of that unusual code name? Was it random, or was he trying to tell them something? She typed out a response.

> Ahab as in the captain of the whaling ship in
> Moby Dick or as in King Ahab in the Bible?
> Check both of these out, as well as any other
> Ahab that leaps to mind. Look inside the
> agency first. Have we ever had an operation
> called Moby Dick or anything similar that we
> can tie the name Ahab to? The Avenger strikes
> me as someone who has a detailed purpose for
> everything he does. There **must** be a hidden
> message there. Find it.

Candace sent the message and plopped down in her office chair. Any plans for the gym or television this evening had just gone out the window. It looked like she needed to brew a strong cup of coffee and start reading *Moby Dick* again.

CHAPTER FIVE

Angel Sinclair

Mom took it better than I expected. She asked me all the same questions that Gwen did, plus a lot more. She scoured over every inch of the forms and brochure and made me look up the academy online. It had the same photos and information from the brochure and nothing more.

"I don't understand why they want you to start right away." Mom pushed her fingers through her hair, which was as red as Gwen's and mine. "You're already a month into your senior year of high school. There could be academic repercussions for pulling you out like this."

"Mom, I love you, but we both know I won't be missing out on anything at Excalibur. It's too easy for me and you know it. Slash told me the curriculum at the academy is quite advanced. It's like a first year at college. It's just what I need to challenge me academically."

"But you're not even sixteen yet."

"I will be in a couple of weeks. This isn't about my age, Mom. I know I can do this, and Slash thinks so, too. I'm excited to check it out. Please let me give it a try. If it doesn't work out, I'm back here in a snap. But if I don't try, I know I'll regret it."

Mom looked over at Gwen for support, but to my surprise, Gwen said, "If she wants to try, let her do it. We both know she can handle it academically. Slash nominated her, so he must believe she has what it takes to do well there. Besides, Angel may be just sixteen, but she's got more common sense than most people I know my age. She'll also have friends there to keep her in line. Even better, she won't be far away. We can check up on her as often as needed."

"Hey," I protested, but Gwen just grinned.

My mom blew out a breath and stood from the table. "I'm sorry, but I have to think about this. It's quite unexpected."

It was the best I was going to get for now, so I didn't push it. Instead I rose from the table, following her toward the kitchen. "Mom, can I go to Wally's after dinner?"

Wally had texted Frankie and me, telling us we had to come over after dinner to discuss "it." We both knew what "it" he was talking about.

Mom turned on the stove and pulled a casserole out of the refrigerator. "Sure. I'll have Gwen drop you off on her way home. You can call me when you're ready to come home."

I returned to my room and quickly texted Wally and Frankie I could come. Frankie responded with a half-dozen brain explosion emojis, said she'd also gotten a visit from "you know who," and she was coming, too.

Mom, Gwen, and I talked about everything at dinner except for the academy, although that's all I could think about. When we finished, I offered to do the dishes so I could get to Wally's as soon as possible.

When I finally arrived at Wally's, Frankie was already there, chatting with Wally's mom and dad.

Wally took us to his room and closed the door behind him. For a moment I just stood there.

"What's that?" I said pointing at the middle of his room, where a huge battlefield was set up with dozens of soldier figures, tanks, and airplanes.

Wally looked pleased that I'd asked. "That? Oh, that's Operation Barbarossa from World War II. It took place from June to July 1941. Hitler's attack on the USSR was the bloodiest of the war, and as a battle it covered the largest area. It didn't cause the USSR to collapse, but his victory destroyed the Red Army in western Russia. The Soviets had to retreat and spend years rebuilding their army."

I circled around the table, intrigued. "I didn't know you liked this stuff."

"Oh, he does," Frankie said. "He's a military buff. He can recreate hundreds of the great battles of history right from his head."

Wally's cheeks reddened slightly. "Yeah, obviously I have a lot of free time on my hands, so I store a lot of random facts up here." He tapped his head.

"That's totally cool, Wally." I meant it. Sometimes, he *was* like a walking encyclopedia. "What else is stored in that head of yours?"

He shrugged, the color in his face fading as he stood a little straighter. "Tons of stuff. The constellations, the periodic table of elements, all the bones and muscles in the body, and a lot of geographic facts like longest rivers, largest deserts, etc. Some of it's useless trivia, but I'm hoping to try out for *Jeopardy!* someday. I'll make myself a nice little nest egg and start investing in cryptocurrency."

"Perfect." Reluctantly, I tore my gaze from the battlefield and got right to the point of why we were here. "Okay, White Knights, let's get real. Who's going for UTOP?"

"You mean the academy," Frankie corrected me.

"No, I mean UTOP. The academy is what we use in mixed company, meaning nonclassified. We're alone here, so we can say we're trying out for UTOP. Operative status. If we don't make it, we're back at Excalibur within four weeks."

"Well, I've got mixed feelings about UTOP," Wally admitted, sitting on the corner of his bed. "Slash said there would be some physical challenges. That would sink me before I even got started."

"He also told me it wasn't going to be boot camp," I countered. "According to Slash, no one fails because they can't do a push-up."

"Oh, thank God," Frankie said with feeling.

"Seriously, it's not a military academy." I wondered if I were trying too hard to convince myself of that. "They're looking for other stuff."

"What other stuff?" Frankie asked.

"Skills. Mine and Wally's in cybersecurity, and your mad graphic abilities on the keyboard."

"Does that make us good spy material?" Frankie wondered.

"Maybe. It was enough to get us nominated. I guess we'll find out. Are you guys going for it?"

Frankie nodded, excitement flashing in her eyes. "I'm going for it. My dad is in the military, so that should let you know how much money there is in the bank for me to go to a four-year university without taking on crippling debt." She leaned against Wally's dresser. "This is my shot at a free education and a solid job as soon as I graduate. It's worth it, even if I need to figure out how to do a push-up."

I didn't think it would be as simple as a push-up, but I looked at Wally anyway. "In or out?"

"Well, if I'm not going to wash out because of the physical challenges, then heck yes, I'm in. Are you kidding me? Harris. Wally Harris—spy. Girls would totally be into me."

"You're going to try out for UTOP because you think it will get you girls?"

"Heck yes, I'm doing it for the girls. And for national security, of course. I assure you, both are great motivators."

I rolled my eyes. "Well, we don't get a lot of time to prove our worth.

"Four weeks doesn't seem like a long time," Frankie mused. "Are your parents okay with it, Wally?"

"Why wouldn't they be?" He shrugged. "They're rightfully seduced by the possibility of a free, four-year university education. In fact, I think they stopped listening after I said the word *free*. Plus, if I wanted to try it, I don't think they could think of a good reason I shouldn't."

"I think my dad suspects it's something other than a training academy," Frankie said. "He knows it's connected to us bringing down that Iraqi hacker. But he's been quiet about it. What about you, Angel? Is your mom cool with it?"

"I wouldn't exactly say she's cool, but I think she's going to agree. Personally, I'm intrigued by the challenge. But more importantly, I'm glad you guys want to give it a go. I don't want to break up the White Knights." Embarrassed by my unexpected and emotional declaration, I looked at the floor, my cheeks heating.

"Awww, that is so sweet, Angel," Frankie said. "All for one, and one for all?"

She held out her hand, palm down. After a moment, Wally put his on top of hers. They both looked at me. Feeling kind of stupid, I put my hand on top of Wally's.

"Let's do it," Frankie said with a grin. "White Knights forever."

CHAPTER SIX

Angel Sinclair

When I returned home from Wally's, I got ready for bed. After my mom kissed me good-night, I waited until the sound of her footsteps faded down the hall, then climbed out of bed, pushed all thoughts of UTOP and spy school aside, and sat down in front of my laptop. It was time to continue the search for my father.

The disappearance of my dad is perhaps the greatest mystery of my life. One day he woke up, went to work, and never arrived. His car was parked out in front of the building where he worked, and his wallet, filled with cash and credit cards, was placed atop his neatly folded jacket in the passenger seat. The car was locked from the outside, the key thoughtfully tucked under the front tire. No evidence of violence or robbery. He hadn't cleaned out his bank account or taken his passport.

He just vanished without a trace.

A brilliant cryptologist, mathematician, and computer programmer, my father had worked as a security engineering analyst at King's Security. According to the police report—which I read after hacking into the department when I was thirteen—he had a happy home life with a wife and children he supposedly adored, no debt, and a bright future. He was well liked by his colleagues and had no enemies. After searching for him for several months, the police gave up. They weren't able to confirm there'd been foul play, which eventually led them to believe it had been a willful disappearance. As the years passed, it was almost as if his existence was wiped from the face of the earth.

Except for us—the family he'd left behind.

Even though I hadn't known my father, I'd never forgotten about him. Neither had Mom or Gwen. Mom still wore her wedding ring, which I used to think was crazy, but not so much anymore. Because now I believed my father was still alive.

For years, I'd compiled tons of information on him, creating a trail that just a few weeks ago led me right to the doorstep of the NSA. That's when I received an anonymous email warning me away from trying to find him and suggesting "criminal elements inside the NSA" were monitoring me.

It was a shocking and exhilarating development, because it seemed to confirm my father was still alive. It also made me wonder if my search for him was on target. Had my father worked for the NSA? If so, was he a spy? Was that why he'd abandoned us?

Whatever the reason for his disappearance, I was determined to find him and get to the truth, regardless of whether I was being watched or not. I'd just be more careful. It was risky, but it was important. Perhaps the most important thing in my life.

I flexed my fingers and rested the tips on the keyboard. I didn't care what anyone said. This was my life, and I was *never* going to stop until I uncovered the truth about my dad.

CHAPTER SEVEN

Isaac Remington

Executive Director, Research Directorate ED/RD, NSA

Crypto-Secure Phone

> From: Executive Director, Research Directorate
> ED/RD
> To: DIR NSOC
> Classification: Top Secret, No Foreign
> 0206 GMT
>
> Message Follows:
>
> Any updates regarding the status of the negotiations with the HA? Do we know what he wants yet?
>
> End of Message

Crypto-Secure Phone

> From: Director NSOC, National Security
> To: DIR ED/RD
> Classification: Top Secret, No Foreign
> 0210 GMT
>
> Message Follows:
>
> This couldn't wait until tomorrow? Meet me in my office in the morning for full briefing. Negotiations are proceeding. Avenger is promising more information on terrorists and has given us relevant leads that are panning out in exchange for his demands. I'm still seeking clarity on what kind of immunity he wants, and talking to the Justice Department. Think they will agree to some kind of deal. More tomorrow.
>
> End of Message

Deal? Isaac slammed his phone on the kitchen counter. Stalking across the room, he yanked open a cabinet and pulled out a bottle of gin. He poured some into a glass, adding tonic and ice. He shook the glass a couple of times before taking a large swallow and picking up a burner phone. He tapped in a number and waited.

After four rings, it was picked up by a man with a curt voice. "Who's this?"

"Update me," Isaac said. "And it'd better be good."

There was a slight pause. "You're in luck. We think he might have contacted the daughter."

Isaac sat straight up and almost spilled his drink. "What? When?"

"A couple of weeks ago. We noticed a significant drop in what she was saying on her cell and home phone, as well as what she was doing on her computer. Right about the same time, we intercepted a heavily encrypted message going in. After that message went in, we were getting so little information, we switched tactics. We rented a house on the same street as her apartment complex to keep the family under twenty-four-hour surveillance."

"You think Sinclair contacted her?"

"I think that's the most likely scenario. We traced the message, but it went nowhere. We're still trying to break the encryption, but it isn't looking good. The daughter seems to have taken whatever message she received to heart. Given her subsequent actions, it was probably a warning. She's been crazy careful with all outgoing information, including phone calls. She's still using her computer but has been tunneling out using encrypted VPNs that she changes daily. We don't know what to make of the fact that, if it were Sinclair, why he feels threatened enough to reach out to her. Is he worried about her or himself? We have no indication that he's tried to contact his wife or the older daughter."

That was interesting. What was Sinclair thinking, and why the focus on the younger daughter? Maybe she was getting closer to him than they thought? "So, he's watching the daughter closely. Good. That's our conduit, then. What are we doing to manipulate this to our advantage?"

"Well, we were able to plant a few bugs in the common areas of the house last week when no one was home. That's why we're pretty sure Sinclair's wife has not been contacted. Unfortunately, most of what's being said in the house is inconsequential, other than the daughter has been nominated to go through the UTOP trials. I bet he knows that, too."

Isaac's annoyance rose at the news. "Let me guess. Slash nominated her. He's already called me asking about the Hidden Avenger investigation. I've held him off for now. I want Slash and his department shut out of this investigation entirely."

"Why are you so worried about Slash? He wasn't around when Sinclair left fourteen years ago, and he knows nothing about Lando. IAD has no bone to pick in this fight. I would think Candace Kim would be more of a threat to us."

Isaac let out a grunt of disgust. "Candace Kim is a bureaucrat who thinks she has things under control when, in fact, she doesn't have a clue." He tried to temper his irritation that he had to explain himself. "She's walking blindfolded, swinging wildly with a stick and hoping she somehow hits the piñata, when she isn't even in the right part of the room. She's not being obvious about it, but I'm certain she's having fantasies about becoming the first woman director at the NSA. She is annoying but predictable. I can manage her."

He paused, considering his next words. "Slash, however, is another story. He's a bit of a mystery and appears to be too good to be true. His meteoric rise in the NSA is concerning. Always seems to be in the right place at the right time to save the day. He's either really lucky or really dangerous, because no one is *that* good. But he's definitely by the book and has successfully cultivated a close relationship with the director. I don't want to put our years of planning for this opportunity at risk to Slash's good luck or unwillingness to do what is necessary to keep our nation safe. Let's not give him a reason to get involved."

"Agreed. Yet, he nominated Sinclair's daughter and two of her friends, which is odd. Is this a coincidence, or does he have some connection we don't know about to the Hidden Avenger? We really have no idea where his loyalties lie, but approaching him to try and find out might either raise his suspicions or have unfortunate consequences if we're wrong."

Isaac set his glass down, the condensation creating a small wet ring on the counter. "It has to be a coincidence. It's just unfortunate that Slash and his fiancée have a personal connection to the girl. It only adds another layer of complication to a delicate operation."

"Yes, it does, sir."

While it was a disturbing development and merited continued observation, it was not crisis-level. Isaac took another drink and mentally went through his options. "How do you think UTOP plays into this?"

"Honestly, I don't think we have anything to worry about. The daughter may have mad skills at the keyboard, but she's not UTOP material. If she accepts the nomination, she'll be the first to wash out."

"Good. Because I need her focus on finding her father, not on the UTOP trials. She'll be nearly impossible to monitor ensconced at the UTOP campus. We're running out of time to get the Avenger before Candace Kim does." That, thought Isaac, was the crux of their problem.

"You're right about that, sir. She has a lot invested in bringing him in. Think about it. People like success stories, and giving them a woman would be icing on the cake. Not saying she'd be a lock for the directorship, but it sure wouldn't hurt."

"The directorship is *mine*." Isaac tightened his hand on his glass. "We've worked too long and invested too much in it, which makes it imperative that we bring in the Avenger first. I want you to step up our efforts. Do what you need to do to find the Avenger and make it fast. Are you clear on that?"

"Crystal, sir."

CHAPTER EIGHT

Angel Sinclair

One week later, I waited nervously on the couch inside my apartment with two small suitcases, my laptop bag, Mr. Toodles, and my mom.

"I feel like you're forgetting something," my mom said, jumping up for the hundredth time and looking around the apartment.

"We've had this same conversation a dozen times in the past hour, Mom. They said they're providing pretty much everything for us. They are even sending a driver for me. Look, I promise I'm not forgetting anything. I've got everything I need."

"What about your phone charger? Extra batteries? Your gloves?"

"I've got all those things. Besides, if I did forget anything, you can bring them to me. I'm only going to be two hours away, remember?"

"But they said it will be at least four weeks before I can visit."

My heart skipped a beat nervously. In four weeks I'd know whether I was in or out. If I failed, my mom wouldn't have to visit. I'd be coming home on my own. "They just want us to get acclimated. It will be fine. I can survive four weeks without whatever I forgot."

She sighed, pulling me in close for a hug. "I'm not ready for an empty nest. It's all happening so fast."

"I promise I'll call and text as often as I can, okay?"

"You'd better."

"I will."

The doorbell rang and Mr. Toodles barked like the fierce dog he is, with tiny little yaps and yips. My mom scooped him up as I opened the door.

A man in a white dress shirt, dark slacks, and sunglasses stood there. "Good morning. Ms. Sinclair, are you ready?" he asked.

I never once imagined that I would be escorted to college by a US government driver. It was both super cool and super weird. Still, I tried to act like it was no big deal. "Yes, I'm ready. Thank you for coming."

He nodded, then tipped his head toward my mother. "Good morning, ma'am. I'm here to escort your daughter to the academy."

"Oh, it's so nice to make your acquaintance. Would you like to come in? Do you have time for some coffee?"

He smiled slightly. "Thank you. I appreciate the offer, but I've got two other students waiting in the car." He pointed to my suitcases. "Are these yours?"

"They are," I confirmed.

He nodded once more at my mom and rolled my suitcases out the door. I slipped my laptop bag and purse over my shoulder and gave Mom and Mr. Toodles one last hug. My mom looked dangerously close to tears.

I headed for the door but hesitated, suddenly not sure what to say, or if I could say anything to make my decision to leave any easier. Was I suddenly having doubts?

"I'll text you when I get to the campus and get settled in, okay? I promise."

My mom suddenly straightened, giving me a smile. "Of course you will. You're so smart and strong—you'll do great. I love you, Angel."

"I love you, too, Mom."

It was harder than I thought it would be to walk out the door. I had to swallow hard a few times to keep my composure. Luckily, I was distracted when I saw the limo and Wally and Frankie in the back, practically bouncing off the seats.

"Angel, will you look at this?" Wally said as I climbed in with them. "We're riding to school in style. It even has a refrigerator and free snacks." He opened the door, pulled out a Coke, and shoved one at me. "Drink up."

"I've never been in a limo before," Frankie said, pushing some buttons. "There's a television here."

"No alcohol, though," Wally said. "Dang."

"We're all underage," I pointed out.

"Thank you, Captain Obvious." He pouted, but Frankie and I just laughed.

The trip was supposed to be about two hours, but it took at least forty minutes longer, mostly because the traffic on I-95 south was a killer, even on a Monday morning. It didn't bother us at all. Sitting in a luxurious limo with every comfort (except a bathroom) was not a hardship. We drank soda and ate potato chips, Cracker Jacks, and gummi bears while we traveled.

Finally, our driver pulled off at an exit and drove for a while longer before turning onto a rural road. The only sign of life was a small gas station that looked closed. As we went deeper down the road, the area became increasingly wooded. Finally we came to a stop in front of a white stone arch that hung above an enormous, black, wrought-iron fence. A brick wall, about fifteen feet high, connected to the gate and disappeared into the forest. I'm not sure who the wall was intended to keep out in the middle of nowhere, but it did seem kind of ominous. Our driver pulled to a stop in front of the fence and typed some numbers on a small keyboard on the dashboard. Curious, we pressed our faces to the windows to get a look at the words carved into the arch.

"*Si vis pacem, para bellum,*" I murmured.

"What does that mean?" Frankie asked.

Since I was the only one in the car who'd taken Latin, I translated. "If you wish for peace, prepare for war."

"Oh, that's not scary at all," Frankie whispered, leaning back in the seat.

The driver spoke to us through a microphone. "We're here. Welcome to UTOP, kids."

The gate began to open slowly, and we drove into the compound. We all strained to get a look at the campus, then I turned around and watched as the heavy gate closed behind us.

Wally whistled softly and pointed ahead. "Get a load of that."

He pointed toward a series of precisely arranged colonial-style brick buildings arranged around a large courtyard and shaded by several towering trees. An impressive array of antennas covered the roofs.

I could imagine students sitting on the benches that dotted the landscape or on the grassy areas, studying or working on their laptops. It would have been an idyllic setting, except for one thing—it was a Monday morning and the place was deserted. It looked like a ghost town.

"That's odd," I heard the driver say. I'm not sure he realized his microphone was still on.

"What's odd?" Wally asked, alarm crossing his face

as he leaned forward and pressed the microphone button to the front of the limo. "Where is everybody?"

"I'm not sure. Something isn't right." The driver pulled into a parking place in front of a large courtyard, the sides of which were occupied by several small buildings, and pulled out a cell phone. He tapped on the phone and waited. We could hear ringing, but no one picked up.

He punched the phone off. "Well, that's not good."

"What's not good?" Wally said, his voice squeaking. "What's going on?"

The driver opened his door, his hand reaching under his jacket. "You kids stay here. I'll be right back." He slammed the door and walked cautiously toward the courtyard.

Frankie gripped my arm. "Where's he going?"

"I don't know," I said, pressing my face to the window.

The driver was halfway across the quad when a sound like a firecracker went off. He fell to the brick walkway and didn't get up.

For a moment, all three of us stared in horror, our mouths open.

"What the what?" Wally shouted. "Did someone just shoot him?"

"OMG!" Frankie gasped, squeezing my arm so tightly I was sure I'd have bruises. "We have to help him."

"Help him? Are you crazy?" Wally slid to the floor, grabbing me and Frankie and trying to pull us down. "There's someone with a gun out there. Maybe he won't see us."

Frankie and I immediately joined him on the floor in a jumble of limbs. I snapped the door lock on, then snatched my cell out of my purse to dial 911. I had no bars. Wally and Frankie both checked their phones.

"Where the heck are we that we have no cell signal?" Wally said. "This is crazy."

"What are we going to do?" Frankie whispered.

I tried to stay calm, despite the rapid pounding of my heart. "I don't know. We can't just sit here."

"Why not? The driver told us to stay in the car," Frankie said, her breath catching. "We should listen to him."

"Yeah, but what if whoever shot him comes after us?" Wally argued. "We'll be sitting ducks in here."

"Maybe the limo is bulletproof," Frankie said.

"Maybe it isn't. You want to stick around and find out?"

Frankie's face was turning purple from breathing too fast. "It doesn't make sense. Why would someone want to shoot us? We didn't do anything."

"These days, no one needs a reason to shoot someone," Wally said. "We're all targets."

I didn't like what he'd said, but I didn't disagree with it, either. I lifted my head to peek out the window. A figure dressed in all black and wearing a ski mask emerged from behind one of the buildings and was cautiously making his way toward our downed driver.

My heart lodged in my throat. "I see the shooter. He's dressed in black and holding a handgun. He's headed toward our driver, who's still on the ground and not moving. That's not a good development."

"You think?" Wally hissed. "It's time to get the heck out of here."

"What about our driver?" Frankie asked. "We can't just leave him there. He was so nice."

"We can't do anything for him at this point," I said. "But maybe we can find help."

"We have to get out of the car," Wally said. "If we stay here any longer, we won't have a choice." He flipped the door lock open and cautiously cracked the door on the side opposite of where the dark figure was still bent over our driver. Pushing it open just enough to exit, he slid out of the car and motioned vigorously for us to follow.

I wasn't crazy about the plan, but I agreed action was better than inertia. Frankie wiggled across the limo floor and slid out of the car next to Wally. Seconds later, I joined them. We partially closed the door and crouched there, our backs against the car, our hearts beating hard.

"What now?" Frankie whispered.

I pointed to an area between the buildings and kept my voice low. "That way. Maybe one of the doors are open and we can get inside and find help or a weapon."

"What if the bad guys are already inside?" Wally said. "I say go for the woods."

"Three geeks in the woods," I said. "That would not end well. We'd be easier to target than a herd of elephants."

"Good point," Wally said. "Okay. To the buildings, it is. On the count of three. Zigzag as you run, and keep low."

"How do you know zigzag works?" I asked.

"I play a lot of first-person shooter games. Trust me, okay?"

There was no more time for discussion. We nodded, and Wally started the countdown.

"One, two…three."

Fueled by adrenaline, we burst out from behind the car toward the buildings, nearly tripping each other as we zigzagged. I quickly pulled to the front, my legs pumping harder than they ever had before. Something pinged off the brick sidewalk near my left foot as I hurtled between the buildings with the others on my heels.

OMG! He's shooting at us!

I took a hard left the first chance I could, Frankie and Wally right behind me. We tore around another corner, a second ping hitting the wall just above my head. The second I turned the corner, I saw an old-fashioned wooden door with a small iron window and a latch handle. I slammed into it, pressing down on the handle, but it was locked. We ran on, taking the first turn we could. Another door was there, and I pushed on it. To my relief, this one opened, and the three of us tumbled in, nearly taking each other down. I slammed it shut behind me, but there was no lock.

"Hurry," I gasped, tearing off down a hallway, not knowing or caring where I was going, so long as it was away from the guy with the gun.

Wally and Frankie followed me. Our harsh breathing and tennis shoes hitting the tile floor echoed in the empty hallways. To my dismay, no security guard, military escort, or adults of any kind to help us appeared.

My heart was pounding so frantically, I thought I might have a heart attack. I took a hard left down another corridor and tried the first door on my right. It opened, and I pushed Wally and Frankie inside. There was no lock on this door, either, so I grabbed a chair and jammed it under the door handle to keep it from being opened. Slowly, I backed up, holding a finger to my lips.

A quick glance around indicated we were in a staff break room with a few round tables and a vending machine. Wally was already looking through the drawers for a weapon or anything that might offer protection. He held up a metal cake cutter and a couple of plastic forks. Frankie pulled out a bottle of bleach. I did my own quiet search, finally pouring a handful of salt into both hands. It wasn't much, but it was either that or trying to brain the attacker with a paper plate.

The three of us huddled together in a corner, hoping the attacker would pass us by. Moments later we could hear the handle on the door being jiggled. It was silent, and then a loud crash sounded.

Frankie screamed as the door flung open and the shooter, dressed in black, stepped over the chair I'd jammed beneath the handle.

To my utter shock, Wally acted first, shouting a battle cry and hurtling the cake cutter like a knife, right at the guy's head. To my astonishment, the guy caught it one-handed just before it reached his head. Before I could react, Frankie jumped toward him, throwing the open bottle of bleach at his head. While he was busy swatting the bottle away, I launched myself forward, latching onto his arm with the gun and tossing the salt directly into his face.

I must have gotten some in his eyes, at least partially, because he cursed and stumbled. I struggled with his arm, trying to get him to release the gun. I leaned over to bite his arm, using the only weapon I had left at my disposal, when he snaked an arm around my neck, holding me tight against him and rendering me immobile. If I struggled, he tightened his hold on my neck, cutting off my breath. For a moment, we all stilled, looking at each other. The acrid smell of bleach permeated the air, making me gag. Wally and Frankie, out of weapons and options, froze and watched me with frightened eyes.

Slowly, the guy lifted his gun and pointed it at them. I squeezed my eyes shut, bracing for the shots.

They never came.

"Bang," he said. "You're all dead."

CHAPTER NINE

Angel Sinclair

To my astonishment, the shooter suddenly released me. I staggered backward, grabbing my neck as our driver—apparently not dead—entered the room, climbing over the discarded chair. He patted our attacker on the shoulder. The attacker pulled the ski mask off his head. He was young, blond, and had a friendly smile. He gave us a quick smile and salute, disappearing out the door.

Frankie, Wally, and I stared in shock.

"Y-you're not shot," Wally finally stammered, stating the obvious.

"I am not. Let me introduce myself." He took off his sunglasses and tucked them neatly into the pocket on his white dress shirt. "I am Dexter Donovan, training director of UTOP."

He held out a hand, but none of us stepped forward to shake it.

"Wait. None of this was real?" I exclaimed, looking around. "This was some kind of test?"

He turned his attention to me. "That's correct, Ms. Sinclair. We like to have a baseline for every potential candidate before they receive any actual training."

"A baseline?" I repeated, still trying to wrap my head around the situation. We hadn't even been on the campus for five freaking minutes and they threw us into the middle of an active-shooter drill? What kind of baseline did they expect from three kids?

"Wow." Wally pushed a hand through his hair. He was still shaking. "Okay, so we're all technically dead. What does that mean? We failed our first test?"

"There's no winning or losing at UTOP, Mr. Harris," he said. "There's only response and counter-response. We're simply collecting data."

"But...he said we were all dead," Frankie exclaimed.

"Oh, he was right. If this was real, you'd all be dead." He wrinkled his nose at the bleach smell and motioned with his hand. "Let's move to more comfortable quarters. The smell is getting to be too much in here."

He turned and left the room while Wally, Frankie, and I exchanged worried glances. How was this possible? We'd just arrived on campus and had already failed at something? I wasn't used to failing, and I didn't like how this had played out. Swallowing my anger and frustration, I followed Mr. Donovan. I should have suspected something like this. It *was* a spy school, after all.

Mr. Donovan led us down a corridor and up two flights of stairs before he stopped in front of a door. A plaque on the wall near the office read *Dexter Donovan, Director, UTOP*. He pressed his thumb to a pad on the door and then tapped in a code before the door swung open. He motioned for us to enter, so we did.

A huge wooden desk dominated his office. Three chairs were placed side by side in front of his desk, and he indicated we were to sit, so we did, like three obedient children, with Frankie in the middle. Mr. Donovan didn't sit but leaned back against his desk, folding his arms and studying us like lab specimens. I wondered if he were going to tell us he'd be driving us home now.

He didn't speak for some time, presumably giving us time to reflect on our failure. We sat in silence, awaiting our fate.

Finally, he asked us a question. "What do you think was your first mistake?"

"Leaving the car?" Frankie immediately volunteered. She glanced uneasily at me, then Wally. In my opinion, she got bonus points for having the courage to answer first. "You told us to stay put, after all."

"But the shooter was coming toward the car," Wally countered. "We could have been trapped with no easy exit, if he came to investigate it."

"What if the car windows were bulletproof?" she suggested.

"What if they *weren't?*" Wally's fingers drummed anxiously on his thigh. "We'd be trapped and dead."

"True, but we ended up dead anyway. Right, Mr. Donovan?" Frankie looked at him for confirmation, but he just asked us another question.

"What else did you do wrong?"

Another stretch of silence ensued before I finally spoke. "We went into the buildings. The woods would have been safer."

Wally and Frankie gaped at me in astonishment.

"But going toward the buildings was your idea," Frankie finally said.

"I know." I wished I could take my decision back, but I couldn't. What had been done, was done. "In hindsight, it was a mistake. I ended up trapping us in a room, which was basically the same thing as trapping us in the car. We should have headed into the woods just like Wally suggested."

"Anything else, Ms. Sinclair?"

I hated these feeling of inadequacy. It was a direct hit to my intelligence, the one thing I thought I had going for me. "We should have split up."

"Ah, hindsight is quite useful, isn't it? Why would it have been better to separate?"

"Because three targets moving in different directions are harder to track down and hit. We lost any advantage by sticking together."

"Exactly. Now, let's examine your actions once you were trapped inside the staff room. While it was admirable you all found items with which to protect yourself, you didn't have a cohesive plan of action."

We didn't respond. What could we say? He was right. We'd been three scared kids.

Mr. Donovan pushed off the desk and walked in front of us. "For example, Ms. Chang, you chose a bottle of bleach, which was perhaps the most useful weapon gathered between the three of you. But you were too far away to use it properly. If you would have stood closer to the door, you might have been able to disarm your attacker when he crashed into the room. The same with you, Mr. Harris. While your aim with the serrated cake cutter was surprisingly accurate, the distance gave your attacker plenty of time to be prepared to catch it. It likely wouldn't have taken him down, either. Just annoyed him more."

He paused and looked at me. My cheeks were still burning with embarrassment. His scrutiny only made me flush more. "You, Ms. Sinclair, were the only one to use your so-called weapon correctly. You waited until you were close enough to get the salt in his eyes. However, if Jonas had been a real attacker, you would have been shot as soon you lunged at him. So, you would have been dead, too."

I looked down, clenching my hands in my lap, mad

at myself for not anticipating any of this. If I got another chance, it wouldn't happen again.

"But it happened so fast," Frankie protested. "It wasn't fair. We weren't expecting it."

"I'm aware of that, Ms. Chang." Mr. Donovan stood and walked over to the window, looking down at the grassy quadrangle area. "That's part of your training here at UTOP. An operative must *always* be expecting it."

He stood there quietly for a long time. Finally, he turned around.

"You're dismissed. Jonas is outside, ready to take you to your dorms. You're located in the special KIT area, which is in the back of the campus. You'll have everything you need there, including a library, a gaming room, television, a gym with a swimming pool and a basketball court, an open field for sports, a walking garden, and your own cafeteria. Other areas of the campus are restricted to current UTOP students only, unless you're specifically guided there by a staff member. Fraternization with other UTOP students is forbidden for obvious reasons. They're future US operatives. But you're not prisoners here. Once a week, on Saturday, we'll take you into town for a few hours to hang out, shop, and decompress. I don't need to repeat that you're not allowed to talk about any of your activities here to anyone outside the establishment. You can, however, discuss normal activities, classes, friends, course load, etc., with your friends and family, of course."

"Is there even cell service here?" Wally asked. "We were going to call for help when we were in the car, but we couldn't get any bars."

"We blocked it for the purposes of the exercise. It should be fine now." He walked to the door, opened it. "As I mentioned before, we wanted a baseline—to see how you handled yourselves in an emergency. You're free to call your parents to let them know you arrived.

However, before you do that, I want to offer you a chance to go home. I assure you, it only gets harder."

"You want us to go home?" Frankie asked, puzzled. "We just got here."

"I'm offering you the option, no questions asked. An exercise, like the one we just conducted, can be quite traumatic for some students. If you feel uncomfortable with this kind of thing, now is the time to say so. Therefore, I'm offering you a chance to go home. I would completely understand if you feel this kind of thing isn't for you."

Wally glanced at me with questioning eyes. Frankie looked between both of us. I lifted my chin, gritted my teeth and said nothing. Neither did Frankie and Wally.

Silence stretched on.

"Well, does your silence mean all three of you wish to continue?" Mr. Donovan asked.

We nodded.

"Then it's settled. Please spend the afternoon unpacking, making yourself familiar with the KIT compound, and meeting your fellow UTOP nominees."

"There are other nominees?" I asked.

"There are, indeed." He shook each of our hands gravely. "Welcome to the UTOP trials. I wish you all the best of luck."

CHAPTER TEN
Slash

As soon as the kids were dismissed and had left the office, Slash stepped into the office through an adjoining door. He knew what was coming and had prepared his arguments.

Dexter returned to his desk and sat down, a disappointed look on his face. "She didn't do as well as you expected. I was hoping for a more instinctive response from her and from all of them."

Slash shrugged, careful not to sound too invested. "I wouldn't presume to contradict your impression as to what's important, but Angel took the leadership role, and they followed."

"She would have killed them. Strong leaders who make bad decisions often lose more people than weak leaders who are fearful to do anything."

"Perhaps, but she used salt and was the only one of the three to actually score a hit," Slash pointed out.

"Her instincts were off."

"We're looking for different kinds of instincts." He approached Dexter's desk and put both hands on it, leaning forward a bit. "Perhaps it's time to consider the relevancy of the assessment tools given today's rapidly evolving security environment."

"It's always about computers to you."

"Not always, but it's where the future of espionage is headed." As the newest director of the Information Assurance Directorate at the NSA, the hardest part of his job was helping the current leadership understand and integrate technology into espionage. It had been a difficult challenge to convince many of the old-timers to move forward on this. While progress was being made, it was happening at a far slower rate than he liked.

"Our intelligence agencies are in transition," Slash continued, keeping his tone light. He didn't want to aggravate Dexter, just make a point. "We need to be prepared, and these kids are a step in the right direction."

Dexter didn't look convinced, but at least he didn't openly argue. A clever man and an excellent agent in his own right, Dexter had been in the business long enough to understand the impact technology was having on intelligence activities. How to integrate the old to the new was the stumbling block. Slash's job was helping to smooth the way.

"I understand what you're saying," Dexter said. "Regardless, none of them are what I expected." Dexter shifted in his chair. "They're different than our usual candidate."

"That's a good thing."

"How? No matter how skilled they are in the virtual world, we both know the base qualifications for an operative remain the same. They need to have real-world smarts, too."

Dexter was only partially right. While Slash couldn't speak to the kids' real-world capabilities, he had full faith in their brainpower, technical capability, and creative thinking. Whether they could withstand the pressure, psychological testing, and competition would be the real test. But he was certain that kids like Angel, Wally and Frankie were the kind of talent the agencies needed to cultivate.

"As the requirements for the operative evolve, so must our criteria," Slash said. "We not only need to update the assessment tools we use in looking for the right candidate, but adjust the challenges and trials, too. I'm comfortable in saying the coming challenges will be more in line with their instincts."

Dexter shook a finger at him. "I'm warning you, Slash, computer skills will not be enough. They'll have to show a lot more intellectual flexibility, emotional depth and psychological potential than they just did."

"They will. Give them time to adapt. They're *all* smart, and not just in computers."

"They'd better show those smarts soon or they'll be the first to wash out," Donovan warned.

"They won't."

"You really have faith in them." Dexter studied Slash for a long moment, then let out a sigh and sat back in his chair, crossing his arms against his chest. "I do have to give them credit for agreeing to stick it out. I just hope you're right about them."

"I am." Slash smiled, showing Dexter his confidence. "You'll see."

Angel Sinclair

We followed Jonas, aka the masked shooter, to our dorm rooms. Without the ski mask, he seemed normal. I put him at about nineteen or twenty years old, and he had blond hair and a nice smile. Frankie apologized twice for throwing the bleach container at him, even though we'd thought he'd been trying to kill us. Wally nervously asked him questions like how long he'd been at UTOP and how often he was required to portray an active shooter methodically hunting down kids.

Jonas laughed and brushed off most of the questions with ease. Exactly how an operative should act.

I thought the whole situation was exceptionally awkward, so I kept my mouth shut. We walked past the main buildings and down a brick pathway through the woods. I didn't see another person and wondered if the other nominees had already come in.

"What does KIT stand for?" I asked.

Jonas stopped, perhaps because it was the first thing I'd said since we'd left Mr. Donovan's office.

"Kids in Training," he said. "KIT."

"Oh. Did you train here?" Frankie asked.

He grinned. "I'm not a kid."

She put her hands on her hips, gave him a little frown. I think she wasn't used to having to work so hard to charm anyone. "And that's not an answer."

"That's because the answer is classified, Miss Chang." He pointed in front of him. "Here we are. Welcome to your new home."

Home was a giant, white concrete bunker with small windows. It looked like it could withstand a tornado. It seemed out of place next to the colonial-style masterpieces of the regular UTOP campus. Jonas led us to the front door, entered a code on a keypad, and pressed his thumb to a biometric reader.

"The front and back door codes and the Wi-Fi password are all in the welcome packets in your rooms. You'll be fingerprinted and processed tomorrow."

That sounded more like jail than spy school, but what did I know?

There was beep, and the front door popped open. We followed him inside and down a loud, echoing corridor. It seemed as empty here as the other buildings had. We went up a flight of stairs and down another corridor before coming to a spot in the hallway where it forked off in two directions. Jonas pointed to the left.

"Mr. Harris, room number seven is yours. The password on the door is 7777. Once your roommates arrive, the password can be changed at your leisure, although I suggest doing so as soon as possible. If you think you can find your way by yourself, I'll escort the ladies to their room."

Wally straightened. "Of course I can find my way. See you later." He strode off down the hallway without another look back.

Jonas led Frankie and me down the right corridor, stopping at room four. "Ladies, this is where the official tour ends. The temporary password on your door is 4444. Don't change it until all of your roommates arrive, and then make sure everyone knows the password. You're free to roam around the building and outside as long as you stay on the KIT campus. There's a map in your welcome packet so you don't get lost. The packet also has information on where the laundry room, gym, library, gaming areas, and cafeteria are located. I trust you'll be fine, as long as you remember the restrictions on where you're allowed and not allowed to go."

"Thank you so much, Jonas," said Frankie, shaking his hand like he hadn't just been trying to kill us a half hour earlier. "I hope to see you around."

He shook his head with a smile. "You won't."

He disappeared down the hallway. Shaking my head, I tapped out 4444 on the keypad. The little light on the keypad turned green, and the door popped open. Frankie and I entered into a seating area with a couch, two worn armchairs, and a coffee table that looked as if it had seen better days. Two small side tables held some ugly lamps. That was it for the common room area.

To the right was another door. When we went inside, we saw two military-style bunk beds, four desks, and two tall dressers. Our suitcases and my laptop bag were already at the foot of one of the bunk beds. There were stacks of sheets, blankets, towels, and a pillow on the beds. Across from us, the lower bunk bed had already been taken and someone had made the bed. A dark-blue suitcase had been pushed against the wall, and a laptop, printer, and small lamp were set up on one of the desks.

I wasn't thrilled to discover I'd have to share a room with Frankie and two other people I didn't know, but I swallowed my reservations. Time to deal. I wasn't going to fail again.

"Someone's already here," Frankie said in a hushed voice. She walked over to the closet and held out a hand. "There are clothes in the closet. They're nice."

"Well, we've got one roommate, at least," I said. The upper bunk still looked empty, and the sheets and towels hadn't been touched.

"I call lower bunk," Frankie said, sitting down on the bed. "You're nimbler than I am. You take the top."

I didn't care one way or the other, so I didn't argue. Instead, I stood on Frankie's bunk so I could reach my towels. "I wonder where the bathroom is."

Frankie hopped up. "I bet it's in here," she said, disappearing into an adjacent room.

I followed her into a stark white bathroom with two sinks and a large mirror that stretched across the wall. Two shower stalls with blindingly white tiles and a separate toilet section completed the area.

"Wow. This place could really use a decorator," Frankie observed.

"It's functional," I said, putting my towels on one of the unoccupied bars. "At this point, that's all that matters." I left the bathroom and picked up my cell. "I've got to text my mom."

"Me, too," said Frankie. "My family will be anxious to hear how I'm doing."

After I texted, I picked up one of the welcome packets on my desk. I shook out the papers and sorted through them. "Want to look around? I've got a campus map."

"Let's unpack first. I want to be organized."

"Okay, as long as you can finish before lunch. I'm starving." I sorted through the papers until I found a schedule. "Looks like lunch today is at noon sharp in the cafeteria."

"That gives us forty minutes."

I finished well before Frankie, and that was after I'd made both of our beds and hooked up my laptop and printer to the Wi-Fi, adding extra peripherals like a Wi-Fi enhancer.

Frankie was still unpacking her clothes and shoes.

"I can't fit all my clothes into two drawers," she complained with an armful of clothes.

"Because you brought too many," I said.

"I hardly brought any," she said, frowning. "I just didn't know what we would need."

"Didn't you read the instructions on what clothes to bring? Two pairs of jeans, a couple of T-shirts, one nice outfit and dress shoes, underclothes, a swimsuit, a warm coat, hat and gloves, and a couple pairs of pj's. You've got a lot more stuff than that."

"It's important to be prepared for every occasion."

I sighed. "Fine. You can take one of my drawers. I can fit everything into one." I rearranged my drawer so Frankie could put the rest of her stuff away.

She gave me a hug. "You're the best, Angel. Thanks so much."

"Are you ready for lunch now?" I asked.

"Yes. I'm starving. Is it time?"

"We're five minutes late, and we still have to find the cafeteria. It's a good thing we've got a map."

"Okay, let's go."

We followed the map down two flights of stairs. The cafeteria was in the building in the left wing. Calling the place a cafeteria was a stretch. It was more like a large café with a one-person serving staff and a few round tables that sat about four. Wally already sat at one of the tables, talking with two guys I didn't know. A third guy sat alone at a table with his back to us. A pretty blonde girl with long legs sat at a table with Wally. He seemed relieved to see Frankie and me and nearly leaped out of his chair to greet us.

"Angel, Frankie, you're here. Come meet everybody."

One of the guys sitting with Wally unfolded from the table. He was huge, maybe six foot four, with deep-brown skin, muscular biceps, and brown hair cut nearly to the scalp. Being five foot three, I had to look up…a lot.

"Hi, I'm Bo Coleman," he said gruffly, sticking out a hand and shaking hands first with Frankie.

His hand completely swallowed hers up. "It's nice to meet you. I'm Frances Chang, but please call me Frankie. This is my best friend, Angel Sinclair."

"Angel?" he turned to me. "That's your name?"

"Wait. *You're* a nominee?" I blurted out.

"I am." He grinned. "Why do you look so surprised?"

"Because you don't look like a kid. You're so…" I let the sentence trail off.

"Handsome?" he filled in for me. "Buff?"

"Tall and muscular. I mean…how old are you?"

Frankie elbowed me, probably thinking I was being rude, but Bo didn't seem to mind. "Eighteen. And you?"

"Sixteen." It was a lie since technically my birthday was in a couple of weeks, but both Frankie and Wally wisely kept their mouths shut.

"Seriously?" He laughed. "They're starting them younger every year."

I might have been offended, except he had a kind twinkle in his eyes that put me at ease. He returned to the table, picked up one of the three hamburgers on his plate, and resumed eating.

The blonde next to Wally didn't stand, but she lifted her hand, acknowledging us. "I'm Kira Romanova from Ontario, California. Before you ask, I'm seventeen."

"I thought Ontario was in Canada," Frankie said with a grin. She walked over and pumped Kira's hand like they were long-lost buddies. Frankie was the friendliest and nicest person I'd ever met, and it was all genuine.

"I'm really excited to meet you, Kira," Frankie gushed. "We're going to be roommates. It'll be so much fun."

Kira carefully withdrew her hand, looking a bit freaked out. Thankfully, Frankie didn't notice, because she was already focused on the guy sitting next to Bo.

"Hello," she said to him. "Who are you?"

The guy rose from his chair. He was thin, with stringy, dark hair. His black jeans were too big for him, even with a belt. A baggy black T-shirt with a skull on it hung nearly to his knees. He had a nose ring and a half dozen silver studs in the lobe of his left ear.

He held up his hand, palm out, as if warning Frankie to stay where she stood. A black-stoned ring on his thumb glinted in the light. "Hello, and welcome to the KIT compound," he said. "I'm sure you're going to enjoy your stay here no matter how badly we screw with your head. Good luck and may the odds be in your favor."

"Hey, that sounded exactly like Mr. Donovan," I said. Holy crap, he was good. If I hadn't seen him doing it with my own eyes, I would have believed Mr. Donovan was standing right behind him.

"Wow." Frankie clapped, clearly impressed. "That imitation was so good. Can you do other voices?"

He grinned and in a girl's voice said, "I'm really excited to meet you, Kira. We're going to be roommates. It will be so much fun."

Unbelievable. He sounded exactly like Frankie, right down to the inflections in her voice. "That's wicked skill, dude," I said.

He gave me a grin and a thumbs-up. "Now, this is my real voice. I'm Mike Garcia from the Jersey shore. Seventeen. I'm not hungry and I'm not into chatting, so I'm going to ditch the party. Later." He stood and left the cafeteria without another word.

I watched him go, his black boots clomping on the floor. The fact that he wasn't the talkative type kind of gave him points in my plus column.

The last guy present, who was eating with his back to us, hadn't turned around the entire time we'd been in the cafeteria. I think Frankie had been put off a bit by Mike, so when she didn't try to engage him, I spoke up. "Excuse me. You in the corner, would you like to introduce yourself to the rest of us?"

The guy turned slowly in his seat. My breath caught as I got my first glimpse of his face. Jet-black hair, a square jaw, high, sculpted cheekbones, and the greenest eyes I'd ever seen. I froze, unable to look away. Finally, his mouth curved into a smile.

"You going to stare at me all day, Red?"

My cheeks flushed. Could I act any more like a dork? I'd finally been assertive, something I never did, and then choked when he actually responded. I cleared my throat, trying to regain control. "I'm not staring... exactly."

"If you say so." He dipped his head. "Before you ask, I'm Jax Drummond from Queens, New York. I'm seventeen." His voice held just the faintest touch of a lilt, Scottish maybe. "Now that the obligatory introductions are complete, I hope I can be left alone to finish my lunch in peace." He abruptly turned his back on us.

Another friendly soul...not. This was going to be a strange group dynamic. I'd been hoping spy school would be more like Hogwarts and less Hunger Games, but it certainly wasn't feeling that way to me so far.

Frankie shrugged it off and waved me over to the counter where we could order our food. A young woman wearing a hairnet and plastic gloves sat on a tall stool. She was looking at her phone but put it away when we arrived.

"Hey, girls. What can I get you to eat?" she asked.

Frankie beamed at her. "Oh, thank you so much for being patient while we took time to meet our fellow nominees. We know we're late, and we really appreciate you waiting for us."

"Oh, hey, it's no problem." The woman smiled at us. "Today's menu is behind me. Hamburgers, egg salad sandwiches, and a few different kinds of salads and soups. The sides are listed there." She pointed to a chalkboard. "I've been advised of any and all food allergies and meal preferences, so we have a wide selection of vegan, gluten-free, and nut-free options. Just ask me if you have any questions."

We quickly made our selections and loaded our drinks and sides on a tray. I would have chosen a table for just Frankie and me, but Frankie was determined to be inclusive. She made a beeline for the table with Kira. I didn't see a way out of it that didn't make me seem rude, so I swallowed my annoyance and joined them.

Wally leaned over from his table. "So, girls, what do you think of your room?"

"There isn't enough drawer space," Frankie complained. "Regardless, this will be a real adventure." She actually sounded excited about it, like it was going to be all fun and games and we hadn't just been through an active-shooter scenario.

Wally must have been thinking the same thing, because he leaned toward me. "Hey, Angel, did you know everyone had the same shooter scenario upon arrival?"

"Really?" I looked across the table at Kira. "You did, too?"

She nodded. "Yes. I was in the limo with Bo. We got picked up together from the airport. Bo tried to take the guy down physically. He got the gun out of his hand, but our attacker ended up subduing him. I ran like a rabbit and hid in the woods. They couldn't find me, so they finally had to announce it was a drill, and I came out."

"Wow," I said. "So you beat the scenario?"

She shrugged. "I guess. Wally already told me what happened to you guys. Sounds like it sucked."

"Yeah, I guess so." I tried to shrug like it was no big deal. Apparently we'd been totally incompetent. "Anyone know what happened with Mike or Jax?"

Wally took a slug of his Coke. "Mike said he and Jax were together." He dipped his head at Jax, who had a set of earbuds in and was listening to something while tapping his foot. "Mike said they also ran for the woods, but they stuck together. Mike started a small fire as a distraction, and Jax came at the guy from behind when he came to investigate. Jax and Mike took him down. But only temporarily. They didn't have any way to restrain him, so eventually the attacker got loose and brought them both in. Still, I think it counts as a win for both of them."

My shame deepened. Was I the only stupid one who had insisted on going into the buildings?

Kira sipped what looked like tea and regarded Frankie and me. "You guys seem really friendly. Do you know each other?"

"We do," Frankie said, beaming. "We all go to same high school in DC."

Bo leaned forward. "Wow. Must be one heck of a high school. Three nominees from one location. How many more of us do you think there'll be?"

I shook my head. "I don't know. I thought there would be a lot of us."

Jax snorted, and I realized the earbuds were only a defense against unwanted conversation. I'd done it before myself. He'd been listening the whole time.

"You guys don't know anything. This is highly specialized training. It takes a lot to be invited to something like this. I'm surprised they found seven of us to compete."

I wondered if he was right, and if he was, how did he know that?

"We have one more bunk in our room that hasn't been taken yet," Kira pointed out. "It has sheets, blankets, and towels on it. It could be eight."

"Interesting," Wally said. "Four girls, four guys."

I looked at Jax. "You said compete. Are we competing against each other?"

"What do you think, Red?"

"First, my name is Angel, not Red. Second, I think we're competing against ourselves and a set of standards developed by the intelligence agencies for this kind of work."

"Wrong," Jax said. "They look for whoever rises to the top in the group. Sometimes, if no one rises, they fail the entire class."

Bo leaned forward on the table, frowning and asking the same question I'd had. "Exactly how do you know that?"

"I have my sources. Spy school, remember?"

Kira stood up. "Well, it's been real, but I'm done here. I'm going to go look around."

"Why don't you wait for us to finish, Kira?" Frankie said. "Angel and I will go with you."

She shook her blonde hair. "Thanks, but I prefer to do my investigations solo."

Frankie looked crestfallen but pasted a smile on her face anyway. "Sure. See you back in the room."

One by one, everyone left the cafeteria until it was just Wally, Frankie, and me. Wally took Kira's vacated chair and put his elbows on the table, facing us. He looked upset, so I asked him what was up.

"Did you see those guys? All of them look buff except for Mike. But at least he's skinny. I bet he can do a push-up or two."

"Wally, I told you, this is not boot camp," I said.

"So you say, but did you expect to encounter an active-shooter scenario the first two minutes after we arrived on campus?"

"No," I admitted.

"Exactly. Those guys at least tried to take down the attacker. I threw a cake cutter."

"Mr. Donovan said your aim was pretty good."

"Not helping, Angel." He took off his glasses and polished them using his shirt.

I pushed my tray to the side. "Frankie, what's your first impression of our fellow nominees?"

Frankie finished swallowing her bite of sandwich and took a sip of water. "Honestly? I think they're all cool. Everyone will have a lot to offer to the experience."

I rolled my eyes. "Do you always have to be so positive about everything? What if Jax is right and we end up competing against each other?"

"Then we'll do our best and the right people will be selected, won't they?"

It was not fair that even when she was looking at the world with rose-colored glasses, she was still perfectly logical. "Grrrr. I really hate it when you're right, Frankie."

Wally chuckled as Frankie dabbed at her mouth with her napkin and pushed her tray aside. "You should be used to it by now, Angel."

Maybe I was, but it didn't help my mood. No matter how positive Frankie felt about the situation, I was worried. I didn't want to be the first one to go home, but after hearing how the other candidates handled the active-shooter scenario, I thought that might be exactly what happened.

CHAPTER ELEVEN

Candace Kim

NSA Headquarters, Fort Meade, Maryland

"Three minutes until we have contact with the Avenger. Everyone, stand by."

Candace nodded tersely at the technician who returned to monitoring his computer screen. She began to pace the conference room, her nerves on edge. "Are we ready across the board?"

It was Jim Avers who answered. "Yes, ma'am, we are."

Over the past forty-eight hours, Candace had read *Moby Dick* and all references to Ahab in the Bible. She'd reread Ethan Sinclair's file and scoured through dozens of possibly connected NSA operations, none of which were called Ahab or involved whales or biblical kings. Jim had done the same, and neither of them had come up with anything remotely relatable to the situation. If the Avenger was sending them a coded message, he wasn't making it easy.

Candace did a quick head count of people in the room. Everyone except herself sat in front of a laptop.

Nine people. Six technicians, herself, Jim, and Isaac Remington. She would have preferred to lock Isaac out of the investigation, because she neither liked nor trusted him. Although this operation had become hers to run, Isaac was a director and her equal, as well as the former boss of the suspected Avenger. If he was interested in the case—and he was—she had no choice but to include him. She'd almost invited Slash, too, but decided it would be prudent to keep him working on things behind the scenes. He had an enviable track record of success operating that way, so she'd back-brief him later.

One of the technicians lifted a headphone from his ear. "We're live. We have contact."

The room silenced, and everyone slid into a seat except for Candace. She preferred to stand so she could pace as needed. She could always think better when she could walk.

"The first transmission is in," Jim stated, reading the screen. "It's an email with only one line. It says 'Ahoy Ahab, what's going down?'"

"So it *was Moby Dick*," Candace murmured. "What does he want?"

"He's uploading updates on the terrorist activities he's been monitoring and wants to know if we've confirmed the previous information."

"Tell him we have," Candace said. "And say thank you." She was satisfied the Avenger was delivering on his end, and so she wanted to assure him she would come through on her side.

Jim typed the message and sat back. After a minute, he said, "He wants to know about the request for immunity."

"Tell him the Department of Justice needs clarification on the nature of the immunity he's requesting," she said. "It's a no-go if he's been involved in murder or treason, even peripherally. But they're willing to deal, assuming he follows through on providing more verifiable information on the terrorist threat, turns over the ShadowCrypt patch, and conducts no further criminal activity between now and the time he returns."

After Jim sent the message, a response came back almost immediately. "He says he's never hurt anyone, nor has he ever aided a terrorist or anyone with harmful intent toward any persons or the US. Nor has he engaged in treason of any kind. The immunity is for real or perceived virtual actions, and he agrees to the conditions."

Candace nodded. "Perfect. Tell him I'll contact the Justice Department and get back to him." She frowned when she saw Isaac typing at his station. "Isaac, what are you doing? You're not authorized to respond."

He turned around in his chair. "The Avenger is a liar. He committed treason when he installed the ShadowCrypt patch. He's allowed terrorists all over the world to hide their plans, certainly costing thousands of lives. That makes him a murderer."

Why in the world was Isaac going off plan? It was beyond unprofessional to lose control and get emotional in such a situation, jeopardizing the entire operation.

Still in disbelief, she stalked over to his computer. "What did you do?"

"I sent a message. Short and sweet. I told him there were some of us who knew he was lying and were not on board with the immunity offer."

The room went dead silent.

Anger swept through her. "You did *what?* You were to observe only. You have no authority to make direct contact."

His eyes narrowed at her tone. "I'm a director at this agency, just like you. I have *every* right to protect the agency from this ill-conceived idea of negotiation with a traitor."

Before Candace could respond, Jim spoke. "He's not answering, ma'am. He might not be coming back."

Candace tore her gaze from Isaac. "Can you tell if he's still there?"

"Hard to say at this point."

A thousand thoughts whirled through her head, mostly on how she could fix this, but when she spoke, her voice was cool and controlled. "We wait, then."

While she waited, she considered Remington's reaction and her options. He was clearly trying to sabotage the deal, but why? He'd made it clear he considered the Avenger a traitor for shutting the back door. But she'd also caught him eyeing her to see how she was reacting to his actions. He was putting on a show, but why and for whom?

A few minutes ticked past. "Anything yet?" she asked.

"No. Nothing," Jim replied.

More time passed with no contact. Her mind worked furiously to figure out what was going on with Remington. Was he trying to prevent her from bringing in the Hidden Avenger because he wanted to do it himself? It would not reflect well on her if she failed, even if she was not at fault. Regardless, it was disgusting that Remington would risk people's lives and an invaluable tool solely to advance his own career. Was he really that selfish or stupid? Or could he be afraid of the Hidden Avenger for some reason? Did the Avenger have information that might damage Remington's chances of becoming director...or was it something else?

She was about to call an end to the operation when an email from the Avenger suddenly popped up on the screen. Jim leaned forward, reading aloud.

"He's satisfied we'll see the deal through. The instructions for our next virtual exchange and more information on the terrorists are in an attached file. However, that file will disappear in three minutes."

"Get it," Candace instructed, her voice terse as she started pacing again.

"I've already got it," one of the technicians said. "I've opened it, and the data is intact. It's been saved to another server and is safe."

Thank God, at least something had gone right. "Thank you."

"He also says the next conversation will be code-named Pope 264." Jim glanced at her over his shoulder with a puzzled expression. "Whatever that means."

"I don't know, but it's not random," she answered. "He's trying to tell us something."

"No, he's not," Isaac countered. "He's trying to distract us, send us running down a rabbit hole to keep from focusing on what's real here—that he's a liar, a cheat, and a treasonous former agent gone rogue who doesn't deserve immunity."

Candace saw sympathy and agreement from a few of the technicians in the room. Isaac was stirring up things, and she didn't like it one bit.

She didn't address his words directly, but ice dripped from her voice as she spoke. "From this point forward, only Jim and one technician will have access to a laptop for communication purposes with the Avenger. Everyone else stands back or is not permitted to attend. Those are my orders. If anyone has an issue with that, I suggest you take it up with the director."

Everyone nodded, except Isaac. The smug expression on his face said volumes. The damage had been done. He'd made it known to Sinclair that there were people inside the NSA who weren't going to make it easy for him to come in. If that spooked him and he bolted, the fallout would be pinned to her.

She wouldn't underestimate Isaac next time. But she hoped he'd continue to underestimate her.

CHAPTER TWELVE

Angel Sinclair

"**D**oesn't it seem weird we have all this space and they are making us share one room?" I asked Frankie.

While the KIT campus was cool, not to mention completely self-sufficient, it was a bit strange that all of this was just for seven kids. I guess the government had its reasons, but it was a bit unnerving.

After roaming around the area for a while, Frankie and I parted ways with Wally and returned to our room. According to our schedule, dinner was promptly at five. We had about an hour more of downtime before that. I was exhausted and needed some alone time to process all the things that had happened to me to this point. Unfortunately, sharing a room with other people meant alone time was going to be hard to come by. At least Kira wasn't there, and no one had yet claimed the top bunk across from Frankie and me yet.

Frankie plopped down stomach first on her bed. "It is kind of weird, but I bet they want to see how well we get along with each other. So, what's your favorite part of the campus? The swimming pool? The gym? Wait, don't tell me. The gaming room."

"The gaming room is a pretty sweet setup," I admitted.

"Well, I liked the garden maze the best. The flowers in the garden were lovely. I like how someone had added a few pumpkins and haystacks, too. It makes it feel so welcoming and normal. Although the swimming pool was amazing, too. Not quite as fancy as Excalibur's, but nice just the same."

"Maybe we can go swimming after dinner," I suggested.

"Great idea."

Frankie closed her eyes, declaring she wanted to take a nap. I envied her the ability to shut down. I wished I could do the same, but I was too wired. Instead I sat down at my desk, booted up my laptop.

There was no way I'd be stupid enough to search for information on my dad on a government network, but I could read the information I'd already downloaded.

Although I'd already read it a hundred times, I opened the police report on my dad. I flipped to the page where the police discussed my father's workplace, King's Security. Wally and I had traced it and discovered it was owned by the NSA. I'd never been told my dad worked for the NSA and apparently neither had the police, because it hadn't been in the report. My dad's official title had been security engineer. I knew that meant he would have been responsible for testing and screening computer security software and monitoring networks and systems for potential intrusions. They also implemented and tested strategies to plan and prepare for security threats. But my dad's background was in cryptology and encryption. Cryptologists created and deciphered codes and cryptograms. So what had my dad been working on when he disappeared?

I googled for inventions and advancements in cryptology around the time my dad disappeared and read until I almost fell asleep at the keyboard. That's exactly when Frankie woke up and announced we had to go to dinner.

We met Wally in the cafeteria. Everyone was there except for Jax and Kira. I hadn't seen Kira since lunch, and she lived with us. Where did she disappear to all the time?

After dinner, we invited Wally to go with us to the pool. He declined.

"Are you kidding? I don't want Kira to see me in my bathing suit. As you can see, I'm not exactly buff."

"Seriously?" I crossed my arms, frowning. "You're not going to start pining over Kira, are you?"

"How can I stop myself?" Wally sighed and pressed a hand to his chest. "Have you taken a good look at her? She's gorgeousness times a million. The most beautiful woman I've ever seen in this close proximity. And she's got to be smart if she's here. The perfect woman for me."

I rolled my eyes. "You don't know anything about her. You just met her. Don't lose sight of what's important here."

"Oh, trust me. I know what's important. I know you're going to say I'm overreacting, but I feel like she's my destiny."

"Ugh." I threw up my hands. "It's lust, Wally. Knock it off."

Frankie giggled, but Wally crossed his arms and glared at me. "It's not lust. Well, maybe a little, but you do *not* know what's in my heart."

"Fine," I said, huffing out a breath. "Your loss. If you don't want to come swimming, we'll go without you."

We got dressed in our swimsuits and headed out. When we got to the gym, Jax and Bo were on the mats wrestling. Kira was in another corner lifting weights. Mike was nowhere in sight.

Jax saw me and waved cheerfully. "Hey, Red, you want to wrestle next?"

"Um, no, thanks." My cheeks heated. "I'm going swimming."

"Your loss," he said grinning as he picked up a towel and swiped it across his brow. "Maybe next time."

"Sure, maybe," I called out. Biggest. Lie. Ever. No way was I going to get that close to him.

Frankie and I headed on to the swimming pool, grabbing a couple of towels on our way and dumping them on a chair.

"I think Jax likes you," Frankie announced.

"*What?*" I frowned fiercely at her as I pulled my hair back in a ponytail, securing it. "I just met him. How can you extrapolate that?"

She raised an eyebrow. "He didn't ask me to wrestle."

I didn't have an adequate answer to that, so I dived into the pool. We had it all to ourselves, so we swam a bunch of laps and then splashed around a bit. When we got out, Jax and Kira were gone. Bo was in another corner of the gym using a bow and arrow to hit a target. I wrapped myself in a towel and watched him hit the bull's-eye three times in a row.

Holy crap. He had some mad skills with the bow. He must have felt me watching, because he turned around and gave me a little wave. I waved back, and he resumed his target shooting.

Anxiety swamped me. I'd never used a bow in my life, and I totally sucked at darts. I hadn't held or fired a gun and didn't play on any sports teams, other than when forced to do so in gym class. Other than swimming, I had no ability in anything physical, which was kind of scary after watching Bo nail the target time after time.

Frankie was chatting with the lifeguard, so I went

into the locker room to change. When I came out, Bo was gone and the lifeguard was closing down the pool.

"The lifeguard is so nice," she said. "I thought it must be a boring job watching us swim, but he told me he likes the solitude to think."

"Well, hurry up and get dressed," I said, a bit irritated I had to wait for her. Did she have to talk to everyone? "We're the last ones in the gym."

"Oh, sure," she said, hustling into the locker room.

The fourth bunk in our room was still empty by the time we finally got back. It looked like it was going to be just the three of us. Kira was just getting out of the shower. She walked into the room, toweling her hair.

"Lights out at ten," she said shortly and then turned her back on us.

I had no idea what was her problem with us. Her standoffishness was bordering on rudeness.

"We've still got an hour," I said. "But after this day, I won't have a problem falling asleep."

"Me neither," Frankie agreed.

Frankie took her shower next. I followed and then blow-dried my hair. When I got out of the bathroom, Kira was already lying in bed, her back to the room and us. Frankie was sitting on top of the covers, reading. She was dressed in yellow flannel pj's with green blobs on them. Her wet hair was parted in the middle and rolled up in two socks on either side of her head.

I couldn't stop myself from asking. "What's that on your pj's?"

"Frogs." She set aside her book and tugged on her sleeve so I could see better. "Did you know frogs are considered good luck in China? They're associated with rain. Rain means good crops will sprout. Good crops mean lots of food for the population. Lots of food means happy people. I just figured I could use a little extra luck to start off this new adventure."

"Okay. And why are there socks in your hair?"

She patted the socks. "I'm going for the crinkly-hair look tomorrow." She glanced over at Kira, who was lying as still as a stone. There was no way she was asleep with the light still blazing and the two of us talking, but she seemed intent on ignoring us. Frankie and I exchanged a puzzled glance.

"Hey, Kira," Frankie said. "We didn't get a chance to talk to you much earlier. What's your story? How did you end up here? We're looking forward to being roommates with you."

She was still for a long moment and then she finally rolled over, propping her head up with one hand. "Look, I know you want to be friends, but I intend to stay focused on what has to be done here. So, no offense if I don't want to join your posse. Just leave me alone and we'll be good. Okay?"

"Hey," I said. "No need to be rude."

"We're not a posse," Frankie said earnestly. "We're all inclusive. We can help each other, you know."

"I don't need your help. Perhaps I wasn't clear. Leave. Me. Alone." She rolled over again, pulling the covers over her head.

I clenched my teeth, but Frankie didn't seem upset in the slightest.

"Angel, can you turn off the lights, please?" Frankie said. "Kira is right. We'd better get to bed. We have a big day tomorrow."

I lifted my hands in a can-you-believe-that gesture. Frankie pursed her lips and looked disappointed in me. Huffing, I dropped my hands and stalked across the room, then banged my fist against the switch as I turned it off. I didn't know who Kira thought she was, but she was acting like a princess, and my tolerance for that was exactly zero.

Still fuming, I climbed up to my bunk and settled in.

I thought I'd be up for hours mulling over everything that had happened over the course of the day, but my last thought was I needed to up my game so I could handle whatever they intended to throw at us in the coming days.

CHAPTER THIRTEEN

Angel Sinclair

A soft noise woke me. For a moment, I was completely disoriented. The bed felt wrong, the blanket smelled different, and the room was cooler than I was used to. It took me a couple of seconds to realize I was in the UTOP dorm. I quietly rolled over to my side and saw a dark figure disappear into the bathroom.

My body went on high alert, and I was instantly awake. I didn't know if it was another test, but just in case, I crept down the bunk and grabbed a flashlight from my desk. I tiptoed toward the bathroom and waited, my back pressed against the wall next to the door.

The figure walked out of the bathroom, careful to switch off the light before opening the door.

I flicked on my flashlight, hoping to blind whoever it was. A girl about my age with dark hair and wearing pajamas gasped and jumped backward.

"Whoa. Who are you?" she whispered, squinting at me through the light.

I lowered the flashlight so it wasn't in her eyes, but I could still see her. Just in case.

"Are you our roommate?" I whispered back.

"I am."

I let out a breath, keeping my voice at a whisper. "Oh, sorry. I thought this was another test—like you were coming to slit our throats while we slept or something like that. I guess I'm on edge. I'm also a very light sleeper, unlike the two others here."

"My name is Hala. I'm sorry I came so late. My flight from Cairo was delayed, and then I had to wait to be picked up from the airport. When you said test...I take it to mean you were attacked upon arrival at the campus, as well?"

I relaxed, leaning against the wall. "Yeah, everyone was. They want a baseline for our abilities, I guess. Were you alone for it? The rest of us had partners."

"I was alone."

Wow. I couldn't imagine how scared she must have been. "I bet that sucked. What did you do when your driver got shot? Did you run toward the buildings or the woods?"

She frowned. "Neither."

"What? Neither? Do you mind if I ask what you *did* do?"

"Sure. Once I saw my driver go down, I wiggled through the small opening between the front and back seat of the limo. I pried open the glove compartment and found a gun inside. I lay on my back across the front seat and waited until my attacker showed himself in the window. Then I shot him through the glass."

My mouth dropped open. "You...shot him?"

"Absolutely. My dad always says, if you're holding a gun, you'd better be ready to use it."

"D-did you kill him?"

79

"Of course not. The gun shot blanks. But I passed the test."

"Whoa. I bet. By the way, I'm Angel Sinclair. Frankie Chang is asleep in the bunk below me. We're both from Maryland. You're in the upper bunk, and below you is Kira Romanova from California. Did you say you were from Cairo?"

"No, I'm from Boston. My dad is the head of the FBI bureau there. I was visiting my grandmother in a small town not too far from Cairo. The plane got delayed, so that's why I'm late."

"Your grandparents are from Cairo?"

"Just my dad's parents. My mom's parents moved here thirty years ago from a small town called el-Kosheh."

I held out a hand. "Oh, well, it's nice to meet you, Hala."

She shook it. "Likewise, Angel. I like your name, by the way. It's nice to know I have an angel nearby."

We each climbed up on our bunks, and after some tossing and turning, I finally fell asleep again. This time nothing woke me.

CHAPTER FOURTEEN

Angel Sinclair

The alarm on my cell phone went off at precisely 6:58 a.m. It had been set to vibrate only and tucked under my pillow so I didn't wake anyone. The schedule said we'd receive a wake-up call at seven, but the way things were going, I didn't want any more surprises.

At exactly seven, a male voice was piped into our room from two small speakers located in separate corners of the room.

"Good morning, candidates. It is oh seven hundred, and time to get your day started. Please dress in the clothes that have been provided for you and have been placed outside your door. Eat breakfast, and report to Room 101 for your orientation promptly at oh seven forty-five."

Kira sat up and rolled her neck. She looked up, startled, when Hala started stirring above her. "Hey, did we get a new roommate last night?"

"We did," I confirmed.

As Kira hopped out of bed, Hala sat up, yawning, her

dark hair tousled. "I came in late last night and didn't want to wake you by turning on the lights. I'm Hala Youseff. You must be Kira."

Kira put her hands on her hips and studied Hala. "How did you know that?"

She tipped her head toward me. "Angel heard me come in last night. She filled me in on everyone."

I couldn't be sure, but I thought I saw Kira flush. Embarrassed, maybe, that she'd slept through it.

I climbed down from my bunk. Frankie had the covers pulled over her head and wasn't moving. I tapped her on the leg. "Rise and shine."

Frankie gripped the covers tighter in case I tried to pull them off. "It can't possibly be morning." She peeked out from beneath the covers and saw Hala. Her eyes widened, and she sat up. "Oh, hello. Are you our new roommate?" After a big stretch, she climbed out of bed in her frog pajamas and waved at Hala cheerfully. "I'm Frankie. Nice to meet you."

To her enormous credit, Hala didn't say anything about the wacky pj's. Instead, she grinned and waved back. "Hi, Frankie. Glad to meet you, too."

Frankie peppered her with questions, all of which Hala patiently answered. I headed toward the bathroom, but Kira got there first, so I went through the common room to the front door to see what clothes had been left for us. Four piles of T-shirts and camouflage pants, each of our names neatly pinned to the top T-shirt, were stacked outside the door.

"Hey, guys," I called. "Come look at this."

Everyone except Kira, who was still in the bathroom, crowded around me.

"It's military-issue clothing," Hala said, leaning down to pick up her pile. "Three white T-shirts and three pairs of camouflage pants. I bet they're exactly our size."

Frankie picked up her pile and hugged it to her chest.

"This is the best day ever. I always wanted a pair of genuine camouflage pants."

I had no idea why anyone would want to purposefully own a pair of camouflage pants outside of the military, but what did I know?

I picked up my pile and Kira's, dropping hers on her bed. She came out of the bathroom and I slipped inside, carrying one T-shirt and one pair of pants. Hala was right. The pants and shirt were a perfect fit, even if my reflection made me feel like I was playing soldier.

While I brushed my teeth and washed my face in the outer part of the bathroom, Frankie changed. Hala joined me at the other sink. It felt a bit like being back at home with Gwen, except I hadn't shared a bathroom with anyone since she left for college when I was twelve years old. Given the fact I didn't really know these people, except for Frankie, and I didn't do social well, it was an uncomfortable situation.

I pulled my hair back in a ponytail and put on my socks and shoes. I was tying my shoes when Frankie came out of the bathroom. Fashionista that she is, she'd knotted the bottom of her T-shirt and let it rest on her left hip. Her long dark hair was pulled back into a braid and entwined with what looked like green and brown shoelaces. She stood in front of me and held out her hands.

"So, what do you think?" she asked.

"It's...you," I said. "You really made the outfit your own."

Beaming, she turned around in a circle to show off all sides. "Aren't these camouflage pants the bomb?"

"Um, they're functional."

Hala came out next. She looked about my size, although a little taller. Then I remembered how she'd shot Jonas without hesitation, and I wasn't too worried for her.

Kira was the last to emerge from the bathroom. Somehow, she made camouflage glamorous. Her blonde hair was sleek and smooth and she'd put on makeup. I wouldn't have noticed, except her skin seemed to be glowing and her cheeks looked a lot pinker than they had when she beat me to the bathroom.

We went to the cafeteria together, with Frankie chatting nonstop. The cafeteria smelled like bacon and coffee. Wally and Bo were at one table, shoveling in food, deep in conversation. Mike sat at the table next to them, and Jax sat at the corner table as usual, his back to us and his earbuds in. We introduced Hala to everyone, and even Jax took out his earbuds long enough to say hello. After we got our food, Frankie, Hala, and I sat together, but Kira ignored us and went to sit next to Mike.

Hala leaned over the table, lowering her voice. "What's with her?"

"I think she's scared and lonely," Frankie whispered. "She acts like she doesn't need anyone, but she does. We just have to redouble our efforts to be her friend."

What? Had she lost her mind? "Are you kidding me, Frankie?" Her niceness was getting ridiculous. "That's your assessment of Ms. Prima Donna?"

"Give her a chance, Angel."

I had no intention of doing that, but I pressed my mouth shut and didn't say so. I didn't want to hurt Frankie's feelings, but in my opinion, Kira was nothing but trouble.

"What about the guy in the corner...Jax?" Hala asked.

"He's a loner, too," Frankie offered. "He isn't interested in socializing. But he's sure hot."

"Loners seem to be a theme around here," Hala said.

I was going to confess to my loner status as well, but I wasn't sure it was true now that I had Frankie and

Wally as friends. I didn't expect how happy that would make me.

"So what do you think will happen today?" Frankie asked.

I'd come to breakfast hungry, but now I'd abruptly lost my appetite. I forced down a few bites of oatmeal and some juice, but that was all I could manage. Kira didn't eat much, either. Frankie, Hala, and Bo ate their breakfast without any problem, and I couldn't see what Jax was doing with his back to us. I guess trying out to be a spy wasn't as scary for them as it was for me. Four weeks was already seeming like an eternity if we were going to be on edge the whole time.

Wally pushed back his chair, and I got my first good look at him in camouflage. He looked different, maybe more confident. Maybe the administrators knew what they were doing by putting us in camouflage after all.

As soon as Wally stood, it was like our signal to go. We dumped our trash and returned our trays before heading to Room 101.

I kind of expected something unusual would be in Room 101, like a weapons display, high-tech gadgets, or spy notebooks, but it was just a normal classroom. Several rows of desks, a smartboard, and a teacher's desk. Room 101 could have passed for my English lit class at Excalibur.

We all chose a desk and sat. For a moment it almost seemed as if we were back at Excalibur. I felt the back of my neck prickle like someone was watching me. I turned and caught Jax a couple of desks back, staring at me from the same row.

He lifted a hand and gave me a little wave. "Hey, Red. Hope you're a good student, because I may have to copy off your paper."

I was pretty sure he was a smart guy or he wouldn't be here, so the only logical reason I could fathom for his continued needling was that he was trying to throw me off my game. Maybe he saw me as threat or as significant competition. The only problem—I couldn't figure out why me. I didn't see him doing the same to anyone else, so why had he singled me out?

I didn't respond and turned around in my chair. I wished I'd never insisted he introduce himself, caught sight of his mesmerizing eyes, and stared at him like a star-struck idiot. Maybe just the fact that I'd called him out had made him laser in on me. I made a mental note to never do anything like that again.

I was still thinking about his eyes when Dexter Donovan, aka our limo driver, strode into the room carrying a briefcase.

"Good morning, ladies and gentlemen," he said. "I hope you found your accommodations satisfactory." He looked around. When no one complained, he continued. "I know you're all wondering how we're going to test you for the position of operative. Let me explain. You'll undergo a series of rigorous physical, emotional, and psychological challenges. I won't lie to you—we're looking for a specific type of individual to join UTOP. In order to see how you perform, you'll be given four major trials, to be held every Friday. You're expected to complete them. Testing will be weighted toward those who finish each challenge, but other factors will be considered, as well, though those factors will not be made known to you. UTOP is highly exclusive, which means the challenges will be difficult on many levels. You'll be tested in many different ways. If, at any time, you wish to quit or leave, you have only to let me or one of the trainers know. There's no shame in leaving—as I've told each of you, this job is not for everyone. Your talents may lie elsewhere and be equally as valuable in protecting national security."

He paused and surveyed us. The room was so silent I could hear the analog clock on the wall ticking.

"Just so I'm clear, there's no such thing as failure. About ninety-six percent of UTOP nominees don't make it. Hopefully, your recruiter told you that most of the people unsuited to the life of an operative are excellent fits elsewhere in the community. For example, your testing may indicate you're better suited to the research and analysis sector, computer security, the various language divisions, or communications and surveillance, among many, many other options. Are we clear on that?"

I tried to hide my anxiousness. Those odds were not in my favor, especially after the active-shooter disaster. I had to up my game and keep it up for the rest of my time here.

After we nodded, Mr. Donovan smiled. "Good. Now, what are we looking for in an operative? The answer is simple. Someone who is smart, innovative, can think outside the box, and is persistent. However, the primary goal of an operative is gathering intelligence. It's really as simple as that. So, for the next few days you'll undergo a series of psychological and IQ tests to determine your suitability. I urge you to answer the questions as honestly and as transparently as possible. Say what you think and feel, not what you think we want to hear. Trust me, the nominees who try to fake the tests are the first to wash out. You'll also attend regular classes like the ones you were taking before you came here. We have no intention of letting you fall behind academically."

There were a couple of groans, but Mr. Donovan waved a hand.

"Now, your first trial will be on Friday," he said. "For your downtime, if you have any, feel free to use the gym, the pool, the library, the gaming room, and all the outdoor areas. Equipment can be checked out in the gym. You may not, however, leave the campus until we specifically permit you to do so, which we will every Saturday."

He turned to his briefcase and popped it open. We collectively tensed, having no idea what he had in there, but instead of the machine gun or machete I'd imagined, he pulled out a sheaf of paper. "Your personal schedules are here. Please read them carefully and be on time for all your tests and classes. Everyone has something different to do except for the trial on Friday. Good luck to each and every one of you."

He called out our names one by one, and we picked up our schedules. As soon as we were out in the hall, Wally, Frankie, and I compared ours.

"What do you have first?" I asked Wally.

"Physics," Wally said. "Room 122. I didn't see that one coming. I was sort hoping for Seducing the Enemy or something like that."

Frankie and I laughed, mostly at the idea of Wally seducing anyone successfully. He must have guessed what we were thinking because he looked indignant at our amusement.

"I have Psychological Testing in Room 106," Frankie said. "I wonder what that is. What do you have, Angel?"

"It says Small Group, Room 108. What the heck is that?"

Wally shrugged. "No idea, but I guarantee it will be more exciting than my physics class."

I didn't agree at all. I'd rather read an entire physics textbook than sit in a small group with people I didn't know.

Unfortunately, it looked like I didn't have a choice.

CHAPTER FIFTEEN

Angel Sinclair

"I s this Small Group?" I asked when I arrived at Room 108. Bo and Jax were already seated at a round table. A man with his back to me was sitting with them.

The person with his back to me turned around. He was probably in his fifties, with salt-and-pepper hair and a neatly trimmed beard. He smiled and waved me in.

"Hello, Ms. Sinclair. Please close the door behind you. Our group is now complete."

As instructed, I closed the door and sat in the only chair available between Bo and Jax. My breath hitched in my throat, so I sat on my hands to keep them from showing my nervousness.

"Welcome to Small Group, everyone," the man said. "My name is Jasper Kingston, and I'm your facilitator. What we do today is simple in construct. I'm going to ask each of you some questions. I may ask the same question to more than one person, and perhaps to all three of you. I want you to answer the questions I present as honestly and openly without wondering what I, or your classmates, might think. I warn you, some questions may be personal."

Oh, please no. No, no, no. I wanted to get personal with everyone in this room as much as I wanted a root canal.

Jax leaned forward, frowning. "What's the point of asking personal questions in a group of strangers?"

Mr. Kingston didn't seem perturbed by Jax's question. "Mr. Drummond, I assure you, over the course of the next few weeks, you'll know your classmates better than you ever imagined. Now, shall we continue or does anyone want to excuse themselves from this exercise?"

None of us said anything further, so Mr. Kingston spoke again. "Fine. Mr. Coleman, you get the first question. How would you describe the color blue to someone who is blind?"

"What?" Bo said in confusion.

I exchanged a baffled look with Jax. What kind of question was that? Was this the line of personal questioning Mr. Kingston was talking about? Or was this just to throw us off, to see how we handled the unexpected?

Mr. Kingston patiently repeated his question, either not aware or not caring how bizarre the question sounded. Bo fell silent, likely trying to process. I had no idea how I'd answer the question and hoped fervently I wouldn't have to.

"I guess I would take the blind person's hand and stick it in a bowl of cool water," Bo finally said. "I'd tell them water is blue, the oceans are blue, the sky is blue, and blue is a cool, soothing color."

Mr. Kingston leaned back in his chair. "Interesting. Why did you choose that method of explanation?"

"I don't know. I guess I just figured if they couldn't see, they would have to *feel* the color. That probably doesn't make sense."

Personally, I thought it a clever way to explain color to someone who couldn't see. My respect for Bo went up a notch. But Mr. Kington's expression didn't change, and he didn't say whether it was a good answer or not, so who knew?

"Thank you, Mr. Coleman. Ms. Sinclair, if you were to stack this room in pennies only, what would be the total amount of money?"

"Excuse me?" I stammered. It had only been a few minutes and I was already experiencing mental whiplash. What was with these strange questions?

He repeated the question, adding, "Please explain your calculations aloud."

For a moment, I could only stare at him. It took me a full minute to wrap my head around the question before the rational part of my brain took over. "Um, okay. First I would have to account for the size of the penny. I would estimate the size as nineteen millimeters by nineteen millimeters, with a thickness of 1.5 millimeters. That would make the total volume of the penny 541.5 cubic millimeters."

Mr. Kingston dipped his head indicating he was following, so I continued.

"Then I'd have to determine the size of this room." I turned around in my chair looked at all four corners and the ceiling. "It seems to be about nine meters by nine meters with five meters for ceiling height. Taking that into account, if I divided the penny volume, which is 541.5, into the total volume of the room—I would get the figures of five thousand millimeters times nine thousand millimeters times nine thousand millimeters. That results in a monetary value of $7,479,224.37."

Bo whistled under his breath, but Mr. Kingston's face remained expressionless. "Explain the formula, please," he said.

"The formula is the room volume divided by the

volume of a single penny, divided by one hundred, to get a dollar amount."

"I see. How do you account for the spaces between the pennies?"

"I'm calculating each penny as though it was square, so the space is included in the 541.5 calculation. There's no need to account for it."

"Thank you, Ms. Sinclair." He turned to Jax. "Mr. Drummond, you and your buddies are examining a car engine. The friend to your right says the closed coil end of a valve spring should go against the cylinder head. The buddy to your left says all valve springs use shims to control free-spring height. Who is right?"

Jax snorted and leaned his elbows on the table. "First, all valve springs do *not* use shims to control assembled free-spring height, or any assembled height, for that matter. My buddy on the right is correct. A closed coil end of a valve spring should go against the cylinder head."

"Thank you, Mr. Drummond."

The questioning continued with a series of strange questions to each of us. Bo seemed to get the more odd, abstract questions. Jax got pointed questions about mechanics and engineering. I received math and computer questions. We were never told if we were wrong or right, and Mr. Kingston only asked follow-up questions if he wondered about our method or reasoning.

After at least an hour of this exhausting line of bizarre questioning, the questions suddenly turned more personal.

"So, Mr. Coleman, what would you say is your greatest weakness?" Mr. Kingston asked. "I would like to remind you that we value honesty in this line of questioning, so please keep that in mind when answering."

"My greatest weakness?" Bo asked. He didn't seem as taken aback by the abrupt shift in questioning. Maybe we were all getting better prepared at expecting the unexpected.

"Yes, your greatest weakness," he repeated.

"Well, finally, a question that isn't so hard." Bo relaxed back against his chair. "My family is my weakness. We're a tight-knit unit."

Mr. Kingston clasped his hand on the table. "Explain how a family is a weakness."

"Because they mean the world to me. If someone wanted to hurt them or do wrong to them, it would cloud my judgment, make me susceptible to blackmail."

"Thank you for your honesty, Mr. Coleman." He turned his attention to Jax and studied him. "Mr. Drummond, how would you say your family has handled money and financial matters over the course of your lifetime?"

"Money?" Jax stared at him with disbelief before he broke off laughing. "Wait. That's my personal question? Seriously? You're asking me about money?"

"Yes, Mr. Drummond. I'm asking how your family handled their finances while you were growing up."

"That's the wrong question to ask me." Jax lifted his hands. "There *was* no money. I'm even not sure if my old man had a bank account. If he did, he never shared it with me."

"But the bills were paid, correct?"

"Sometimes. By my mom mostly, and in later years by me. I suppose he handled some of the bills."

"Okay, then I wish to adjust the question. How do *you* handle money, Mr. Drummond?"

"Me? If that's a veiled way of asking me if I have a bank account, I don't. Although you probably already know that. I'm a money-under-the-mattress kind of guy." He snapped his fingers, and a hundred-dollar bill suddenly appeared in them. "I also like to keep spare change in my pocket, just in case."

I gaped at how he'd made the money appear out of thin air, but Mr. Kingston didn't seem surprised in the slightest. "How exactly do you earn that money that goes under the mattress?" he asked.

Jax's fingers tightened on bill, but I might have been the only one who noticed. "Not illegally, if that's what you're asking. I take odd jobs after school and on the weekends. Cutting wood, working on cars, yard work. Sometimes I do construction. Stuff like that."

Mr. Kingston studied Jax. "I see. Are those the jobs that earn you the most money?"

I wondered where Mr. Kingston was going with this line of questioning. Why did it matter whether Jax had money or not?

Jax's face flushed slightly. It seemed like he was struggling with something to say before he finally answered. "No. That's not where I get the good money."

"Where does the 'good money' come from?"

His jaw tightened, and I could almost feel the tension rolling off him. "I get that by tutoring kids after school. Mostly math and physics. Sometimes I help engineering students at the community college. It pays well."

"Do you ever do the homework for the students, Mr. Drummond?"

Jax stiffened but then slowly raised an eyebrow. "Sometimes. If the price is right." His tone was flippant, but I could sense the embarrassment in his words. I swallowed hard, looking down at my hands. This felt wrong, making us expose deeply private things when we hardly knew each other. What was the point?

"Thank you, Mr. Drummond." Mr. Kingston turned to me, and I braced myself for the worst.

"Ms. Sinclair," he said. "Describe yourself at a party that doesn't include a family member. How do you act? Whom do you talk to?"

"A p-party?" I stammered.

"Yes, a social gathering with friends and acquaintances."

"I, um, know what a party is. I just wasn't expecting that question." I hesitated, thinking the best way to approach the odd question. "Well, theoretically, if I had to go to a party, I would probably stand in a corner and not to talk to anyone."

"Okay. Let's not talk theoretically. Give me an example of how you've acted at an actual party in the past."

Dread filled me at having to answer the question. I spoke so quietly, my voice was barely above a whisper. "I've never been to a party before." My cheeks burned in shame.

"All right, then," Mr. Kingston said briskly, as if that embarrassing revelation wasn't worth another moment of his time. "Onto the final round of questioning. Mr. Coleman, if you won a ten-million-dollar lottery prize this afternoon, what would be the first thing you'd spend the money on?"

Bo let out an audible breath, probably thankful he hadn't gotten a weird question. "I'd buy a therapy dog for my older brother. He was in Afghanistan, and he's got some issues. A dog would really help him a lot. We've applied for one, but we're really far down on the list, and it's expensive. But if I had ten million dollars, I'd not only buy the dog, but I'd hire a full-time trainer and a physical therapist to work with him."

"Your nation is grateful for your brother's service," Mr. Kingston said.

Bo nodded his head and pressed his lips together. My heart squeezed in sympathy.

"Ms. Sinclair?"

I jerked my head up. "Yes?"

"What about you? What would be the first thing you bought with ten million dollars?"

Several possibilities flashed through my mind, but they always came back to one thing. Mr. Kingston had asked us to be honest, so that's what I would be. I clenched my hands in my lap and summoned the courage to speak the truth.

My truth.

"I'd use it to find out what happened to my dad," I said. "He, ah, disappeared when I was little. So I'd hire private detectives and spend whatever it took to find out what happened to him. Whatever was left over, I'd give to my mom."

"I see." His tone was nonjudgmental, but I felt mortified and more than a little sick to my stomach. How much further would they crack us open and let us spill out in order to understand what made us tick?

But Mr. Kingston had already moved on. "Mr. Drummond, how about you? How would you spend the ten-million-dollar prize?"

Jax laughed. "That's an easy answer. Fast cars, fast women, and a fast life."

"I see. Is that your final answer?"

"It is, unless you clarify the question."

Mr. Kingston raised an eyebrow. "Explain."

"You changed up the question for me. You didn't ask me what would be the *first* thing I spent the money on. You just asked me what I would spend it on in general."

Mr. Kingston nodded, a flash of interest sparking in his eyes. "I stand corrected. I so revise my question to you. What would be the *first* thing you spent your money on?"

"I'd buy something for my mom." This time around, Jax's voice was oddly devoid of sarcasm.

"And what would that something be?" Mr. Kingston pressed.

"Seriously?" Jax looked at him incredulously. "You need to know *exactly* what I'd buy my mom?"

"Yes. Exactly."

Jax paused for so long I didn't think he was going to answer. Finally, he spoke, his voice so soft I had to lean forward to hear it. "A headstone, okay? I'd buy her the biggest, most beautiful marble headstone in the entire cemetery. Satisfied?"

"Quite." Mr. Kingston snapped his briefcase shut and stood. "Thank you, students. This concludes our session for today. I appreciate your candid answers. I'll see you tomorrow. You're free to go."

He abruptly left, leaving the three of us sitting there in dazed silence, gutted and more than a little embarrassed about what we'd just revealed about ourselves. I had to close my eyes for a moment to regain my composure.

Jax was the first to leave, shoving back from the table and slamming the door on his way out.

Bo reached over and patted my hand. "You okay, Angel?"

It was a kind word from a guy I didn't know, and I while I appreciated it, mortification swamped me. I'd been emotionally exposed in front of strangers, and the way I felt about that was too raw and uncomfortable for me to process at the moment. I nodded at Bo, unable to speak past the lump clogging my throat. Without another word, I left, leaving him sitting there alone with his thoughts.

This UTOP thing was turning out to be a lot harder than I'd expected.

CHAPTER SIXTEEN

Angel Sinclair

I had twenty minutes before I had to report to Room 111 for Psychological Testing, so I headed outside to the garden area. I had no idea what testing would entail, but I needed to regain my composure and get some fresh air to clear my head. It wasn't a good sign that I was so shaky after the first round of testing. I wasn't sure what I'd thought would happen, but getting so personal, so fast was shocking for an intensely private person like myself. I felt weirdly vulnerable, knowing that people were walking around judging me.

It was a lovely fall day and the sun was shining, but the air had a cool edge to it. Instead of regretting not having a sweatshirt, I welcomed the coolness. A couple of deep breaths and I felt better. I walked through the garden and headed into the maze. I hadn't taken but a few steps when I collided with someone.

"Jax?" I said. Apparently we'd had the same idea about where to go to clear our heads.

"Red? What are you doing out here?"

"I'm getting some fresh air before the next class. I…thought I would be alone. I didn't know you were here."

"Sure you're not following me?"

I bristled. "I'm positive."

"Lighten up, I was just joking. Come on. Walk with me." He strode off, not even waiting to see if I'd agree. I hesitated but knew a part of succeeding at the trials would be knowing our peers and how to best compete against them. Maybe that had been the purpose of the personal questioning. The teachers were offering us a glimpse into each other's strengths and weaknesses so we could exploit them. It suddenly made me feel sick. Maybe I wasn't cut out to be an operative after all.

Jax stopped and turned around. "You coming?"

Part of me wanted to walk away, but I couldn't afford to isolate myself from the other candidates. I had to jog slightly to catch up to him.

We walked for a while without saying anything. Suddenly he looked at me out of the corner of his eye and asked, "So, you've never been to a party? Really?"

I froze midstep, embarrassed. Jax, perhaps sensing my discomfort, touched my arm lightly, his fingers warm against my bare skin. When he pulled back from my arm, a pink rose appeared in his fingers. He presented it to me. "Don't be mad. I'm intrigued by you, that's all. You seem so…genuine. In a world of fakes, that's refreshing. By the way, be careful of the rose—it has thorns."

I looked down at the flower, then at him. "How did you do that?"

He snapped his fingers, and another rose appeared. He lifted an eyebrow and handed it over. "It's magic."

"You can do magic tricks?"

His smile melted into a frown. "A true magician doesn't call them tricks. They're illusions."

I sniffed the rose, impressed. It was real. He was good at this sleight of hand. Really good.

"So, what did you think of that question-and-answer session back there?" he asked.

I held on to the roses as we resumed walking. "I don't know. It was different." Actually, it had been more than different. It'd been an emotional stripping down that I hadn't expected and hoped I would never have to endure again. Unfortunately, I had a feeling I wouldn't get my wish.

"They're testing our mental response time and honesty." He reached down and picked up an acorn, skipping it along the ground. "You noticed how carefully they tailored each question to our strengths and weaknesses. I didn't know you were such a math and computer genius."

"I'm not a genius. Well, at least I don't feel like one. Math and computers just make sense to me. Probably in the same way a car engine and certain engineering concepts make sense to you."

"Yeah, well, just when we were getting in the rhythm of the thing, they dropped the personal questions bomb. It wasn't really fair play."

"I agree. They're probably judging our emotional flexibility," I said.

"Perhaps. Whatever you want to call it, it sucked."

"No argument from me there. What class do you have next?"

"Who knows? I'm supposed to report to the gym. What about you?"

I shrugged. "Psychological Testing, whatever that means."

"More mind games." He studied me for a moment. "You held your own back there, Red. Good for you."

"Thanks, but my name's Angel, and you did, too."

His expression abruptly shuttered, as if he weren't

used to hearing compliments. "I've got to get back. See you around."

He started to walk away when I called out to him. "Hey, Jax, I'm sorry about your mom."

He froze, and I wondered if I'd offended him. After a moment, he glanced over his shoulder and shrugged. "Don't be. She got the better end of the deal."

CHAPTER SEVENTEEN

Candace Kim

NSA Headquarters, Fort Meade, Maryland

"Thanks for stopping by, Slash."

"No problem," he answered. "I'm happy to help. Any progress on the Avenger front?"

"A lot, which is why I asked you to stop by."

Candace appreciated his insight on the situation, which she found unusual since she knew him the least of all the directors at the NSA. Slash was new to his position, having only recently been elevated to director, an impressive promotion that had raised more than a few eyebrows given his age, background, and number of years at the agency. But she'd seen him at work firsthand during several sensitive, high-pressure situations, and he'd handled them all with expertise, brilliance, and calm. Her gut also told her that he was a good guy, and she always trusted her gut.

She rose from her desk and shook his hand. "We just had another exchange where we told him we had tentative approval from the Justice Department on the immunity issue, assuming he followed through on our demands. He said he's willing to deal."

"You're convinced the Hidden Avenger is Ethan Sinclair?"

"I'm convinced. I just need him to confirm it for us." She invited him to sit, and he did, but she remained standing and walked over to the window.

"So, what's next?" he asked.

Candace looked out at the view. The autumn colors had turned the forest surrounding the NSA compound into a beautiful riot of yellow, orange, and red, but these days she was too tense to enjoy it. Sighing, she turned around to face him again. "Well, the Justice Department has said that if it *is* Ethan Sinclair, they're willing to arrange protection for his family through the US Marshals' Witness Security Program for a period of up to six months."

"That's good news. How does it affect the daughter Angel Sinclair? She's currently in the UTOP trials."

Candace knew that. She also knew that while Slash would want to keep the entire family safe from whatever threatened them, she wondered if he had a special connection to the girl. She knew Slash's fiancée mentored Angel at her company and that he'd been front and center when the girl had brought down the Iraqi hacker. She also knew he'd personally invited her to UTOP. But just how invested was he in her and her future?

"How's she doing at UTOP?" Candace asked.

"It's just starting, but I have full confidence in her."

"Good for her, and good for you for nominating her. We could use more women operatives, especially tech-savvy ones."

"That we could," he agreed.

She hesitated and then plunged forward with her question. "Do you mind if I ask how you know Angel Sinclair?"

A guarded look came into his eyes. This was not a man who would easily share information, especially personal information, so she was gratified when he responded. "I'm friends with her older sister, Gwen, who works at ComQuest in Baltimore as a microbiologist. Gwen and Angel helped my fiancée and me with a project. I was impressed by Angel's skill and capability behind the keyboard, especially given her age."

That wasn't anything Candace couldn't have found out herself, but she appreciated that he'd offered it. "I'm satisfied she's protected for now at the UTOP compound. Are you?"

"I am," he replied. "But what about the rest of the family?"

"They're already under protective surveillance. But Ethan will need to provide further information about himself before this goes any further."

"What kind of information?"

"For one, why he bolted and why he slapped ShadowCrypt on the back door."

Slash steepled his fingers together, regarded her. "You may not want to hear what he has to say."

She understood what he was getting at. Examining whether or not the NSA—or certain employees within the agency—had overstepped the boundaries regarding spying on US citizens would be a highly delicate matter to navigate, especially internally. "Actually, I do. If we need to clean house, then we're going to do it."

He didn't respond, but she thought she saw a flash of approval in his eyes. Good, because if she had to take a close look inside the NSA as part of bringing Ethan in, she'd need all the friends she could get.

"The director has agreed to the private one-on-one meeting with Ethan," she continued. "He's curious, as am I, as to what's going on."

"There's more to his story," Slash said. "He's going

to want any assurances in writing and will most certainly have anything reviewed and verified by a lawyer," Slash pointed out.

"We'll do it. I'm going to bring him in." She perched on a corner of her desk and folded her arms against her chest. "So, there's something else. He's trying to tell us something. I've got some of our best analysts looking at it, but nothing yet. I've got two code words from him so far—Ahab and Pope 264. Do those things mean anything to you? Any clue what Sinclair is trying to communicate?"

Slash considered. "Ahab from the Bible or of *Moby Dick* fame?"

"My question exactly. *Moby Dick*, I think. I wasn't sure until he said the words 'Ahoy, Ahab,' which, to me, indicates that's the connection."

"Hmmm. Pope 264 is Saint John Paul II. The 264th pope."

She hadn't expected that quick of a response from him. Perhaps she should have. She recalled he had an Italian background, and Italy was a heavily Catholic country. "You're Catholic?" she asked.

"I am." He slipped a cross out from beneath his shirt, kissing it before tucking it back under.

She smiled. "Well, that explains that, I suppose. And, yes, we determined it was John Paul II. Unless there's something else to it I'm not seeing. But what do a captain on a whaling boat and a Catholic pope have in common?" It sounded like a bad joke when she said it out loud, but Slash didn't smile.

"I don't know. I'll give it some thought."

"Thanks. Given your expertise, I'd appreciate it." She walked over to the chair next to Slash and sat down. "I have another problem, as well. Isaac has inserted himself deeper into the investigation. He's a loose cannon. I'd shut him out, but I can't without asking the director to support me, and I don't want to do that except as a last resort. He doesn't need to hear his directors are squabbling. Isaac was there during our last communication and sent a message to Sinclair without my permission. He told Sinclair there were elements in the NSA who considered him a traitor. Isaac is starting to worry me. His dislike for Sinclair seems personal, and I don't like that."

"My guess is Isaac has his eyes on the directorship, and if you bring Ethan in, you could be a threat to that."

She felt her forehead tighten as she acknowledged his words. "That's not what this is about. What Ethan Sinclair knows, and has, is vital to the security of this nation. Regardless of who is director, the mission of the NSA, and its many fine people, will continue. But I'll be devastated for this agency if our internal politics cause us to fail in stopping a major terrorist attack. I couldn't explain that to the president, to my family, or to anyone. We're better than that. We *have* to be better than that."

"We will be." He rested his elbows on his thighs, the expression on his face thoughtful. "However, that still doesn't resolve the problem. Ethan doesn't know who to trust within the agency, which means he thinks there are people on the inside who are not trustworthy."

"Agreed. He doesn't know who is on whose side."

"Neither do we," Slash replied.

That was the core of the problem. No one on either side knew who was trustworthy in or out of the agency.

"If we're looking inward, I wonder how the fact that Isaac was Ethan's boss at the time plays into things," she mused. "I've reviewed Ethan's file multiple times. Other than the fact that Isaac was Ethan's supervisor at King's Security, nothing else has popped."

"Then there's something we're missing. If you'd like, I'm happy to take another look." He rose, so she did, too.

"I'd like that very much. Thank you for your help. I'll send the files over to you first thing in the morning."

He started to leave, but she stopped him. "Slash, there's something going on inside the NSA. It's hard to know who to trust. I want you to know I've made a decision to trust you with helping me find and safely bring in the Hidden Avenger. I hope that trust is reciprocated."

He studied her face for a long moment, as if weighing whether she met his criteria for credibility. Finally he nodded. "It is. I'll let you know if I find anything."

CHAPTER EIGHTEEN

Angel Sinclair

I reported for Psychological Testing and sat stiffly in a chair across from Mrs. Thompson, who had brown hair and a nice smile. I wondered if Thompson was her real name. Probably not, although it didn't really matter. She gave me a bottle of water, which I drank until it was empty, while she chatted about the weather and the Redskins, apparently attempting to put me at ease.

It wasn't working.

We were seated at a table that was too big for us. The lighting was dim and there was a dark window across one of the walls, where I assumed whoever was grading my responses would be watching. I was scared, but of what, I wasn't sure. Regardless, the mere fact that I would be doing this alone and not in front of my classmates was a relief. I put on my best game face, figuring if I were going to be an operative, I needed a better poker face for these kinds of things.

"Angel, I know you're nervous, but I want you to relax," she said. "We're just going to play a game.

Okay?" Her calling me by my first name put me a fraction more at ease.

"Okay."

"Great. I'm going to give you a word, and I want you to tell me the first word that pops into your mind that you associate with it. There are no right or wrong answers. This game just helps us see the way your mind works. But it's quite important you don't stop to consider your answer. It must be the first thing that pops into your mind. You need to answer within a one-second time frame. Do you understand?"

"Yes. I've done word-association games before."

"Excellent. Then you'll be a natural."

I didn't share her confidence, but I clasped my hands on the table in front of me and steadied myself.

"Here we go," she said. "Are you ready?"

"I'm ready."

She glanced down at the paper in front of her. "Attack."

"Hackers," I responded.

"Problem."

"Solve."

"Lead."

"Myself."

She paused, giving me a moment. Or maybe there was another reason she paused. I didn't have time to wonder because she said, "Mother."

"Protect." It slipped out. I hadn't expected that to come out of my mouth, but there it was.

"Beware."

"Liars."

"Alone."

"Safe."

"Friends."

That one was easy for me. "White Knights."

"Government."

"Secrets."

There was another slight hesitation before she said, "Father."

I fell silent and stared at the table. It was as if my brain had abruptly clicked off.

After a moment, she repeated the word. "Father."

I blinked, then looked at her. "Alive."

CHAPTER NINETEEN
Angel Sinclair

The rest of my day involved digital fingerprinting, a quick lunch, a private tutoring session in cryptology—the highlight of the day—then a medical examination by a nice female doctor, a chemistry class with Mike, an English literature class with Hala, Wally, and Kira, and a physical fitness exam with a buff military-looking guy. By the time it was over, I was a hot mess.

When I got back to the dorm room, Frankie and Hala were already there. Frankie was lying on the bed with a washcloth on her forehead. Hala was working on a laptop at her desk. Kira was nowhere to be seen, as usual.

"Hey, guys," I said, perching on the corner of Frankie's mattress. "Everyone okay?"

Frankie lifted the washcloth off her face. "I'm alive, but the physical fitness exam nearly killed me. Did you have to run the mile?"

I nodded. "I did. Don't ask me how long it took."

"As long as you don't ask me. Hala, how did you do?"

111

She turned around from the screen. "The physical fitness test was the easy part for me today. I was on the gymnastics team at my high school. We trained a lot, so I'm in pretty good shape. The hard part for me was all that weird psychological testing."

"It was brutal," I agreed.

"Oh, that was my favorite part," Frankie said, sitting up. "It was fun."

"Fun?" I looked at her as if she'd lost her mind. "Are you nuts? That was *not* fun, Frankie."

"Of course, it was. We just had to answer a bunch of questions about ourselves."

"Did you have a group session?" I asked.

"Yes, it was Mike and me. It was cool. I like Mike. He's a really interesting guy."

Frankie liked everyone, so that didn't mean anything special. She was my closest friend, but her definition of fun and mine didn't always match. I met Hala's skeptical gaze over Frankie's head.

"I have a chemistry class with Bo and Jax," Hala said. "And English lit with you, Wally, and Kira. But I'm by myself in an acting class."

"Acting?" That seemed an odd choice of curriculum to me, but everything seemed strange lately.

"That was my reaction, too," Hala said.

"I have a class by myself, too," Frankie offered. "Graphic design."

"I'm in a class by myself for cryptology," I said. "I wonder what all that means."

"Maybe they're playing to what they perceive are our strengths," Hala answered. "Although I've never had an acting class before in my life."

None of us had answers, so we started our homework. Kira never showed up, and I wondered what she was doing. When it was time for dinner, we walked over to the cafeteria together. Kira was there, deep in conversation with Jax at a table in the back. Their heads were bent together, his dark and her blonde. It was a striking sight, like the two of them could pose for the cover of a magazine. They spoke earnestly, gesturing with their hands but keeping their voices lowered. I forced myself to look away.

Wally was sitting with Mike and Bo. Hala joined them with her food tray. There was no more room for Frankie and me at their table, so we sat at an empty table after we got our food. After a few minutes, Wally came over to sit with us so he could talk to us about our day.

"The physical fitness test was the absolute worst," Wally said. "Kira was being tested in another part of the gym and she did, like, twenty chin-ups. I couldn't even do one."

"Don't worry," I said. "I couldn't do one, either."

"Me neither," Frankie added. "But the trainer was nice anyway. Do you know he has two-year-old twins? He showed me their photos on his phone. They're so adorable, but he and his wife don't sleep much. The poor man has bags the size of Alaska under his eyes. I felt sorry for him until he made me run that mile."

"All I can say is that we're in real trouble, guys." Wally shook his head. "We'll never be operatives if we can't jump from one building to another like James Bond."

"Let's be clear, I'm not jumping from a building. Ever." I picked up an orange slice and ate it. "Let's not blow this out of proportion. It could be they were just getting a baseline, like they did with the active-shooter scenario."

"Which was another disaster," Wally said. "I hope they don't send me packing."

"No one is going home yet, Wally," Frankie said. "It's only been one day. How did the rest of your day go?"

113

"Oh, you mean the part where I answer bizarre questions and spill my guts in front of two pretty girls?"

"You're always spilling your guts to us, and we still like you," Frankie pointed out.

That made me laugh. Leave it to Frankie to keep it real. "Frankie's got a point. We need to calm down and let this play out. Mr. Donovan told us to do our best. It's the only thing we can control."

After dinner, we headed back to our room. I wanted to do some online surfing and go to bed early. Frankie wanted to read, and Hala told us she was going to go to gym and work off some steam. Kira, as usual, was missing.

"What's with Kira anyway?" I asked. "She lives with us, but we never see her. It's like she's avoiding us on purpose."

"She always seems to be missing at the same time as Jax. Did you notice that?"

I'd noticed, but I didn't want her to know I noticed. "Hmmm…" I said noncommittally.

"Or it could be that she's just scared and lonely and Jax is nice to her."

It was possible. Frankie always thought the best of people, but I didn't, so we weren't always going to agree on things like that.

Frankie opened her book, and I booted up my laptop and began reading my father's thesis from MIT, *Asymmetrical Cryptography: Authentication and Encryption.* It was heavy reading, but somehow, it helped me feel closer to him.

Hala came back after her workout, showered, and got into her pajamas. I shut down my laptop and got into my pajamas, too. Frankie was already tucked under the covers, still reading.

I was just going to the bathroom to brush my teeth when Kira walked in. She went to a drawer, picked out her pajamas, and went into the bathroom to change without saying a single word to any of us. Shrugging, I stood at one of the sinks in the outer part of the bathroom and started brushing my teeth.

Kira came out in her pj's and washed her face and brushed her teeth at the adjoining sink. She didn't say a word to me, and I had no idea what her problem was. When I exited the bathroom, Frankie was cheerfully asking Kira questions about her day.

Kira was ignoring her until finally she turned around in exasperation. "Look, would you just stop trying to engage me? I'm *not* your friend. I don't know you, and I don't *want* to know you. We're all forced to share this room, so let's do it as clinically as possible. You can stop all the pretend friendliness crap."

I strode to stand between her and Frankie. "Back off, Kira. It's not pretend for Frankie. She's actually nice."

"It's okay, Angel," Frankie said quietly. "She's right. I can be overly friendly."

"No. It's *not* okay for her to talk to you like that." I glared at Kira. "She can show some common decency. I'm not a people person, either, but that doesn't give me license to be rude."

Hala scaled down from her bunk in a pair of blue silk pajamas and came between Kira and me, holding out her hands. "Look, guys, it's been a long day and everyone is tired and stressed out. How about we get some sleep?"

"Best idea I've heard all day." Kira crawled into her bed and turned her back to us, facing the wall.

I exchanged a glance with Hala, who shrugged. Frankie resumed reading, not seeming upset by the incident whatsoever. Did anything ever bother her?

I climbed up to my bunk and lay on my back, staring at the ceiling, still fuming at Kira's rudeness.

What the heck was wrong with people?

As I lay there, I realized I missed my own bed, my mom, Gwen, and even Mr. Toodles. For the first time, I seriously wondered if I was doing the right thing by trying out for UTOP.

What am I doing here?

What did Slash see in me that I can't see in myself?

Do I really have what it takes to be an operative?

My thoughts drifted to my father. Had he been a spy, and if so, was that why he'd vanished without a word, leaving us behind? If he were alive, why wouldn't he come home?

I rolled over and punched my pillow. Whatever the answers to the questions, I knew one thing. I wasn't a quitter.

I intended to give UTOP my best shot, however far that took me.

CHAPTER TWENTY

Isaac Remington

"We've got a problem," Remington fumed, his fist tightening on his burner phone. He'd have to buy stock in an expendable phone-making company if this blasted situation continued much longer. "The Justice Department and the director have agreed to all his terms. The idiots! Don't they see how he's trying to manipulate them?"

"Sinclair is a dangerous loose end."

"I know. I wish the director had retired years ago, so that someone with the guts to defend our country could take the reins and finally whip NSA into shape."

"That would be hard to do without removing the ShadowCrypt patch. Now the patch is apparently within reach, along with Sinclair."

"It's within Candace Kim's reach," he spit out. He could feel his blood pressure rising. "They're even talking about putting the family in WITSEC, on his request."

There was a moment of silence before his accomplice spoke. "We need to get our hands on Sinclair soon or things could get real complicated."

"Don't I know it. We need to know what he has on us in terms of proof. Do you think he can tie us to Lando's boating accident?" That was the real sticking point, wasn't it? If only he could be sure of what Sinclair had. "Although, if he had proof back then, he wouldn't have vanished. He's bluffing."

"It's a risk to assume that."

"Perhaps, which is why we need his youngest daughter to draw him out. We know he's already reached out to her once, so we should assume he might do it again."

"What about the other daughter or the wife? Can they be leveraged?" There was a noise in the background, a car honking and the squeal of tires.

"They could, and that's the backup plan, but neither of them appear to be actively trying to find him," Isaac explained. "The youngest daughter is poking around places and causing trouble. She's given us some of our best leads on him. Now he's reached out to her and made contact for the first time in fourteen years. That's huge. She's the key to this thing."

"So, what's our next step?"

"Tell the others we need a two-pronged approach." Isaac considered his words carefully. He'd thought everything out and had planned this for a long time. "On the one front, we've got to use the girl to bring him out of hiding. On the other front, I must discredit Sinclair with the Justice Department. It shouldn't be hard. Once everything quiets down, we find him and make him disappear for good."

"How are you going to get at the daughter? She's behind the security perimeter at UTOP."

"Every day except Saturday, when the candidates go into town for their weekly break."

There was a short pause. "Good point. I hadn't thought of that."

Isaac suppressed a sharp retort. It shouldn't be this hard. Did he have to spell everything out? Didn't anyone else share his forward-thinking vision? He kept his voice even, patient. "Yes. So, if we need to do something, we do it then. She's the leverage we need. Then, after a family accident, there'll be no more problems or witnesses left to worry about."

"Oh. Do you think they could connect his disappearance back to us? After all, you've been pretty vocal about your dislike for him."

He hated the weak spirit of his compatriots. Fixing that would be a priority when he became director. "Please. Sinclair has been backdooring terrorists for years. I don't think it would be too difficult to imagine a scenario where certain factions weren't happy with him when he's found out. A sudden, permanent disappearance shouldn't be any surprise at all. We simply blame it on the terrorists, and that's the end of that."

A longer pause and then a laugh. "Wow, that's ingenious."

Isaac smiled. At last they were seeing what he was capable of doing for the nation. "And that's exactly why I'll be a formidable director."

CHAPTER TWENTY-ONE

Angel Sinclair

The rest of the week was essentially the same as the first day. More group sessions with grueling questions, psychological testing, exercising in the gym, and classes with homework. To say it was brutal would be an understatement. Added to the mix were written tests, which I assumed were IQ tests. Those I didn't worry about. I'd always tested well, so that was one concern I felt I could put to rest.

I spent what little downtime I had gaming in the gaming room, doing my homework, washing my clothes, or hanging out with Frankie and Wally. There wasn't much free time to be had, and when we were together, it was obvious we were all becoming increasingly nervous about Friday and the first trial.

On Thursday morning, during the group session with Jax and Bo, Mr. Kingston told us today our session would consist of only one question and we'd have free time until our next class. That was good news to me, because the group session was the hardest for me to manage every day. One question would be a walk in the park.

"So, Mr. Coleman, I have a scenario for you," Mr. Kingston said, adjusting his tie. "Your mother is desperately ill. A pharmaceutical company, located two blocks from your house, has a cure to your mother's illness. The medicine is too expensive for you to afford. If you could break into the company building and steal the medicine without the slightest fear of repercussion, would you do it?"

"No repercussions?" he asked.

"None. You would get away with it completely, and your mother would be cured."

"Oh, man." Bo sighed, rubbed his forehead. "It would be tempting, but I wouldn't do it. It wouldn't be right. It wouldn't be honorable. It's not the way my mom raised me. She wouldn't want me to steal."

"So, is that a no?" Mr. Kingston asked.

"It's a no."

"Thank you, Mr. Coleman. Ms. Sinclair. How about you?"

I considered. "Is it a terminal illness?"

Mr. Kingston shrugged. "That's unknown."

My mind went through a number of scenarios, none with a clean answer. "I have mixed feelings about this," I finally said. "Legally and morally, it's wrong. But we're talking about helping someone I love. I honestly don't know what I'd do unless I was in the situation, at that very moment. But I have to say I'm leaning toward stealing the medicine, especially if there are no repercussions."

"So, is that a yes or a no?" Mr. Kingston tapped his pencil on the table. "I'm afraid I can't take ambiguity as an answer."

I sighed. "It's a yes."

"Okay. What about you, Mr. Drummond?"

"Seriously?" Jax looked in astonishment at Bo and

me. "You guys have to think about your answer? It's a dilemma for you people? I'd take the medicine in a heartbeat. No repercussions, a life saved. The wealthy pharmaceutical company wouldn't even notice."

"That's not the point," Bo said. "You're stealing."

"For a good cause," Jax countered.

Bo shook his head. "It's not honorable."

"Who cares about honor?" Jax's eyes gleamed. "It's about survival. Either you're willing to play to live...or you die."

He had a point, but it was a cold, hard one. Jax remained a mystery to me. Tough, smart, sardonic, yet...I saw a sadness in his eyes. I knew his mother had died, but I wondered about the circumstances.

The room fell silent, and Mr. Kingston stood. "Well, thank you, students. That's it for today. I won't see you until next week. Good luck to each of you with the trial tomorrow."

We were silent as we filed out. These tests were showing us how different we were from each other. I didn't know if that was a good or a bad thing. How were we being scored? Was I meeting the criteria for an operative? It was hard to say when you didn't even know exactly what they were looking for.

I didn't feel like going back to the room, and it was drizzling outside, so I decided to go to the small library. Two comfortable-looking armchairs, three circular tables, and a couple of floor lamps were arranged near the bookshelves. The library was empty, except for a young woman sitting behind the circulation desk who looked up from her laptop when I strolled in.

"Hello, Angel," she said cheerfully. "Let me know if I can help you find anything."

"You know my name?" I asked. I was sure I'd never seen her before.

"Of course. There are only eight of you this session.

What are you looking for?"

"Can I check out any book I want?" I asked.

"Sure. It's just like a normal library."

"Cool. Do you have any books on coding?"

"We sure do. Those shelves over there," she said, pointing. "You'll find everything computer-related in that area."

I thanked her and perused the titles in the area she'd mentioned. When I came out holding a book, Mike was sitting at one of the tables. He looked up when he saw me. He was dressed in the same white T-shirt and camouflage as I was, but the bling on his fingers and the studs in his ears were missing. The nose ring was still in place, however. Maybe that wasn't removable.

"Hey, Mike," I said awkwardly, noting he was reading a manual called *Advanced Lockpicking Secrets.* "How are you?"

"I'm okay," he answered, equally awkward. "Are you, um, doing okay with the chemistry homework?"

"Yeah, it's easy so far."

"I noticed you're really good at chemistry. Me too. Wonder when they're going to start challenging us."

I shrugged. "Maybe we're challenged enough on other fronts."

"Maybe."

"Well, I'll see you around." I started to pass him.

He put out a hand, and I stopped. "Hey, Angel, can I ask you something?"

"Sure."

"Do you have a class by yourself? I mean, we're in chemistry together, and I'm in another class with some of the other kids, but do you have one just by yourself?"

"Yes. I think we all do. I've got cryptology, Frankie has graphic design, Wally is focusing on malware, and Hala has acting, of all things. I don't know about Kira, Jax, or Bo. What do you have?"

"Circuit design with a side of laser and optical engineering. It's awesome."

"Wow," I said, my eyes widening. "That's...different."

"I know, right? You guys all seem to be experts in computers and math, and I'm all about circuits, fuses, and superconductors."

I looked down at the book on the table. "And lockpicking."

He followed my gaze and laughed. "Nah, that's just for fun. You know, I may not be an expert in computers, but I love to play chess and I can navigate a mean game of *Hidden Realm*, if you want a challenge sometime. You're quite the gamer."

I stared at him. "How did you know that?"

"I've watched you play." It suddenly occurred to him that maybe that sounded more than just a little creepy. His face turned a shade of scarlet. "I mean, I wasn't stalking you or anything. I was headed to the gaming room once, but you were already there playing. So, I watched you play through the window without interrupting you...and okay, and that *does* sound stalkerish. But I swear, there was no creep factor involved. I just didn't want to break your concentration, that's all. You're really good."

"Thanks. Next time, if you want to play, just come in and let me know."

"Deal."

I left him, thinking he wasn't anything like I'd expected when I first saw him, and went to my next class. The rest of the day passed without incident. After dinner, Wally talked Frankie and me into going to the gym to work out, which in itself was a shock. Wally convincing us to go to the gym. Would miracles never cease?

When we got to the gym, Bo and Jax were wrestling each other again. Both guys were in muscle shirts and soft shorts. It looked like they'd been at it awhile, because they were both sweating heavily.

Kira was running on the treadmill with earbuds in. Wally stopped to watch her. It occurred to me that *this* was why Wally had wanted to go to the gym—to watch Kira. Apparently this was where she spent most of her free time, driving herself to physical perfection.

Still keeping an eye on Kira, Wally and Frankie went to check out the hand weights, while I stayed to watch Jax and Bo go at it for a few more minutes.

Bo was bigger and stronger, but Jax was fast. A couple of moves later, Bo had Jax nearly pinned to the ground. Jax reached up and yanked hard on Bo's ear.

"Ouch," Bo roared, his grip loosening. Jax was able to slip out of his hold. "That's cheating."

Jax laughed and tossed his dark hair out of his eyes. "Only if we were playing a legal match. That's not what we're at this school for. If I'm an operative and I'm wrestling someone, I'm trying to survive. You need to learn how to play dirty, Bo. I'm not playing by your or anyone else's rules."

Bo shook his head indignantly and grabbed a towel before leaving the mat and heading over to the weights.

I thought about what Jax had said. Survival at all cost—wasn't that an important thing for all of us to learn? But just what would he be willing to sacrifice for that? It was a question to which I didn't have an answer.

Jax saw me watching and crooked the fingers on one hand at me in a come-hither motion. "Hey, Red, want to give it a go?"

I crossed my arms against my chest. "No."

"Too bad. I could teach you some helpful self-defense moves, you know."

When I stood my ground, he shrugged, grabbed a towel, and headed for the men's locker room.

Did he want to help me or learn my weaknesses? He had to have seen me at work with the weights and know

I couldn't wrestle my way out of a paper bag. Why couldn't I figure out what he wanted from me?

After a moment of contemplation, I looked around the gym and decided to jog on the treadmill. I chose the one the farthest away from Kira, who didn't even glance my way when I got started.

An hour later, I was soaked in sweat and dead tired. My legs were shaking. Frankie and Wally looked worse than me. They'd lifted weights for a while and then spent time on the treadmill and elliptical machine. Kira had disappeared, probably to take her shower before we got back to the room, so she could get in bed and safely ignore us.

When the gym closed, we walked back to our rooms, groaning and complaining the entire way.

"They're going to dump me," Wally said, wiping his beet-red face. "Frankie can lift more than me."

"No one cares about that," Frankie said.

"I care!" Wally protested.

I rubbed the back of my neck. "Look, guys, I sincerely doubt tomorrow will be a weight-lifting exercise."

"It better not be." Wally swung his arms around. "Or I'm toast. On the upside, I'm so exhausted, I shouldn't have any trouble falling asleep tonight, despite my crippling insecurity about my physical prowess. Waking up may be a problem, though."

"You'll both do fine," Frankie said. "We all will. You're worrying too much. Whatever comes, we'll figure it out. We always do."

I wanted to contradict her, but the truth was, I liked her optimism. I *needed* her faith in me, now more than ever.

We were the White Knights. Together we could conquer all.

"Thanks, Frankie," I said. "What would we do without you?"

CHAPTER TWENTY-TWO

Angel Sinclair

D espite my exhaustion, I didn't sleep well Thursday night. Kira and Hala were both tossing and turning, too, so I suspected they were also anxious. Only Frankie slept blissfully. When she woke, she was her usual cheerful self, although she mentioned her muscles were a bit sore.

We ate breakfast, although most of us could barely choke anything down, then assembled in Room 101 for orientation.

Once we were present and seated, Mr. Donovan entered the room. "Good morning, candidates. Today will be your first trial. We wish you the best of luck. Now, I ask you to please rise and remain still while we prepare you."

I stood up hesitantly, not sure what he meant by "prepare." Jonas, the student who had pretended to be the assassin in the active-shooter scenario, came up behind each one of us and arranged blacked-out goggles tightly over our eyes.

"From this moment until we reach our destination,

you're not to remove the goggles or speak to each other," Mr. Donovan instructed us. "If you're caught doing either, you're immediately disqualified."

Someone took my hand and led me down the hallway and outside, where I could hear the birds chirping. "Watch your head," a woman said, as she lifted my leg and helped me up into what was likely a bus or a van. I was instructed to sit, so I did. Someone slid in beside me. I had no idea who it was.

When we were all loaded, the vehicle took off. I calculated a less than five-minute ride, so wherever we were going, it was close. I suspected we were being brought somewhere on the UTOP campus.

The vehicle halted, and we were taken off the bus one by one. We must have walked into a building, because a blast of cool air hit my face. We walked a bit more before I heard a door open and I shuffled forward.

We abruptly stopped. "Put your arms out, please," a female voice instructed me.

I did as she said, and she secured something on me— a heavy vest or shirt. Something cool was fastened to my wrist.

"Hold on to me," she said, placing my hand on her arm. "I'll take you where you need to go."

We walked until she suddenly stopped. I nearly fell over her. "Stay here. Do not remove the goggles or leave this spot until instructed. Once you remove the goggles, you can talk to the other participants as needed. Do you understand?"

I nodded, my mouth dry, still afraid to talk. I waited for what seemed like hours, but time passed differently when you couldn't see. Finally a voice came over what sounded like a loudspeaker. It was Mr. Donovan.

"Students, you may remove your goggles."

I reached up and pulled mine off, blinking a couple of times as my eyes adjusted to my surroundings. I stood in a dark cavern with fake plastic rocks and weird strobe lights flashing. Laser tag was the first thing that leaped to mind. Glancing around, I looked for the other students but didn't see anyone else. I examined my outfit—a vest with lights and a belt with a laser gun. I removed the gun, holding it in my hand and pressing back against a fake rock.

My initial assessment was this wasn't going to be so bad.

I'd played laser tag a few times in my life. I wasn't great at it, but I didn't suck, either. I figured Wally would be pretty good because he played online shooting games all the time. Physical maneuverability could be a problem for him, but I wasn't too worried. He could hold his own. Frankie, however, might be in real trouble, not that I even knew where she was. I had a feeling laser tag wasn't her thing.

"Your mission is to get out in under fifteen minutes," Mr. Donovan continued. "Every successful shot is worth five points. Minus five points to whoever gets shot. Be careful if you get shot, because your sensor will light up for five seconds, making you a beacon to others. The timer on your wrist lets you know how much game time you have left and how many points you have in terms of your personal score."

I glanced down at the plastic timer secured around my wrist. The top line, in glowing green numbers, read *Game Time 15:00*. The bottom line read *Points 20*. So, we started with twenty points. That meant we could get hit no more than four times without scoring against someone else. This wasn't going to be easy.

"Your chest, back, shoulders have hit boxes," Mr. Donovan continued. "Your gun also has a hit box. You must score in the hit box to get points. Here are the rules. This is a noncontact trial. No tackling, fighting, or hitting. You'll receive an immediate disqualification if you do not observe this rule. Also, no spawn killing and no stalking. Your primary objective is to get out in under fifteen minutes with the highest score. You shoot another player only if you want more time or you want to come out ahead in terms of points. If you lose all your points from getting shot, then the game ends for you. The person who comes through the exit first gets a large bonus. Each successive person who makes it through the exit will receive extra points as well."

I inhaled a deep breath, wishing I could see more than just the closest area. But it was too dark beyond my immediate circle, and the momentary flashes from the strobe lights didn't extend very far.

"If you get hurt, stop your play immediately and announce it," he continued. "Health and safety are our top priorities. Remember, your sensors must be visible during game play. You may not cover your light or sensor. Also, no shooting the face. If you hit someone with a face shot, even if it's accidental, you lose fifteen points. Too many mistakes with shooting, and you'll be disqualified. That's left to our discretion. Now, good luck, and may the best student win."

The cavern fell into silence. I considered my play. First order of priority was to find the exit and avoid being shot. I slunk around a corner and ran right into Jax. He shot me immediately, and my vest lit up.

"Watch out, Red," he said melting back into the darkness. I swore, fumbled, and shot at him but missed.

Crap.

Running in the opposite direction, I slipped and half crawled behind a rock, trying to think. I was down five points, but the exit had to be my priority. Feeling along the wall, I inched my way forward. I felt nothing. No door, no exit. I could hear shouting in the distance, a bit to my right. I took a chance and dashed to the opposite wall. A head popped up, and Mike shot me. He scored a hit on my left shoulder. I rolled right at him and shot him in the back as he made a run for it. I saw a flash of surprise on his face as he glanced over his shoulder. Perhaps he hadn't thought I could be so accurate in nonvirtual reality.

Good for me.

I was at fifteen points. Quickly and methodically, I continued my search along the wall, feeling for a door. I glanced at my watch. Four minutes had passed, so I'd better get a move on. I crept forward and collided with someone.

I barely kept from pulling the trigger. "Wally?" I hissed.

"Angel?" He pressed a hand to his chest and lowered his gun. "You scared the crap out of me."

I yanked him down into a crouch, keeping my voice to a whisper. "Have you seen Frankie?"

"No. Just Kira. She was the first one to shoot me. Someone else hit me, but I didn't see who."

I looked down at his arm. "What's your point situation?"

He turned his wrist over and showed me his watch. He had ten points. Two more hits and he was out.

"We've got to hurry and find the exit," I said.

"No kidding. Where do you think it is?"

"Hard to say." I considered. "Most laser tag games have clearly marked exits. I hoped that maybe they kept the door but just hid the exit sign. But I have a feeling they aren't going to make it that easy."

"I agree."

"So, it's going to be hidden somehow." I considered the possibilities. "We're probably looking for a latch or a lever, something that will pop it open."

"Maybe." The strobe lights distorted his face, and it was freaking me out. "You got a plan?"

"There's nothing in the rules that says we can't work together, right?"

"Not that I heard."

"Good. We'll have a better chance if we stick tight. I'll keep feeling along the walls for a hidden door, just in case, and you check the rocks and floor for a lever or something. Keep your eyes open for shooters and Frankie. I'm not sure she can do this on her own. But we have to hurry. Time is ticking."

I heard Jax shout something several feet away, and Bo bellowed back. Apparently they hadn't found the exit yet, either. I hadn't heard a female voice yet, but it could be the girls were being quiet. Or maybe they were already out. It was hard to know.

We started moving along methodically, feeling for anything. Wally and I watched each other's backs. Someone shot at Wally and hit him in the shoulder. I shot back, and someone's vest lit up as they ran away. Wally was down to five points and I was back up to twenty.

"We need to get you healthy," I said. "Let's wait here a minute and see if you can score a hit."

Seconds after I said that, we spotted Bo creeping around the corner. I elbowed Wally to alert him, but Wally was already poised to fire. He squeezed the trigger and scored a hit on Bo's chest plate.

Bo started to fire back at Wally, but I shot at him. I missed but came close enough to ruin his shot. Lit up like a beacon, Bo cut his losses and moved away.

"Thanks," Wally said. "I'm back at ten points."

"No problem."

We continued searching. Time was slipping past at a scary-fast rate. I patted the wall as fast as I could, trying to hurry, when my hand hit something hard and cold. I reached out and wrapped my fingers around a pole.

"Wally, I've found something," I whispered. "It's a ladder. We've got to go up. It's either the exit, or there's another level of play."

CHAPTER TWENTY-THREE

Angel Sinclair

"**C**over me." I slipped my foot onto the first rung and started to climb.

I was almost to the ceiling when there was a shout and an explosion of light below me. Wally was firing at someone who was firing at me. The sensor on my back lit up, but I didn't stop climbing. My head hit the ceiling and I reached up, groping around for a way out. I could feel a seam, so there was a trapdoor of some kind above me. Using both hands, I pushed upward with all my strength. The door slammed open with so much force, I was certain everyone below could hear it. But the way the door opened also convinced me I'd been the first to find this exit.

I pulled myself up and rolled onto the floor before I got shot again. This floor was also dark, and the strobe lights were still flashing. No exit, but another level of play. I scrambled behind a rock with a perfect view of the trapdoor and waited to shoot whoever came through next. Unless it was Wally or Frankie. I'd protect them.

I glanced at my watch. We were low on time, and I was down to fifteen points.

A few seconds later, I heard someone shouting and the sound of clanging feet on the ladder. I expected Wally to pop up, but Jax appeared instead. He must have been expecting me to be waiting, because his gun came through first, firing wildly. Unfortunately, I ducked in the wrong direction and he scored a hit on my left shoulder. But as soon as his shoulders and chest appeared, I landed a perfect hit on his chest. He hit the floor and rolled behind a rock, swearing loudly.

Wally appeared moments later, breathing so loudly I knew it was him before I even saw his face. I kept my gun trained on where I'd last seen Jax, but Wally came through without incident. Jax's chest plate would be lit up like a Christmas tree, so I figured he didn't dare expose himself to another hit.

"Over here," I hissed as Wally heaved himself onto the floor. He came to a crouch and waddled over to me, taking refuge behind a rock.

"You got hit," Wally whispered.

"Twice," I confirmed. "Someone got me on the way up, and then Jax scored a hit on me coming up. But I hit him back so I'm steady at fifteen points. How many do you have left?"

"Five."

That wasn't good. One more hit and Wally was out. I squinted at my watch. The strobe lights were giving me a headache. "We've got nine minutes to get out."

"Maybe I should wait here and try to hit someone coming up to get more points."

"Your call, but time isn't our friend, Wally. I'd suggest sticking together and trying to find the exit."

"But what if there's another level of play after this one?"

"Three levels of play in fifteen minutes is ambitious, even for spies. But if there is, we'll deal with it. I say we stay together."

He looked once more at the trapdoor. No one had appeared. "Okay, let's go."

We searched a lot faster and a bit more recklessly. At this point in the game, speed was more important than caution. Time had become our number one enemy.

"Six minutes left and we've got nothing," Wally whispered after we finished searching the wall and rocks on one side of the cavern and came up empty. "And we don't know where Jax is."

"He's up here somewhere, along with the exit." I bent down to check the lower part of a rock, then someone shot me. My vest lit up.

I whirled and shot in the direction of my attacker. I missed but saw Bo duck behind a rock.

"Get down," I screamed at Wally as Bo shot in his direction.

I glanced over at Wally, sighing in relief when Wally's vest stayed dark. One more hit and he'd have been out. Unfortunately, I hadn't hit Bo, but at least we'd pinned him down behind a rock and the wall. That was good for us, because Bo was at a disadvantage as a result of his size. He wouldn't be able to extract himself without exposing himself to us.

I moved toward Wally to regroup and stepped on something. A grinding noise filled the cavern, and a door slid open just behind Wally's left shoulder.

The exit!

Wally whirled, staring at the opening, dumbfounded.

"Go," I shouted, throwing myself forward and shoving him through the door. He stumbled across the exit, but I tripped and fell on my knees just as someone fired a volley at me. I rolled sideways several times, miraculously avoiding getting hit.

I expected it to be Bo, but Jax lifted a hand in a salute to me and launched himself through the door. Firing at the last second, I scored a direct hit on his back just before he went through. The bell rang again, signaling two players had now exited.

I rolled to my feet, looking around and breathing hard. I was now a good fifteen feet from the exit, and unfortunately, I'd lost Bo. I crouched low, keeping my gun out and moving back and forth as I carefully inched forward. I was about five feet away from the exit when I thought of Frankie. I hadn't seen her since the game started.

Where the heck was she?

Maybe she had gotten shot too many times and was already out. Or maybe she was hiding. Either way, she'd never make it without help. I looked down at my watch. Four minutes and ten points. I could afford to take a look.

I changed direction and headed back to the trapdoor. The bell rang, signaling another player was through. Probably Bo.

The trapdoor to the level below was open and deserted. I had no idea who had come through and who hadn't. I waited for a few seconds and crept toward the door.

Mike popped up from behind a rock and shot at me, but I moved sideways at the last second and it missed. Hala leaped out from an adjoining rock and hit Mike in the shoulder box. His vest lit up as they both sprinted away from me.

I checked the time. We had less than two minutes.

Throwing caution to the wind, I shouted down, "Frankie. Where are you?"

"Angel, is that you?"

"Yes! The exit is up here. There's a ladder. You need to follow my voice to find it and climb it now."

"I know. I'm on the ladder right now. But thank you for helping me. That's really kind of you."

"Will you stop being nice and move it?" I yelled.

I looked around but didn't see anyone else.

"Hurry, Frankie!" I shouted as the seconds ticked past. "How many points do you have left?"

"Five," she said.

She was puffing by the time she finally got to the top and I pulled her to her feet. We turned to run for the exit when a shot fired from the trapdoor. We dived for cover separately as Kira leaped through the trapdoor, rolled once, and shot me in the back.

My vest lit up, but my hand with the gun was steady. I fired and hit her on the shoulder. She fell, her gun slipping from of her hand and skittering a few feet away. I lifted my gun, ready to finish her off, when she held up her hands.

"No, don't shoot," she said. "Please, I only have five points left."

"You didn't ask me how many points I had before you shot me," I pointed out.

Frankie stepped out from behind me. "Don't shoot her, Angel. We can all go across together."

"What?" I said incredulously. "You're helping her? Why? She doesn't even like you."

As we were arguing, Kira rolled to her side, grabbed her gun, and aimed at Frankie's back. Without thinking, I pushed Frankie out of the way and took the shot instead.

The laser gun went dead in my hand, and my chest plate turned from green to red.

Both Kira and Frankie stared at me, frozen in shock. After a moment, Kira scrambled to her feet and bolted for the exit.

"What did you just do?" Frankie shouted at me.

"I saved you. Run, Frankie. You can't save me. I'm

already dead. You have seventeen seconds to get out. Come on, let's go."

I pulled her to the exit, pushing her across. Half stumbling, she made it through just as a loud klaxon sounded and the lights abruptly came on.

Shielding my eyes against the sudden light, I walked out of the cavern and into a waiting room. Everyone stood staring at me, mouths agape. A glance at the wall showed a scoreboard on a television screen bolted to the wall. It flashed our final scores, including points made for accurate shots.

Wally had come in first, obviously helped by the bonus of finishing first, followed by Jax, Hala, Bo, Kira, Mike, and Frankie. The letters *DNF* were posted after my name. Did not finish.

Wally looked stricken. "Angel, what happened? Why didn't you go through after me?"

"He shot at me," I said, dipping my head toward Jax, who wouldn't meet my eyes. "I had to take cover. Then I lost Bo's position, so I was trying to be careful coming out."

"That's not all that happened," Frankie interrupted. "She came back for me and then took a shot meant for me. It's not fair. I should be the one who didn't finish."

"Angel, you should get extra points for finding both exits and the trap door," Bo insisted. "None of us would have gotten out of there if you hadn't found them."

"I got lucky," I said.

Bo raised an eyebrow. "Both times?"

We didn't have time for more discussion because Mr. Donovan entered the room, congratulating us on the completion of our first trial. He avoided eye contact with me, which I took as a bad sign.

We filed out of the building, which thankfully we didn't have to do blindfolded, and climbed on the bus. Instead of celebrating, everyone was quiet on the bus. A quick glance outside confirmed we'd been at an unmarked building on the UTOP campus.

I sat next to the window, looking out. Wally sat next to me, bumping shoulders with me, as if trying to cheer me up. I finally had to tell him to knock it off. I'm pretty sure he thought I was upset that I'd lost, but I wasn't.

I was furious.

And I was completely done with Kira Romanova.

CHAPTER TWENTY-FOUR

Angel Sinclair

After we got off the bus, the guys trudged to their room, and we went to ours. Kira even accompanied us for the first time in forever, which was surprising, because every time she dared to look my way, I glared at her.

If looks could kill...

Frankie, as usual, chatted cheerfully as if nothing had happened. Hala, Kira, and I let her talk. For once, I was thankful for her constant stream of chatter so no one else had to say anything. I got to the door and tapped in the code for our room, pressing my thumb to the pad before it clicked open.

Kira went straight to the bathroom, while I sat down on Frankie's bed and started taking off my shoes.

"Hala, your score was amazing," Frankie said. "You had the most accurate hits out of all of us. Totally impressive. How did you do it?"

Hala pulled out her desk chair and sat down, shaking her hair out of a ponytail. "My dad took me shooting for the first time when I was eight. He's with the FBI, so we have guns in the house. He wanted to make sure I understood how to use them and what it meant to be safe around guns. We went to the firing range quite a bit. Shooting with a laser isn't quite the same, though. The beam spreads out in a cone, so it affects your accuracy. I tried to account for that. I wish I'd found the exit, but Wally got there first and scored the bonus."

Frankie sat down on her bed next to me. "Wally wouldn't have gotten out at all—none of us would—if it hadn't been for Angel."

"I told you, I just got lucky," I said, although at the moment, I wasn't feeling remotely lucky at all.

"I'm sorry, Angel," Hala said. "Frankie told me what happened. It was really nice what you did."

"I didn't do *anything* nice," I said testily. "Just so we're clear, I would have shot Kira if Frankie hadn't stopped me."

Hala looked away, and my anger dissolved. Now I was feeling depressed. Two tests, both failed. Things weren't looking good for me.

Kira came out of the bathroom, her eyes red and face blotchy. She carefully avoided eye contact with me. "Frankie, can I speak with you privately? Please?"

Frankie glanced at me. I narrowed my eyes, but Frankie, being Frankie, stood up. "Sure, Kira. See you guys later."

Just like that, Frankie went off with Kira—the girl who'd tried to bump her out of the game and had caused me to fail a trial. My anger flared again and then settled into a slow, uncomfortable burn in my stomach.

One thing was clear. Kira wasn't going to get off that easy with me.

"So, what did Kira want to talk to you about?" I asked Frankie when she returned. Kira hadn't returned with her and Hala had gone for a walk, so it was just the two of us.

Frankie sat in her desk chair and started braiding her long black hair. "She apologized for trying to shoot me. It wasn't personal and I understood that. She also thanked me for saving her. She has a lot going on in her life, Angel, which is why she's not been that friendly. She thinks you don't like her."

"I don't," I confirmed.

"Don't say that," Frankie admonished me. "I told her you were just prickly."

"I am *not* prickly."

"I also told her you would come around."

"I won't." I fumed inwardly until it bubbled over. "How can you just forgive her like that?"

"What's the point in being angry?"

"Maybe the fact that she's a backstabbing, self-centered, untrustworthy threat makes it worthwhile."

Frankie patted me on the arm. "Oh, Angel. You'll come around." She sat next to me on her bed. "Now it's time to talk about us. Why did you take that shot for me?"

"Why do you think, Frankie?" I blew out a breath in exasperation. "You're my best friend. One of my *only* friends. I want you to stay."

"Hmmm." She finished braiding her hair and secured it with a tie. "You know what I think? I think you need to stop trying to save me and stay focused on you. You're the best candidate out of all of us for UTOP."

"*What?*" Had she completely lost her mind? "No offense, Frankie, but you couldn't be farther from the truth. I almost killed us in the first test, and I killed myself in the second one. That does *not* make me a good candidate for an operative."

142

She sighed and shook her head like I was completely dense. "If you don't believe me, I guess we'll just have to see, won't we?"

I had no idea how to answer that one. While I appreciated her faith in me, it hurt to realize how misplaced it was.

CHAPTER TWENTY-FIVE

Angel Sinclair

I was looking forward to Saturday and our trip into town more than I'd thought I would. I needed a break from all that was UTOP, even if it was for just a little while.

The bus dropped us off on Main Street and the driver told us they'd be back for us in four hours. Frankie and Wally tried to talk me into seeing a movie, but I really wanted some alone time.

When we got off the bus, all of us scattered. The air was cool but not cold. My blue sweater kept me comfortably warm, so I walked around for a while, enjoying the fresh air and figuring out what was available in the town. Virginia's fall foliage was in full display, in gorgeous shades of red, gold, orange, and brown.

All the buildings were in the colonial style, and I felt like I'd stepped back in time. A pretty redbrick courtyard with benches and a statue of a former local politician completed the look. The courtyard was relatively empty, so I sat on one of the benches and

144

called my mom. We spoke for a good thirty minutes, mostly with me answering her questions the best I could without violating my promise of secrecy regarding the specifics of what I was doing. I promised to call her again soon, and she hung up happy.

I stood and decided to return to a cute little bookstore café I'd seen earlier. A tinkling bell sounded as I opened the door. Books of all shapes and sizes were crammed into heavy wooden shelves and took up nearly every inch of wall space. There was a small fireplace and a couple of warm, cozy armchairs facing it. The entire room smelled like coffee and chocolate. It was fairly crowded, but the line was only three people deep. I stood in line, drooling over the croissants and delicious-looking pastries before making my selection.

"Hot chocolate, large, and a chocolate croissant," I said when it was my turn. I dug into my purse and suddenly realized I'd forgotten my wallet. I closed my eyes. "I'm so sorry. I forgot my wallet. Please cancel my order."

"Not necessary," said the person behind me. It was an elderly gentleman, dressed in a gray sweater and holding a cane. He had twinkling blue eyes. "It's on me."

I shook my head. "Oh, no. I couldn't," I said.

"You can." He handed the cashier the money. "I insist. My treat."

"Oh, thank you so much," I said. "I really do have money, I just forgot it."

"It's no problem."

The cashier handed me a hot chocolate and a croissant on a plate. I thanked the man once more, and carried my goodies to a small empty table near the fireplace. I'd just sat down and picked up my hot chocolate when Jax stood behind the empty chair at my table holding a cup of coffee.

"Hey, Red. Mind if I join you?"

I almost spilled my drink. Had he just appeared out of thin air? I was pretty sure I would have noticed him before this, but apparently not. That didn't speak well to my spy abilities. "Um, sure, have a seat. What are you doing here, Jax?"

"The same thing as you." He slid into the chair and lifted his cup in a mock toast. "But, unlike you, I brought my wallet."

"So, you saw that?"

"I did." He grinned, his dark hair windblown and cheeks ruddy. He blew on his coffee and took a sip. "You know, you intrigue me. I can't figure you out."

"Excuse me?"

"You're a mystery to me."

That was weird, because I'd thought the same thing about him. But now my curiosity took over. "Why would you want to figure me out?"

"Why? You know why. It's smart to keep an eye on the competition. There's just something about you, Red. I can't put my finger on it, and that bugs me."

"Maybe you haven't met anybody who can resist your charm," I said drily.

"Ah, so you admit I'm charming."

My cheeks heated. "I'm not admitting anything." But his smile widened, and I hated that my heart did a little leap.

"So, why didn't you go to the movies with Wally and Frankie?" he asked.

"How did you know about that?"

He leaned across the table, lowering his voice to a whisper, his face close enough to mine so I could feel his breath against my cheek. "Spy school, remember?"

I rolled my eyes at the dramatic tone of the whisper. "Well, why didn't *you* go to the movies?"

"No one asked me."

"Oh." I fell quiet. I'd always been on the outside, and

now that I wasn't, I'd forgotten about those who were. I wasn't sure what that said about me.

He wrapped both hands around the mug, watching me thoughtfully. "You know, I've been thinking about what you did in the maze. Sacrificing yourself for your friend...that took guts."

"Not really."

"Yes, really. Didn't peg you for that, which is part of your intrigue. You're not going to quit the trials, are you?"

His question made me wonder why he'd asked. "Why would I quit the trials? I'm not a quitter. They'll have to boot me out first, which I admit could happen. Are you quitting?"

"No way. I wouldn't give up. But that doesn't mean I won't get kicked out."

"Why would you get kicked out? You're probably the best suited of any of us for this kind of work. You don't seem intimidated by anything."

"Is that so?" He raised an eyebrow. Pushing aside his coffee mug, he leaned forward, his elbows on the table. "What else have you noticed about me?"

"You're not afraid to challenge authority, you're smart, quick on your feet, and you have a loose code of honor, which is probably a good thing for an operative. You're also physically fit and not bad-looking, either. Seems a perfect fit for the criteria of an operative to me."

He laughed. "Really? That's what you see in me? Most of the other candidates would say I'm a trouble-maker."

"You are. Kind of." I lifted my hands to soften the blow. "You purposely seem to look for trouble. Why?"

"It isn't hard to find trouble when you don't have to go far to get it." His voice was light, but I could hear something else just below the surface.

I shook my head. "I don't believe that. I think that's just an excuse. In fact, there's something about *you* I can't put my finger on." Having played back his own words, I gave him a self-satisfied smile.

He seemed impressed, and his smile widened. "Touché."

Taking my croissant, I split it in half, handing a part over. It was a peace offering of sorts. "Here, have some."

He reached out and took it, his warm fingers brushing mine. "Thanks."

He took a bite, regarded me thoughtfully. "So, you're good at math, and even better with computers. What else can you do?"

"I like chemistry." I took my own bite of the croissant and chewed before speaking again. "How about you? Other than math and engineering, what's your specialty?"

He finished off the croissant. He'd left a little spot of chocolate on his lower lip. Not that I was staring at his mouth or anything.

He looked around the café and then lowered his voice. "My specialty is deception. And because I'm so good at it, I'm also excellent at spotting deceivers and liars."

I wasn't sure if he was teasing or serious. "That's definitely a useful skill to have if you want to be an operative."

"Yes, it is. Let's just say I have a good understanding of human psychology. Within a minute, I can tell a lot about a person—marital status, occupation, hobbies, desires and needs."

"That's a pretty bold claim. You sound like an armchair psychic."

That made him chuckle. "I can back it up. Let's take you, Angel Sinclair. Red hair, the prettiest blue eyes I've ever seen, a cautious nature, and a mind like a steel trap. That's a lot packed into a small body. You're a careful observer, but you don't say much. Add to that, you have unswerving loyalty, naïveté, stubbornness, and a logical perspective on the world. You've also got a temper when pushed—the red hair gave that away—and you're slow to trust."

"Wow." I clapped. Definitely an armchair psychic. "Anyone can play that game, Jax. But you get points off because the red-haired claim is stereotypical."

"Okay, then tell me it's not true. Just remember, I'm good at spotting liars."

I pursed my lips at him and stayed silent.

He grinned. "But you…what is it about you, Red?"

"You may not be as good at psychology as you think. I'm an open book."

"Not completely. I'm exceptionally sensitive to moods, facial expressions, and even mutual feelings of attraction. But there's a wall around you."

I let my gaze rise to his, meeting the fiery green of his eyes. "What do you really want from me, Jax?"

He finished his coffee and set down the mug. "I'm not sure yet. But trust me, when I figure it out, you'll be the first to know."

CHAPTER TWENTY-SIX

Candace Kim

NSA Headquarters, Fort Meade, Maryland

Candace caught Slash's eye as they were walking out of the director's weekly stand-up meeting. He gave her an imperceptible nod. After chatting with a couple of assistants, she returned to her office and waited. Ten minutes later, Slash sat in her visitor chair.

"You've got news?" he asked.

"Yes, and not the good kind," she replied. "We have a problem. The terrorist networks given to us by Sinclair in his last communication have suddenly vanished. They stopped returning to the two hideouts they were using and faded away. We were following one individual who took a sudden flight to São Paulo and then eluded our contacts there. The others were going about their normal business and never returned. They were tipped off."

"By whom?"

"I don't know, but people are speculating it was Sinclair."

"Why would he do that?" Slash frowned. "That makes no sense. He wouldn't jeopardize the immunity deal when he's so close, and he's never done anything like that in the past."

"I know, but people are arguing this is proof that they can't trust him, and with the evidence of good faith gone, we should cancel the deal. The Justice Department is getting jittery about the latest development. It's taking everything I've got to calm everyone down. What do you think?"

"I think it stinks."

"I agree. Someone is purposely sabotaging our efforts to bring him in, and my number one suspect is Isaac Remington. Did you come up with anything involving the Ahab/pope connection?"

"Nothing." Slash rubbed his hand against his stubbled jaw, thinking. "Would you send me the transcripts of all the correspondence we've had with Sinclair? He's a cryptologist by training, so we should think like one when we're trying to decode whatever message he might be sending."

"I'll have everything to you by tomorrow morning."

"Thank you. When's the next communication scheduled with him?"

"Four days. I don't even know if I should tell Sinclair what's happened. Right now, I'm leaning toward keeping it quiet and seeing if he brings it up. It may give us some insight as to his mind-set."

"Sinclair isn't behind the leak." Slash expression turned grim. "Our problem is in-house. I'm more convinced of that than ever. We should trust Sinclair until he gives us reason to doubt him."

She liked that their thinking matched on this issue. It didn't often work that way when she worked with other colleagues. "I concur, but staying the course will be hard with the others arguing to the contrary."

He fell silent for a moment, thinking. "See if you can stall them. In terms of this investigation, I've got a much lower profile than you. If you're in agreement, I'll do some investigating behind the scenes."

"I'd appreciate that. Thank you."

He stood, crossing his arms against his chest. "Just keep in mind, if I don't find anything, we'll have to rely on Sinclair to flush them out on his own. That could be dangerous for him."

"I know." She'd considered that, and knew it was a risk, but they'd have to take it. They didn't have any other choice. "Let's just hope it doesn't come to that."

CHAPTER TWENTY-SEVEN

Angel Sinclair

After Jax left the café, I looked around. The elderly man who'd bought me my hot chocolate and croissant was sitting near the fire reading the newspaper. He must have felt me staring at him, because he looked up and smiled. I gave him a small wave. Other than him, I didn't know anyone else in the café.

That was a good thing.

I opened my laptop, keeping my back against the wall so there was no one behind me to look over my shoulder. I wasn't going to hack in a café full of people and slow Wi-Fi, but that wasn't going to stop me from pulling up a list of employees at my father's last known place of employment, King's Security, for the period of time he'd worked there. I'd already hacked the list when I was still at home. During that hack, I'd discovered King's Security was a cover for a NSA satellite office, which led me to believe my father might have worked for the NSA.

Methodically, I began to google the names on the list, starting with the security engineers, as I assumed he would have had the closest contact with them. I created a folder and began compiling dossiers on each person. Nothing seemed unusual about any of them until I came to an engineer named Joseph Lando. He'd died in a freak boating accident about two weeks before my father disappeared.

I typed in his name and pulled up an article with a photograph from a newspaper. The article was about his funeral, which had taken place at a local church and been attended by sixty-two people. The eulogy had been given by a man named Isaac Remington. Joseph Lando had been thirty-six years old. There was no other information about the accident, other than it had happened on the lake near his house. He was survived by his mother, Sally Lando, his brother, James Lando, and his wife, Maria. Apparently, Maria and Joseph had no children.

The photograph accompanying the article featured a group of men carrying a coffin. The caption underneath the photo only named the first two men in line, Misha Peterson and Isaac Remington, the man who had delivered the eulogy. I enlarged the photo, and my breath caught in my throat. The second man behind Isaac Remington was my father. I'd seen enough photographs of him to recognize his face. So, my dad had known Joseph Lando well enough to attend his funeral as a pallbearer.

I quickly cross-referenced the names Misha Peterson and Isaac Remington with my list of employees at King's Security. Only Remington came up as having been an employee of King's Security. He had been Joseph Lando's and my father's boss. I did one more search that took me nearly an hour, but I discovered Lando's wife was still alive.

I didn't know what she could possibly tell me after all this time, but I planned to give her a call next

Saturday. I'd take any scrap of information about my father that I could get.

Wally and Frankie sat in the seat behind me on the bus and chatted all the way home about the movie. Mike sat next to me even though there were several empty seats.

"So, Angel, you up for gaming after dinner?" he asked.

"What game did you have in mind?"

"*Quaver Legend.* You know it?"

"Of course I know it. I've made it to level seven already."

He whistled. "Level seven? I'm at level five."

"Noteworthy," I said. *Quaver* was hard, so to be at level five was decent. "Anyone else in?"

"So far, you, me, and Jax. Does Frankie play? Hoping to pull in at least Wally for one more."

"Wally will play," I confirmed. I would have interrupted him to ask for certain, but Frankie was in the middle of explaining an important part of the movie to him. "I think he's a level six in *Quaver*. Frankie isn't into gaming, but you can invite her anyway. Personally, I could use a little stress relief. It's a great idea, Mike."

It turned out that only Wally, Mike, Jax, and I wanted to play. Bo wanted to head to the gym, and none of the other girls were interested in playing. So the four of us headed to the gaming room to get started.

Jax was a so-so player, so it was really a battle between Wally, Mike, and me. Mike and I fought tooth and nail, but Wally edged both of us out to win, using some unconventional moves that left the rest of us in the dust.

"Dang, I'm impressed," Mike said, setting down the controller. "Wally, dude, you can game. All of you have wicked skill. I didn't expect that level of expertise."

Jax tossed his controller on the coffee table. "I was clearly out of my league on this one."

I stretched my arms over my head. Gaming with these guys had felt good. It was strange, but I'd become comfortable in their company. Their appreciation for my skill and smarts was real. I appreciated it, although I didn't need it. Perhaps that was part of the UTOP strategy—creating grounds for accepting and respecting the strengths and weaknesses of others.

In fact, the more I got to know my fellow candidates at UTOP, the more I liked them—minus Kira, of course. For a loner like me, that was a huge and startling personal development.

I wasn't sure what to think of it.

CHAPTER TWENTY-EIGHT

Angel Sinclair

"The next series of questions will be true or false, Angel. I want you to answer as quickly as possible, within a two-second time frame. Do you understand?" Mrs. Thompson sat patiently, her hands folded on the table, and waited for me to answer.

It was Monday morning, and I was cranky and tired. The previous group session with Bo and Jax, where we'd fielded bizarre challenges and spilled our guts, confirmed that the routine was going to be the same as last week. Now I was back undergoing more psychological testing.

Fun, it was not.

"Did you say true and false questions?" I asked to make sure I'd heard her right.

"Yes, that's what I said. No matter how strange the question, I want you to go with the first answer that comes to mind, okay?"

I let out a breath. "Fine. I'm ready."

She looked down at a sheaf of papers in front of her and began to read. "True or false. I'd rather be a florist than a fireman."

"What?" I said.

She patiently repeated the question.

"False," I said. "I totally kill plants."

"Please don't provide reasoning," she said. "Just true or false, okay?"

"Sure. Whatever."

"I've never lied to anyone in a position of authority."

"False."

"I'm a confident person."

"Uh…false."

This strange line of questioning went on for an hour before she was finally done. She made a couple of notes, and I stood to leave. To my surprise, she asked me to sit down and stay for a few more minutes.

Apprehensive, I returned to my seat and waited for her to speak. She leaned forward, resting her elbows on the table.

"Angel, I want to talk to you about Friday's trials. Would you mind if I ask you a couple of questions about it?"

My hands tensed in my lap. I didn't really want to revisit the disastrous trial, but I nodded. "Okay."

"In reviewing the footage, I noticed you were the first one to find the ladder to the trapdoor on the ceiling and realize the game continued on another floor. Why didn't you climb the ladder and immediately move quickly to find the exit on the next level?"

"Well, I sort of did."

"Explain 'sort of.'"

"I told Wally to cover me as I climbed the ladder. I was vulnerable there and needed his protection. Unfortunately, I still got hit going up. Once I opened the trapdoor, I went through and waited for him."

"Why did you wait for Wally?"

"Because we were working as a team. It wasn't in the rules that we couldn't."

"True." She sat back in her chair. "So, on the first floor, was it was your idea to search along the walls, looking for the exit?"

"Yes. It was dark and hard to see. I figured the exit would be concealed, so it seemed logical to search for a door seam or a lever that would open it. That's kind of a standard thing in games online."

"Okay, once you got through and were waiting for Wally at the top, what happened?" she asked.

"Wally didn't come up—well, at least not at first. Jax came next. I think he must have shot Wally or forced him away from the ladder to make his way up next. I was expecting Wally, but I managed to hit Jax when he came through. He probably expected to take the hit. He hit me, too. He didn't bother with me after that. He ran off right away, looking for the exit, I guess."

"So, Jax stayed focused on the assignment."

I didn't miss her point, and my face flushed. "Yes, I guess he did."

"Okay, so once you and Wally were on the second floor, you resumed looking for the exit."

"Yes. That was the goal. I eventually stepped on the door trigger by sheer luck," I explained.

"Not just sheer luck," she pointed out. "You were methodically clearing the level, looking for the exit."

"True, but I stepped on the button by accident."

"Fine. So, the door opened, and what happened next?"

"Wally was closer, so I pushed him through."

"Why did you do that? You knew the first person to go through would get the bonus."

"I know, but if he got shot one more time, he'd be dead. I was healthier, so I let him go first. I was going to follow right after him, but I tripped and Jax showed up firing. I had to roll away from the door to avoid being hit. That's when Jax went through."

She nodded, watching me carefully. "But you hit him."

"I hit him as he went through. Apparently, he had enough points to take the hit and still make it through. It also took my score to a healthy fifteen points."

"Why didn't you go through after Jax? You had enough points to risk getting shot by anyone, including Bo, who was still in the area, and make it through safely."

I looked down at my hands. "I know. I was going to, but…"

"But what?"

"But I knew Frankie was still out there, and I thought she could use some help."

"You didn't think Frankie could hold her own."

"No, she could. I mean, I think she could. I wasn't sure how experienced she was at laser tag. But I figured I had extra time and points, and there was nothing in the rules that said we had to come out *before* fifteen minutes. Just *by* fifteen minutes. I already knew I wasn't going to get the top score because Wally had already secured the bonus, so I went back to see if I could give her a hand and maybe rack up more points before I came out."

"But you got hit."

"Yes, but Frankie found the ladder and got to the second level safely."

"Until Kira appeared."

I stiffened, my fists tightening at the memory of it. "Until Kira appeared. She scored a shot on me, but momentarily lost her gun. At that moment, we're all down to five points. I was going to finish off Kira, but I didn't."

"Why not?"

I hesitated. "Because Frankie asked me not to, which was nuts. Kira doesn't even like us, and especially not Frankie."

"Why doesn't Kira like Frankie?"

"I have no idea. Frankie is nice to everyone. But Kira flat out told us she didn't want to be friends with any of us."

"I see. So, while you were arguing with Frankie, Kira somehow retrieved her gun and shot at Frankie. You saw what happened and put yourself between Frankie and the laser, thereby saving her. Why did you do it, Angel?"

My cheeks heated. "I don't know. I didn't want her to fail."

"So you're her leader, then?"

"What? No." I was taken aback by the comment. "I'm just her friend. I want her to succeed."

"At your own expense?"

I looked down at my hands and then back at her. "I guess so."

"Okay, thank you, Angel."

I stood, feeling like I'd messed up more than I could have imagined. Slash would be so disappointed in me, and that hurt a lot.

I had a bad feeling my time at the trials was coming to an end faster than I expected.

CHAPTER TWENTY-NINE

Angel Sinclair

The one bright spot in terms of physical fitness was my time in the pool. Hala and I were the fastest swimmers, though I was faster for shorter races and Hala had better stamina for longer distances. Unfortunately, my performance in the pool didn't help me with the ups—the pull-ups, chin-ups, and push-ups. Our trainer, Mac, got me started on weights to strengthen my upper body. Everything hurt after one session. Subsequent sessions indicated I was weaker than a wet noodle.

Frankie was delegated to the treadmill, rowing machines, and working with some stretchy band things. All of us had a group yoga session on Wednesday that confirmed I had the flexibility of a sheet of steel.

Ugh.

Slowly we got into a routine with our classes, testing sessions, workouts, and each other. Frankie and Hala started foreign language testing—Frankie in Mandarin and Korean, and Hala in Arabic. The only foreign languages Wally and I knew were computer ones, and they were testing us out on them. I didn't know what everyone else's capabilities were.

Everything seemed fine until Thursday, when all of us—except Frankie—started to stress out about the upcoming trial on Friday.

Maybe in an attempt to distract me from my anxiety, Frankie started talking to me about Jax out of the blue.

"I like Jax," she announced Thursday when we were on our way to lunch. "He's smart and tough, but I bet he's a softie beneath that rough exterior."

"Why are we talking about Jax?" I asked. "The next trial is tomorrow. We have to pass it or we're toast. That's what should have our focus right now."

"Oh, forget about the trial for a while. I'd rather talk about Jax."

"I don't want to talk about him." I glared at her.

"Stop being so grumpy. You never want to talk about anything. Come on, you have to admit he's super cute." Frankie slipped her arm through mine and smiled. "And he does seem to have his eye on you."

I had no idea how to respond, because I wasn't even sure what she meant by that. Asking for clarification would only encourage more discussion on this topic. The truth was I didn't want to talk about *anything*. I wanted only to embrace my sky-high anxiety and shut everything else out, but Frankie wasn't going to let me.

She wiggled her eyebrows at me. "He has that bad-boy vibe."

"That's not a vibe, Frankie. It's real."

"Ooh, is it? Well, I like him anyway." Frankie gave an exaggerated sigh. "Too bad he's not my type."

"You don't have a type. You like everyone."

"Of course I like everyone." She looked at me in exasperation. "That doesn't mean I want to *date* everyone."

"See, what does that even mean?" I. "This is exactly why I don't like to talk about boys with you."

"You don't talk about boys with anyone." She laughed again. "But don't worry. You'll get better at it. I promise."

"Happy birthday, Angel!"

It was Thursday evening and I'd just walked into the cafeteria for dinner to find Frankie holding a cupcake with a candle on it. Bo, Mike, Wally, and Hala stood around her clapping and smiling. Jax and Kira were missing, as usual.

"You remembered my birthday?" I said stopping in the doorway.

"Of course we remembered. Come on and blow out your candle."

Embarrassed by all the attention, I walked forward as they sang "Happy Birthday." After they finished, I blew out my candle. Everyone wished me a wonderful birthday and then Frankie brought out cupcakes for the rest of the group.

"Where did you get these?" I asked Frankie, biting into the cupcake. Chocolate exploded on my tongue.

She took a bite and sighed, closing her eyes. "Oh, I conspired with Suzanne a week ago. She was so kind and agreed to make some for me. Wasn't that sweet?"

I frowned, puzzled. "Who's Suzanne?"

"What? You don't know Suzanne?" She looked over her shoulder. "She's the sweet girl over there who serves us dinner every evening. She's twenty-one years old and studying forensic anthropology. She works part-time here, helping to pay for school. She has three younger brothers and a dog named Rex."

"Do I need to ask how in the world you know all that?"

"We see her every day, for heaven's sake, Angel. Why wouldn't I talk to her?"

"You really do talk to everyone," I said, sighing.

I looked over my shoulder at Suzanne. She noticed me staring, so I pointed to the cupcake and mouthed *Thank you.*

She grinned and gave me a thumbs-up.

Although we'd eaten our dessert first, we got our dinner and sat at the tables. This time Bo pushed together a couple of tables so the six of us could eat together. Other than Jax and Kira, the rest of us were becoming a solid unit.

Frankie whipped something out from underneath the table and handed it to me. "Happy birthday, Angel. I hope you like it."

It was wrapped in tissue paper. I unwrapped it and pulled out a blue T-shirt that read *Have you tried turning it on and off?*

I held it up against me and everyone laughed. "Thanks, Frankie. I love it."

She gave me a hug just as Wally passed me an envelope. "It isn't much, but I know you'll like it."

I ripped it open and found he'd bought me thirty dollars of credits on *Hidden Realm.* Whistling, I gave him a high five. "Sweet."

"Thought you'd like it."

As we ate, the conversation turned toward tomorrow's trials.

"What do you think the trial will be this week?" Wally asked around a mouthful of fried rice. "Skydiving? Fighting terrorists? Playing poker?"

Mike snorted. "I hope it *is* poker. I'm unstoppable at poker and even better at chess."

Wally dipped his head toward me. "If I were you, I'd

be scared of Angel. To her, everything is a mathematical calculation. She'd be formidable in a game of cards."

"No way could Angel be formidable," Frankie said. "She has a terrible poker face."

"Hey!" I said in mock outrage while everyone laughed.

"Yeah, and she'd still have to get the cards." Mike speared a piece of sweet and sour pork and ate it. "Luck does play a role, you know."

We threw out a couple more ideas until Hala held up a hand. "Guys, I think we're on the wrong track here. I bet it's going to be an intelligence test of some kind. Strategic thinking or teamwork."

"Reaction and response," said Mike, nodding. "A series of events we have to react to and respond."

"How we react in dangerous situations," Bo offered.

"We already did that in the laser maze and the active-shooter scenario," I pointed out. "I think Hala's right. It's going to be something totally different."

"Like what?" Wally asked.

"I don't know," I said. "I just think the attacking-and-avoiding-the-adversary thing may have played out already."

We guessed for a while longer until we split up to finish homework and turn in early so we'd be rested for the trial.

Later, after all the lights were out, I lay in bed staring at the dark ceiling and working myself into a nervous wreck. After tossing and turning for about an hour, I climbed down from my bunk, put some clothes on, and grabbed my shoes, a coat, and a flashlight. I needed some fresh air to clear my head.

The lights were dim in the hallway. Instead of going out the back toward the basketball court and garden maze, I decided to go out the front door. The moon shone brightly in the clear sky. I took a breath of the cool air. I zipped my jacket to my neck and strolled around the grounds, finally sitting on a bench under a tree to the side of the building. Clicking off my flashlight, I sat looking at the stars. I sat in peace, revealing the solitude when I suddenly heard a cracking sound.

Without thinking, I slid off the bench and behind a tree. After a moment, I saw what had made the noise. Someone was creeping through the forest, trying to approach the building as inconspicuously as possible.

There was something familiar about the way the figure was shaped. When it passed closer to me, I clicked on the flashlight.

"Jax?"

He jumped. "Whoa. You scared the crap out me, Red. What are you doing out here?"

"I could ask the same of you." I looked over his shoulder at the direction from which he'd just come. "Were you just at the UTOP campus?"

He leaned one arm against the tree and grinned, his teeth gleaming white in the moonlight. "You going to tell on me?"

"Don't you know UTOP is off-limits?" I glared at him. "We're confined to the KIT compound."

"Yes, Mother."

"Knock it off. What were you doing there?"

"Oh, I never kiss and tell."

I rolled my eyes in exasperation. "Do you *want* to get expelled?"

"Of course not. I'm just pushing the envelope. No harm, no foul. Unless you tell on me, of course."

I sighed and sat down on the bench. "I'm not going to tell."

"Good." After a moment, he sat down next to me. "So, why are you out here?"

"I couldn't sleep."

"Worried about tomorrow?" When I nodded, he tapped my head. "Quit overthinking. It will be fine."

"It won't. One more misstep and I'm pretty sure I'm out."

He laughed. "You? Girl genius? I don't think so."

"I'm *not* a genius," I said. "Well, my Mensa scores say I am, but a high IQ doesn't necessarily translate to real-world knowledge."

He chuckled softly. "Red, I'm going to let you into a little secret. Every single one of us is trying to figure out how to get ahead of you. You, of all people, have the least to worry about."

"*Me?* I've already lost two trials. Mr. Donovan said the scores are weighted heavily toward those who finish."

"Yeah, they say a lot of things. This is spy school, remember? Deception, trickery, evasion. They'll say whatever they want, manipulate us in ways we can't imagine, until they get or see what they want from us."

"Which is?"

"The makings of a good operative. That's endgame, right?"

I studied him, considering. His voice had lost its cockiness, and those amazing green eyes were looking at me in a way that seemed different from how he usually looked at me. Was he right? It *was* hard to know exactly what they wanted or expected from us.

"Just keep being yourself, okay?" he murmured.

The intensity in his gaze made my breath catch. Slowly, he lowered his mouth to mine and stopped just short of my lips, as if waiting for me to do the rest. For a moment, I just froze. I'd never kissed anyone before. Then, throwing caution to the wind, I lifted my mouth and pressed my lips to his. He kissed me back, far more tenderly than I ever would have expected from him. Warmth, dizziness, and softness curled through me.

He finally broke the kiss and leaned back on the bench, blowing out a breath and pushing his fingers through his hair. He looked like he was already regretting the kiss. I flushed as he abruptly stood and took my hand. "Come on, they do a check around midnight."

I didn't know what to say or do so, still holding his hand, I followed him across the lawn. Jax didn't head for the front door. Instead, he tugged me toward the side of the building.

"Where are you going?" I whispered.

He led me to a side window that had been propped open with a book. "Girls first," he insisted.

He held his hands together and told me to put my foot in his hand. I did as he instructed, and he boosted me so I could grab the sill and pull myself up. I straddled the windowsill awkwardly before falling inside. Seconds later, he hopped in easily, like he'd done it a dozen times.

Maybe he had.

He shut the window behind him. "Let's go."

We sneaked down the hallway, stopping where the hallway split with the girls' room down one hallway and the boys' room down the other.

"Night." His cool hand touched my cheek. "Happy birthday." He gave me a heart-stopping grin before disappearing down the hallway.

He knew it was my birthday?

Before he turned around and saw me staring like an idiot, I quickly returned to my room, careful not to wake anyone when I came in. As I climbed up into my bed, I thought about Jax's kiss. It had been…amazing. But what did it mean? He'd probably kissed dozens of girls like that.

Did it mean he liked me? Was trying to manipulate me? Confuse me? It was hard to say. I was at spy school, after all. Every action, every word, seemed to be part of a larger game.

But as I snuggled under the covers, I couldn't erase the smile on my face.

CHAPTER THIRTY

Angel Sinclair

Bright and early, we dressed in our white T-shirts and camouflage pants and headed for breakfast. We were all present and accounted for except for Jax, who arrived late, looking remarkably rested and in good spirits, despite his late-night adventure. He gave me a wink as he grabbed a bagel and coffee and sat at a table by himself. Frankie chatted happily with everyone, seemingly oblivious to the extreme nervousness of the rest of us. I envied her ability to be so relaxed about everything.

At exactly 7:40, we met in Room 101 for the briefing on our new trial. To our surprise, we hadn't sat for more than a minute when Mr. Donovan instructed us to move upstairs to the gaming room for our briefing.

As we headed up the stairs, Wally grabbed my arm. "Finally," he whispered. "Gaming! Something I'm going to be good at."

"Don't get cocky," I said. "Wait until you see the challenge."

"If it's virtual, I don't *care* what the challenge is. I'm all over it."

My spirits were also rising, despite my warning to Wally. Gaming was my domain—my strength. From what I'd seen of the others while gaming them or watching them game, this was going to be mine or Wally's to lose. I'd had enough failing in the last trials, so there was no *way* I was going down on this one.

We filed into the gaming room and sat. Mr. Donovan stood in front of us, arms clasped behind his back.

"Today's trial is a role-playing game of management and strategy," he said. "Your avatar will have characteristics like strength, intelligence, and charisma, as well as feelings of happiness, fear, and hunger. You can die if you don't eat, get sick, or fall prey to crime or battle. When you die, all your points die with you. You'll also have to maintain your reputation and confidence level by acting honorably, or not, depending on the situation. Those numbers are given to you based on your actions and interaction with your kingdom population." He spread out a hand at the large screen behind us. "You'll need to build and manage a kingdom, including overseeing activities like farming, construction, protection, economic management, and spiritual and entertainment resources."

My spirits soared. So far, so good. I'd played dozens of games like this and had kicked butt in most of them. I glanced at Wally and saw the smile on his face as well.

Ours to lose.

"The strategy aspect of the game involves the ending," Mr. Donovan continued. "The ending happens when your kingdom conquers your opponents. So, how do you get to the top? Strategy, teamwork, diplomacy, cunning, ruthlessness, money, and/or force are all on the table. Just remember that hits to your health, reputation, as well as discontent from the masses and the economic health of your kingdom, play an important role." He fell silent for a moment, looking at each one of us. "Typically, role-playing games can take weeks, even years, to play out. Obviously, we will be acting on an accelerated timeline. You have eight hours to win the game. Lunch and snacks will be provided in the back of the room."

"Yes." Wally raised a fist. "Let's get this going."

"I appreciate your enthusiasm, Mr. Harris." Mr. Donovan smiled at Wally. "Now, I'm aware that some of you may not have participated in a role-playing game before. No worries. You'll not be playing the game individually. Not exactly."

"What?" Wally's bliss turned to dismay. "Why not?"

"You'll be playing in teams. Men against women."

My mouth dropped open. "Four on a team?" I uttered. "But…role-playing should be individual."

"Oh, no worries, Ms. Sinclair. Each of you will have your own avatar. But the four of you will have a collective, not a singular, goal and accumulated points. Gentlemen, you have an identical setup in the room next to this one. Both teams will be linked to each other virtually. However, strategy and information can be called out and discussed aloud, and in real time, without fear of your opponent overhearing. Please keep in mind that everyone's scores, movements, and mistakes are factored into your overall team score. The game can be played to its conclusion, which is the acquisition and control of both kingdoms. If that hasn't happened by the end of the game—which is eight hours—the team with the highest combined score will be declared the winner."

Wally exchanged a worried glance with me. I understood everything he feared in one look. Dread swelled in my stomach. It was hard enough to manage your own score, actions, and movements in a role-playing game. Directing and coordinating others in a fast-moving scenario, with a ton of different aspects, all while keeping a focus on your own actions and the end goal, would be a nightmare. And that was *if* the others would even agree to direction. Arguing, unforeseen mistakes, and refusing to follow directions could be a real problem. I suddenly had to face the real possibility that I could tank this trial, too. If that happened, I would be a washout for sure.

Before I had time to fully consider the consequences, Mr. Donovan ushered the guys out of the room. Wally gave me a last worried glance over his shoulder. I managed to give him an encouraging thumbs-up even though I didn't feel confident in the slightest.

Right after the guys left, we got another visitor. John showed us the controls, gave us an overview of the rules, and left. We watched a seven-minute introduction video to the game before a digital timer on the wall started the countdown and it was game on.

For a moment, the four of us just stared at each other.

Frankie finally broke the silence. "So, Angel, what's the plan?"

"Me?" I said. "Why are you asking me?"

"I've never participated in a game like this." She glanced at Kira. "What about you?"

Kira shook her head. "Me, neither."

I looked hopefully at Hala, who shook her head. "I'm a novice. I've played a few games with my brothers, but they killed me. Looks like you're in charge by default."

I leaned back, pressing my hands to my head and blowing out a breath. This was far from ideal. I was stuck with essentially three newbies. At least Wally had Jax and Mike, both of whom I'd seen in action. They were experienced and decent players. I had no idea how much Bo gamed, but at this point, it didn't matter.

We were totally screwed.

I inhaled a deep breath. It wasn't in my nature to go down without a fight, so I had to tackle this logically, just like I did any other problem. I stood and walked over to a table that had loose pieces of paper and a few pencils. I brought them back to the group and placed them on the coffee table, smoothing down the paper.

"Okay, I've never played this specific game," I said. "That's because this is likely a scenario custom-made for us. But I've played plenty of online role-playing games similar to this. Usually, you make alliances and form strategies to get ahead. Alliances don't last, because someone you helped at one time will likely have to betray you down the line so they can win. However, since we're bundled together, we must form one strategy, and all of us need to stick to it to work toward the goal of defeating the guys in their kingdom of—" I had to glance at my notes "—Ironhaven. Apparently our kingdom is called Alygarth. Are you clear so far?"

Everyone nodded.

"Okay, then before we start, we have to consider our opponent. I know Wally, and I also know his style of gaming. I've also gamed once with Mike and Jax, so I have a decent feeling of their level of expertise, too. Mike is good, but I'm fairly confident he would relinquish executive control to Wally. Bo is the dark horse. I have no idea whether he plays well or not. But my feeling is that he won't be anywhere near the same level as Wally."

"So, Wally will be the leader?" Frankie asked.

"I think, given the knowledge we have, we should assume that."

"But what if Mike turns out to be the leader?" Kira protested. "Would it change our strategy?"

"It might." I lifted my shoulders. "But this point, we have to act on certainties. Anything else could lead us down a rabbit hole."

"I agree," Hala said firmly. "We should assume Wally is the leader. So, what's our plan, Angel?"

I studied the giant screen where our avatars stood waiting to be assigned. "My gut tells me Wally will pursue a military strategy. It's his go-to scenario, and he's very good at it. He'll build an army and fancy weapons, using them to crush us into submission. However, it also means he'll have to force a lot of his people into conscription, which will cause damage to his reputation, charisma, and the happiness levels of the people. He'll look for ways to offset that, but I bet he's willing to take that risk. Whether he'll be successful is up to us."

"Can we do the same?" Frankie asked.

"We could, but I think that's what *he* thinks I'll do. So, in that case, their strategy will involve preparing to meet us one on one in a military face-off. Because of that, I think we should do exactly the opposite."

"Like what?" Kira exclaimed.

"Like form diplomatic alliances with other nations. We get them to help us, lend us their armies, meaning we don't have to take on the guys on our own. Two or three armies against one are better odds in our favor. Especially if we're scoring points elsewhere."

"Wait. There are other kingdoms?" Frankie asked.

"I'd be surprised if there aren't. Wally will certainly check them out to see what they would be willing to offer, but I doubt he'd put a lot of resources into it. So, we'd have to do better and have more to offer our potential allies."

"But…if we fail to secure allies, we're dead," Kira said. "They'd crush us."

"They'd probably crush us anyway. I'm sure we could build an army with equitable strength and weapons and fight it out. But in this case, the odds favor the guys, as Wally is better in tactics than I am. Given that he's also got Mike and Jax to assist, I'd rather go with the diplomatic solution."

"How do we get other kingdoms to fight for us?" Hala asked.

"We'd have to give them stuff, I assume," Frankie said.

"Yes," I agreed. "A *lot* of stuff. That means everything is on the table. The only thing that is nonnegotiable is the leadership of the kingdoms. That's our endgame."

"Okay," said Hala. "I think I see where you're going with this."

"We'll all have a job," I continued. "But first, we combine our funds to get started. Frankie, you'll be our farmer, but also our church pastor. Our first purchase will be seeds to start growing crops. I'm also going to allocate funds for fertilizer so we can have food early. Spread the crops out to benefit the entire kingdom, but also so that we don't have everything in one place in case of attack or fire. I also want you to start a coffer in the church. I'll give you an allotment to help the kingdom's poor and to raise our point count in terms of reputation and confidence."

"Okay. Got it."

"Hala, you'll be our blacksmith and our carpenter. You need to make the items with which we will barter. The more things you can make, the better."

"I'm good at crafting," she said.

"Excellent." I looked at Kira, my voice cool. I was going to have to put aside my dislike of her for the sake of teamwork. "Kira, you're our diplomat. You need to visit the other kingdoms and create alliances. Feel them out, see what they want, what we can give them. Coordinate with Hala to see if we can provide them with what they want in exchange for military assistance."

"Why me?"

"Because I have a feeling you'll be good at getting others to give you what we need."

She seemed unsure how to take that but said nothing.

"What are you going to do, Angel?" Hala asked.

"We need a military of our own, even if it isn't our focus. We'll need conscripts and weapons. I'm also going to be the kingdom leader/politician, going among the people to see what they need. Keeping them happy is vital to our point count. I will also keep an eye on the overall economic health of the kingdom and see what we can leverage in terms of natural resources. Keeping the kingdom citizens in good spirits and prosperous will help us jack up our score."

"Until we get crushed by the military," Kira said under her breath.

"Not if you do your job," I said shortly. I needed Kira to perform well or we were sunk. I wouldn't put it past her to fail on purpose just to sink me. "Not if we *all* do our jobs. Let's get things underway."

I quickly took stock of our inventory, resources, and money and got to work. Frankie started seeding and watering. Kira went off to the first neighboring country, and Hala started building and crafting items. I signed up conscripts and went to the villages, listening to what the people wanted.

Not surprisingly, food was foremost on their minds.

"How much longer until that first crop is ready?" I asked Frankie.

"Another ten minutes, maybe. Don't worry, it will give me time to plant three more crops and maybe hear a confession or two."

I grinned. "Good girl."

Hala secured two apprentices to help her. One set up weapons, staffs, swords, while the other worked as a blacksmith. Frankie corralled people to work in the field to harvest the crops faster. I kept the army growing slowly but surely and held numerous town meetings, giving people a voice and boosting their confidence and our points.

Hours passed. Frankie pulled me aside. "Angel, I've been offered a box by one of my parishioners. At this point, I can't open it or see what's inside. It's supposedly programmed to open after a certain amount of time. The offerer won't tell me what's inside and whether it's good or bad. If I want it, I have to pay for it. Not a lot, but my resources are stretched pretty thin right now. I'd have to borrow a little money from the kingdom coffer to accept it."

"What do you think it is?"

"I have no idea."

"Have you gotten other items from the parishioners?"

"Yeah. Food, livestock, and clothes. But I think this one is different, especially since I don't know what it is. It could be something good or something bad. However, having said that, I think I should buy it anyway."

I blew out a breath. My head was filled with the dozen of things I needed to spend money on. "I don't know, Frankie. We're in short supply of money. Besides, it could be bomb or a plot by Wally to infiltrate the kingdom somehow." My irritation rose. "I don't like the timing on this."

"Please Angel. I really want it."

I sighed, unable to refuse her anything. "Fine. Hope it turns out to be something worthwhile."

"It will. If it doesn't, I'll take full responsibility."

Kira returned from her diplomatic assignment abroad and reported on her alliance efforts. "There is a kingdom to the west called Draycott," she said. "They want swords and food in exchange for military support."

"I can spare two hundred swords, six of them gold," Hala reported. "I can throw in a dozen cannonballs and one cannon."

"Do it," I told Hala.

"They also want a piece of land here." Kira pointed to a spot right in the heartland of our farming area.

"No. That's our most fertile land," Frankie protested. "That's not a good idea."

"Angel said everything is on the table," Kira said. "That's their price."

I studied the land. "Tell Draycott they can have the piece of land they want if they raise their conscript numbers by a hundred."

Kira's eyebrow lifted. "You want me to barter?"

"Exactly. Do what you need to. Promise what you must, but we need that army to win. Get everything you can."

"Okay. I'll head to Illragorn after that."

I found Illragorn on the map I'd sketched out. "Good thinking, Kira. One army from the east and one from the west. Give the Illragons what they want, too, but Frankie is right. We have to be careful. We can't give away all our resources, or we can't keep our own citizens happy."

"Understood."

For the next few hours we worked furiously, building our kingdom, fortifying our land, keeping our inhabitants happy, and building alliances. Less than four and half hours later, Wally's armies attacked.

I watched the large screen in shock. "He's attacking already? What the heck?"

Hala came to stand beside me. "Element of surprise, I suppose. It's just like you said it would be, Angel. The guys have a massive army."

For a moment, I could only stare at the enormous rows of conscripts marching our way.

Holy crap. They were going to crush us.

"Angel?" Frankie asked, snapping me out of my thoughts. "What are we going to do?"

I blinked until the big picture came into focus. "I'm going to mobilize our forces. We have enough to hold off the initial surge. Kira, I'm going to need those neighboring armies right now."

"I'm on it," she said.

I scrambled around the kingdom organizing the conscripts while Frankie fed them and Hala fit them with weapons and magic potions. At some point, Frankie pulled me aside to talk to me privately.

"You've got this, Angel. So, they came early. Nothing changes in terms of our strategy, right?"

I took a deep breath. "Right." The accelerated timeline was freaking me out, but I could handle this. "Thanks, Frankie."

She smiled and patted my arm. "Now, let's go beat them. I'm one hundred percent certain this win is ours."

I appreciated her optimism, even if I thought it misguided, as I returned to my post. After a complete review of what was happening and where, I called out to Kira. "Where are my armies?"

"Coming soon."

"Soon better be *now*," I said.

"They're on the move." She typed madly on the keyboard. "Stand by."

Hala called out to me. "Angel, the first group of soldiers is almost at our border. Do we fire on them?"

"Not yet," I said, maneuvering more forces into place. "We don't have unlimited ammunition, and I need to get a division of archers to the eastern flank first. Wait for my order."

"Okay. I'll wait."

Four minutes later, Wally's forces hit. "Fire!" I shouted.

The battle raged hard. I kept up with Wally's initial attack, but it was clear that it was only a matter of time before we would be overrun.

"We're getting killed to the east," Hala yelled.

"Kira, where is my Illragorn army?" I said.

"Almost there," Kira called out.

"They aren't going to make it in time," Hala said. "Collapse on the eastern side is imminent."

She was right. I was busy holding off Wally on the northern and western borders. I would never get enough conscripts there in time—not that I had them anyway.

"Collapse isn't imminent," Frankie said in a quiet voice. "We have a secret weapon."

We all whirled around to face her. "We do?" I said.

"Herman."

I looked at her, completely lost. "Herman? Who's Herman?"

"Herman the dragon."

My mouth fell open. "We have a dragon?"

She pointed to the large green dragon now positioned behind the church. "The box. There was a really pretty egg inside and it hatched. What do you want Herman to do? I think he'll only respond to me."

I didn't have the luxury of being surprised or grateful. "Attack Wally's east flank immediately. Tell Herman to rain fire and destruction or something like that."

"I'm on it."

Moments later, a giant green dragon swooped over Wally's eastern flank, breathing fire and taking out a fourth of his force with one pass. The rest of his force scattered just as Illragorn's army arrived, finishing off the rest of them.

We cheered. Kira and Hala exchanged a high five with Frankie, while I directed Draycott's army, which had just arrived, to reinforce us in the west. Slowly but surely, we began pushing the boys back into a defensive position. Herman flew over the opposing forces, breathing fire and causing them to flee periodically. However, he required a lot of food in between missions, so Frankie had her hands full.

I imagined Wally was cursing me at this very moment.

The armies fought hard, the battles were bloody and tough, but we eventually beat them into submission. Exactly seven hours and four minutes from the moment the game started, we won.

Exhausted, but exhilarated, we shouted wildly and hugged each other.

Mr. Donovan walked in, bringing the boys with him. We all shook hands and showed good sportsmanship before Wally gave me a clap on the shoulder. "Dang, girl, I wouldn't have figured you for the diplomatic solution. You took a huge risk with that, but it paid off. The dragon thing was sheer genius."

I pointed over my shoulder. "The dragon was all Frankie."

"Frankie?" Wally looked at me in astonishment. "She's never played a role-playing game in her life."

"I know, right? But she totally kicked it."

Frankie walked over and gave Wally a hug. "You guys played a good game. What did you think of Herman?"

"Herman?" Wally threw a baffled glance at me. "Who's Herman?"

Frankie put her hands on her hips, looking at him like he was completely dense. "My dragon, Herman."

"Your dragon has a name?" Wally asked.

"Of course Herman has a name. Why wouldn't he?"

"Ah, I don't know. We were building a potion to destroy him, but we didn't finish in time," Wally admitted.

Frankie's mouth opened in outrage. *"What?* Poison Herman? How *could* you?"

Wally held up his hands as if protecting himself. "Fake dragon, fake potion."

She narrowed her eyes at him. "Wally Harris, don't you *ever* call any of my creations fake again." Turning on her heel, she stormed off.

I burst out laughing at his stunned expression. "I think we've created a gaming monster."

He puffed up his chest with pride, grinning. "Dang, Angel, I think you're right."

CHAPTER THIRTY-ONE

Angel Sinclair

Saturday morning, we were dropped off in town, and everyone went their separate ways. I told Frankie and Wally I needed to talk to my mom and I'd meet them later at the bookstore café. They went off to do some shopping, and I returned to the same park bench in the town square I had sat on before when I'd talked to my mom. Except this time, I didn't call my mom.

I pulled up the number I'd found and took a deep breath. The phone rang four times before anyone picked up.

"Hello?" a female voice said.

"Hello, is this Mrs. Maria Lando?"

There was silence for a long time and then a soft chuckle. "Oh my. I haven't been called that for a long time."

"I'm sorry to bother you. My name is Angel Sinclair. I think my dad and your husband were friends or coworkers a long time ago."

"Sinclair? Ethan Sinclair?"

"Yes. That's my dad."

"He had two daughters, right?"

"Yes, I'm the youngest. Gwen is my older sister. He...left us when I was just eighteen months old."

"Oh, I'm so sorry. I didn't know he had passed away."

"He didn't. I mean, I don't think so. He disappeared, and I'm trying to find out why. Is it okay if I ask you a couple of questions about my dad?"

"Of course."

"Your husband worked at King's Security like my dad, right?"

"Right. J. P. and Ethan were friends as well as coworkers."

"J. P.? I thought his name was Joseph."

"It was. Joseph Patrick. But his family and friends called him J. P. for short."

"Oh, okay. Anyway, I saw a newspaper photograph of my father at your husband's funeral. That's how I found out about you and looked you up. Do you mind if I ask how your husband died?"

"He died in a freak boating accident. It was the craziest thing, because J. P. was afraid of the water. He couldn't swim. I'll never understood what possessed him to take the *Ahab* out on the water that day alone."

"Ahab?" I asked puzzled.

She chuckled, the memory obviously a good one for her. "Yes, that's what we called our boat—after the captain in the novel *Moby Dick*. I was an English literature major and also the mariner in the family. So why J. P. decided to go out on the *Ahab* without me that day, I'll never know."

It did seem unusual that a man who couldn't swim would take a boat out on the water alone. "He didn't have a life jacket on?"

"No, he didn't. Apparently, the boat capsized and he drowned."

"I'm so sorry," I said, sadness filling me. "The police didn't suspect any foul play? Your husband didn't have any enemies?"

"Oh, Lord, no. J. P. was the most soft-spoken, sweetest man I've ever known. He never raised his voice to anyone, not even me."

I shifted on the bench, wrapping my coat tighter around me. "The article I saw online from the newspaper said a man named Isaac Remington gave a eulogy at the funeral. Do you know who he was?"

"He was my husband's and your father's supervisor at King's Security. It was kind of him to give the eulogy. I appreciated it."

I wondered how to word my next question, wondering if she'd even answer it. "Mrs. Lando, do you know if your husband ever worked for the NSA?"

"The NSA?" Her voice sounded surprised. "No, he never worked for the government. I suppose it's possible they worked on a project for the NSA. J. P. did have a top-secret security clearance, but he rarely spoke about his work, and he never said anything about working for the NSA."

"Do you happen to know what project he was working on when he died?" I asked.

"I believe it was some kind of top-secret encryption project."

"He was a mathematician, like my dad, right?"

"Yes. Computers, coding, cryptology—those were J. P.'s first loves." She sighed, and her voice sounded sad. "He was such a good man. I miss him."

"I'm sorry for your loss." I, better than most, understood the pain she felt. She'd lost her husband, and I'd lost my dad. So many lives hurt and altered irretrievably.

Why? Were J. P.'s death and my father's disappearance connected?

I thanked her for her time and hung up. I felt like I was making progress on finding out what had happened to my dad, but I had no idea where the trail was leading. What had happened to cause my father to so suddenly abandon his family and promising career and vanish off the face of the earth? What did the NSA have to do with it?

I didn't have the answers. Yet.

But I felt closer than ever.

CHAPTER THIRTY-TWO

Isaac Remington

"**G**ive me some good news."

Isaac and Glen Sampson stood at the edge of a lake in a secluded park about thirty miles from the NSA. It was a Sunday afternoon, but the forest around the lake was surprisingly devoid of people. They'd both taken significant steps to ensure they weren't followed and their meeting would be protected from prying eyes and ears. Isaac hadn't seen anyone at all during his hike to the spot. The air was cool, so Isaac flipped up the collar of his trench coat and adjusted his scarf to ward off a chill on his throat.

"I don't have any," Sampson said. "The girl hasn't washed out of UTOP, at least not yet. No one has."

"That's surprising. Do you think they're watering down UTOP?"

"Who knows? Don't worry. This coming week will be the toughest. The third week always loses the most students."

He studied the dark ripples on the water, his shoe just a few inches away from the edge. "How are we monitoring her?"

"Obviously, we can't monitor her while she's in UTOP. But I doubt she's doing any serious hacking there. She's not stupid. She knows everything electronic will be filtered. But there has been an interesting development."

"Which is?"

"She contacted Maria Lando."

Isaac turned toward Sampson. *"What?"*

"She made a call yesterday while they were in town on their Saturday break. We weren't able to tap the call, but when we traced the number from her cell phone, that's where it went. Her name is Maria Gonzalez now. She's remarried."

"How in the world did the girl put that together?"

"I have no idea. She's smart. Or maybe her father is feeding her info inside UTOP."

"No. That would be way too risky. He'd never put her in harm's way like that. Somehow, she's putting it together herself."

"Perhaps. But the trail will lead to us."

Isaac reached down and picked up a flat pebble. He ran his thumb over the cool, smooth surface. "So what? She's a child. What would she do with it?" But there was one potentially troubling aspect. "Do you know if she's had any contact with her mentor, Lexi Carmichael?"

"Carmichael? Why does that name sounds familiar?"

"She's the significant other of the director of IAD. Slash has been sniffing around, and I don't want him involved in this, even peripherally."

"No contact with either, as far as we know."

"Good. Hopefully she'll wash out and we can put our plan into motion. And if she doesn't, I have something else in mind to get the Avenger's attention."

"Such as?"

"Snatch her. All of the UTOP candidates go into town on Saturday, correct?"

"Correct. We've been closely observing her on Saturdays, as requested. She usually calls her mom or sister as soon as she gets into town, but yesterday she called Lando's wife instead. After talking on the phone, she typically goes to a local bookstore café and works on her laptop. Just so you know, we tried spoofing her to log on to our fake wireless hot spot from the café, but she's been careful and avoided them. She's avoiding any hacking, and when she uses the internet, she tunnels out using a secure and encrypted VPN. We haven't been able to crack it yet."

"Well, if she were to disappear, Saturday would be the day for it to happen."

There was a long pause. "Define disappear."

Now was the time to judge the commitment of the group. He took the rock from between his fingers and skipped it across the water. The stone bounced five times before finally sinking. "That depends on the Avenger. Regardless, this ends soon...one way or the other."

"Better sooner than later, in my opinion."

Isaac nodded. "Agreed."

"How's the other part of the plan going?"

"Exactly as planned. The terrorists abandoned their plan and disappeared, along with Sinclair's authenticity."

"You tipped off the terrorists?"

He could hear the unease in Sampson's voice, which irritated him. Was he the only one in the entire agency to have long-term vision? "Yes, but by doing so, I actually saved lives. Whatever they were planning, it isn't going to happen now. Then, once we get our hands on the back door, we'll take them down our way. No harm, no foul."

Sampson didn't say anything, but he reluctantly nodded his head. Isaac took careful note. Sampson was squeamish, and he didn't like it. That wouldn't work well with what he had planned for the NSA. At some point Sampson would have to be reassigned or shuffled out.

"I've got a meeting with the director tomorrow to argue against moving forward with Sinclair," he said. "If all goes well, we'll move on to the next stage. If I run into trouble, we always have the girl to fall back on. Report back to the core that all is proceeding as planned."

"I will," Sampson said. "We'll all be glad when this is settled."

"Yes, we will. Change this significant never happens without risk. Risk that is expertly handled by forward-thinking and intelligent men. We'll manage it. We've managed it for sixteen years, and now our fruit is ripening. It's ours to take."

CHAPTER THIRTY-THREE

Angel Sinclair

Another week passed at the trials, and somehow I wasn't kicked out. In fact, no one had been released from the program, and no one had quit. We just continued with our studies, endured the weird psychological testing and questioning, and kept up with the grueling physical testing in preparation for the next trial on Friday. None of us had any clue what it would be, but my best guess was that it would have to do with our physical capabilities. It was the one big area where we'd not been tested yet. It was also the area I was the weakest.

I started spending every day after dinner at the gym. Running was difficult, and my endurance sucked. To say I was pathetic at weights would be an understatement. Rope climbing, push-ups, or anything requiring physical flexibility would be certain to sink me.

But I didn't want to go home, so I pressed on.

Wally and Frankie came with me to the gym most nights, but on Thursday night, the night before the next trial, I went alone. Frankie was helping Hala run through her lines for her acting homework, and Wally was working on a paper for English lit.

When I got to the gym, Jax was in the pool swimming, and Kira was on the elliptical machine. I watched Jax swim for a few minutes, judging his skill, before heading to the weights to warm up.

After about twenty minutes, Jax joined me. He'd changed from his swimsuit into shorts, but wore a cutoff white muscle shirt. His dark hair was still damp. I was careful to keep my eyes averted as he picked up some light weights and started his reps next to me.

"Aren't you going to use the bench?" I finally asked after a few minutes. I wished we didn't have the mirror in front of us, because it put him front and center in my line of vision, no matter how hard I tried not to look at him.

"Nope," he said. "I rarely lift heavy weights. I start with a small amount of weight and do hundreds of reps. That builds long, lean muscles, not large, bulky ones. I'm in it for the strength, not the physique."

His physique looked just fine to me. Not that I had noticed. Much.

My face started to get hot, because talking about a guy's body was not a typical area of conversation for me, so I abruptly changed the subject. "Jax, why are you afraid of the water?"

"*What?*" He stopped lifting. "Why would you ask that? I was just swimming laps."

"I know. I've seen you swimming several times. But you always swim on a side lane. If those lanes are taken, you don't swim at all. You wait for a side lane to open. You also have this habit of touching the side wall every six to seven strokes. Except it's not really a habit—it's methodical. Every seventh stroke."

"You were *watching* me?" His voice had risen slightly, his cheeks flushed.

"Well, yeah. I watch everyone. I just happen to be really observant."

He started lifting weights again, although a bit faster than he had before. His brow was drawn together in a frown. "I'm *not* afraid of the water. End of discussion."

"Okay. I'm sorry if I upset you. I was just wondering."

He lifted for a few more minutes and then left without saying another word. Apparently I'd hit a nerve, but why he'd be so upset about his swimming habits, I had no idea. Reminding myself to never try to initiate casual conversation again, especially with a cute guy, I finished my repetitions and headed back to the room for a shower.

Hala and Frankie were already in their pajamas and finished with their homework, because they were chatting. Kira was in bed reading a textbook, her back to the room, ignoring us as always. I hopped into the shower and also came out ready for bed. Kira had put aside her book and was trying to sleep; Hala was in bed, and Frankie lay on her back wearing a gel eye mask. I turned off the light and climbed into my bunk.

I couldn't sleep. Again. After an hour of tossing and turning, I sat up in my bed and hugged my knees, sighing.

Frankie must have heard me, because she whispered up to me, "Angel, are you okay?"

"I'm sorry if I'm keeping you up," I whispered back.

"You're not. I can't sleep, either. Are you worried about the trial tomorrow?"

I considered the question. I felt good coming off last week's trial. I hadn't been booted yet, so in terms of anxiety, I wasn't as stressed out as I had been before. There was a lot going through my mind, including the conversation with Jax, but it was a cumulation of everything.

"I'm okay," I lied. "How about you?"

"I'm fine. We'll do as well as we can, you know."

I lay back and slid my elbow behind my neck, resting my head on it. "I know. It just amazes me how nothing ever fazes you."

"Well, there's no sense in worrying about what hasn't happened," she said. "But you're so logical, you already know that, right?" I could hear the smile in her voice.

"Knowing and accepting that are two different things. But you're right. Again."

"Of course I'm right. Again. Good night, Angel. Don't worry. You'll be awesome tomorrow."

I couldn't help but smile. "Good night, Frankie. So will you."

CHAPTER THIRTY-FOUR

Angel Sinclair

"For today's trial, we'll be grading you on physical fitness, mental toughness, and mobility, as well as evaluating your problem-solving skills," Mr. Donovan told us as we sat in Room 101 as part of the briefing before the trial. We were dressed in our usual camouflage outfits, but today we'd been told to bring sunglasses. We'd also been instructed to put on sunblock, which was a strong indicator we'd be outside for the trial.

"The trial will be an obstacle course of sorts. Some are straightforward physical obstacles; others require teamwork and puzzle solving. There will be instructions for what you should do at each obstacle."

What little breakfast I'd eaten churned in my stomach, ready to come back up. I'd known a physical test of some kind would be coming, but I'd been in denial it would be an entire trial. I'd *never* pass something like this. I was about to get a giant boot out of the compound.

"The fastest person to finish gets a bonus," Mr. Donovan explained. "However, *everyone* fails if even *one* of you doesn't finish in the time allotted, which is exactly two hours. *Everyone* must complete *every* challenge. No exceptions. Plan your strategy accordingly."

Well, that totally threw a wrench into things. I considered the implications. If I had to finish for all of us to win, it meant, I would probably get assistance of some kind. That was reassuring, at least to a point.

"One more item," Mr. Donovan said. "You, as a group, get one question, and one question only. One of you may ask it during the obstacle course, but everyone must agree on the question and who will ask it. I will observe you at each obstacle but will not interfere or speak unless it is in response to your one question."

"Are there any other rules?" I asked.

He smiled at me. "None, Ms. Sinclair. So, everyone, please follow me to the grassy area in back of the compound, where the obstacle course has been set up. The clock starts in five minutes."

The minute we arrived at the first obstacle, the clock started. Bo quickly assembled us. It was clear we'd have to work together to help those of us who were physically challenged, myself included, if we were to finish the course as a group.

The October air had a cool tinge to it, but the sun was warm on our head and shoulders. Autumn colors of gold, red, and orange burst from the trees around us. The grassy area had been transformed into an obstacle course as far as the eye could see. Monkey bars, nets, mud pits, the whole thing. Mr. Donovan stood under a tree, his arms crossed against his chest, watching us without expression. My stomach twisted with anxiety, wondering how I would finish this course.

If I failed, everyone failed.

"Okay, everyone, let's talk about how to do this."

I glanced over at Wally. He was holding his stomach, his face deathly pale. I knew he was thinking the same thing I was. The White Knights were the weak link in this operation, and we could easily take everyone down with us. Somehow, this possibility didn't occur to Frankie, or if it did, she didn't seem bothered by it. She chatted animatedly with Mike, appearing not to have a care in the world.

How did she do that?

While everyone was circling around Bo, I studied the first obstacle. It seemed straightforward, not that I thought I had any chance of completing it. Monkey bars over a mud pit.

"Walk in the park, baby," Mike said, following my gaze. "They don't call me Mike the Monkey for nothing."

"They call you Mike the Monkey?" I asked.

Mike's cheeks got red. "Well, they did in elementary school. I've always been good at jumping, climbing, swinging, the monkey bars—you know, that kind of stuff." He made a chattering sound like a monkey, and I laughed, easing my anxiety slightly.

Seeing we were all assembled and listening, Bo got started. "My suggestion for this trial is we stick together. We help each other finish, and at the end, we vote which one of us gets to cross first. We all have to help each other or we won't make it. Agreed?"

We all nodded our heads, so he turned to Mike. "I heard you tell Angel you could cross. You go first. Kira, can you make it across?"

She shielded her eyes and looked at the bars. "Sure. Shouldn't be a problem for me."

"Good. You follow Mike."

"I can do it, too," Hala said. "I'll go after Kira."

"Wally?" Bo looked hopefully at him.

Wally sighed. "The odds that I can cross that without falling into the mud pit are a million to one."

"I can't do it, either." Frankie lifted her hands. "Not without help."

Bo glanced my way with the unspoken question.

I shook my head. "I'm sorry, Bo. I don't think I can make it without slipping off."

"Why would they give us a task like this when they know several of us can't do it?" Frankie wondered aloud.

"Problem solving," Jax offered. "Strategic planning. Time management. Take your pick."

Bo blew out a breath. I noticed he hadn't asked Jax if he could manage it. Guess that meant he could. "Okay, Wally, Frankie, and Angel, if you can't make it on your own, Jax and I are going to have to help you. We'll have to partially support your weight, and as Jax and I are the largest, we'll take turns helping you over. Mike, get going and the rest of you follow."

Mike scrambled to the bars, jumped up, and started across, his legs swinging. When he got about halfway, Kira started. A minute later, Hala followed her. They made it look easy as they hopped off and waited for us.

Bo dipped his head toward Wally. "All right, you're first. Let's go."

"Me?" Wally said, his face paling further. "What about girls first?"

"Get your butt over there," Bo said. "Let's go."

"Wait." Wally looked panicked. "How *exactly* are we going to do this?"

"We'll go across together." Bo said, motioning for Wally to come with him to the ladder on the monkey bars. He reached up and grabbed onto the first bar. "Get on my back."

"You're going to carry me?" Wally said incredulously. "That can't be safe."

"I'm going to *partially* carry you," Bo clarified. "You need to help me by holding on to the bars and carrying some of your own weight. Got it?"

"Not really," Wally started backing up.

"Get on his back, Wally," Frankie said. "You'll be fine."

"I really think we should discuss this further."

"There will be *no* more discussion," Bo said. "If you don't get on my back, I'll knock you unconscious and carry you."

Wally gulped. He may have been the general in the virtual world, but Bo was in charge here. "Fine." He held up his hands. "No need to go all *Halo 5* on me."

Wally walked up to the monkey bars and jumped, catching the first monkey bar inside Bo's hands. "There. Satisfied?"

"Not yet. Put your legs around my waist and wait for my command. I'll tell you when we're moving to each bar. Ready?"

Wally's face was ashen. "Not really, but what choice do I have?"

"None. Jax, get moving. You're next."

"Yes, sir." Jax turned to me and Frankie. "Okay, ladies. Who wants to go next?"

Frankie immediately pointed to me. "She does. I'll watch her and get important tips on what to do."

I was going to protest, but Jax grabbed my hand and pulled me toward the ladder. "Up you go, Red."

Bo and Wally were moving slowly across the bars, but they were hanging on. The muscles in Bo's arms were straining. I couldn't even imagine how hard it must be for him.

Jax snapped his fingers in front of my face. "Red, are you paying attention? Grab the first rung and get on my back."

I looked up. He was tall enough to reach the bar and still have his feet on the ladder. "I have to climb on your back?"

Jax studied me from behind his sunglasses. "While it might be a lot more fun if you held on to me from the front, it would be kind of hard to cross the monkey bars like that."

My cheeks heated. "Fine." I was too short to reach the first rung, so I'd have to jump. I bent my knees when Jax suddenly realized my problem. Bracing his back against the pole, he put his hands on my waist, lifting me up so I could grab the first bar.

"Thanks," I said. "Short-person problem."

"Got it." He repositioned himself by grabbing the second bar and hanging. "Wrap your legs around my waist and wait for my command to move."

I could see the corded muscles in his neck and arms. "I'm scared," I admitted.

"Just get on and trust me, okay?"

"Okay." I wrapped my legs around his waist and said a prayer that I wouldn't slip off. My hands were already sweaty from nerves.

"Reach for the next bar...now," he said.

I reached for the next bar. We were a little off in terms of timing, but he moved on. My hands stayed nestled between his, but after just a few bars, my arms were shaking from the effort of hanging on, and I wasn't even holding half my weight.

He must have felt me shaking. "Take it easy. Red. Just keep your legs tight. I don't want them in the way. We need to keep moving as one, okay?"

"Okay." My face rested slightly against the back of his head.

"Keep going," he urged me. "One bar at a time."

On and on we went. It seemed never ending, although Kira, Mike, and Hala had crossed in what seemed like seconds. Every bar we moved, the harsher his breathing became. I couldn't imagine how Bo had fared with Wally. Bo was bigger than Jax, and he had to lift his own body weight in addition to Wally's, which was heavier than mine.

At some point, I realized Wally and Bo were already across. They'd made it. If they could do it, so could we.

Finally, we were at the last rung. We crossed in sync, Jax getting his feet onto the ladder and letting out a sigh of relief. I unfastened my legs from his waist, and he helped me down. Once on solid ground, I collapsed. It wasn't pretty, but I'd made it. One obstacle down and who knew how many more to go.

"Good job, Red."

I shaded my eyes from the sun as I looked up at Jax. "Thanks. I couldn't have done it without you." He flashed a smile and walked away.

Bo had already gone back across the bars for Frankie, who was waiting on the ladder for him. When he got there, she stopped him.

"I have an idea," she said. "Can you give me a boost up to the first bar?"

Bo obliged and lifted her up. She hung precariously on the rung before starting to swing her legs. To my surprise, she lifted them and hooked them on the next rung. Before I knew it, she'd pulled herself to the top of the monkey bars and started crawling across.

"I think this way will be faster for me," she called down to Bo.

"Woohoo!" I shouted. "Great idea, Frankie."

"Why didn't I think of that?" Wally said, lifting his hands.

Bo went across below her, and they made it across at about the same time.

Bo helped her down, and I gave her a hug. "You're brilliant, Frankie. I can't believe I didn't think of that."

She whispered in my ear, "I actually thought about it *before* you went off with Jax, but I bet you enjoyed your way a *lot* more than mine. You're welcome."

I rolled my eyes but was so happy I'd actually made it across that I didn't say a thing.

"Guys, that ate up seventeen minutes," Bo said. "Let's move to the next obstacle."

We jogged as a group to the next setup.

"It's called the Zombie Mud Crawl," Bo read. "The instructions say the wire is live. It won't shock you if you touch it, but red light and siren will go off and you must crawl out sideways and start over again. We don't have time to play around, people. Do it right the first time."

"I'm small, so this should be easy for me," Hala said. "I'll go first." She stopped at the edge of the obstacle. "Whoa, what's that in the mud?"

Frankie peered over her shoulder. "Worms. Oh, no."

"Frankie, worms are good for the environment," I said. "They don't bite."

"Nope. Not doing it," she said.

"We don't have time to argue," Bo said. "Hala, go."

Hala inhaled a deep breath and crawled under the wire. She was small and fast, but when she popped out the other side, she was dripping in mud and slime.

"Ewwww…" she said, shaking her hands.

"Mike, you're next," Bo said. "Kira, you're after him, and then Wally and Jax."

When Mike started, Bo turned to face us. "Frankie, you're going to get under that wire."

"I don't like worms."

"I don't like losing." He frowned at her. "You're going to do it."

"I'm not."

"Frankie, I'll go first," I offered. "I don't like bugs, either, but I am going to hold my breath, squint my eyes, and just do it. You have to stay calm, because if you jerk up, you'll set off the wire alarm."

"I don't think I can be calm."

"You *can*. You're *always* calm about everything."

"Except bugs and worms. Will you do it with me?"

I glanced at Bo. "Is there any reason we can't do it together?"

He shrugged. "None I can think of. But you run the risk of kicking or flicking mud into each other's face as you squirm. Plus, if the wire lights up, you both must start over. Time is ticking."

"I'm not going without Angel," Frankie said.

"Well, that settles it," I said. "We're doing it together."

We walked to the edge of the pit. Frankie, Bo, and I were the last three. So far, everyone else had made it across without tripping the alarm. Even Wally looked triumphant as he dripped disgusting stuff.

I took Frankie's hand and knelt at the edge of the pit. "Ready?" I gave her hand an encouraging squeeze.

She looked at me uncertainly but nodded. "I'm ready."

CHAPTER THIRTY-FIVE

Angel Sinclair

"You're going to wiggle on your stomach, kind of like a snake," I explained. "Not that there are any snakes in here. Just don't jerk your head up or you'll set off the wire."

She looked alarmed by the snake comment, so I decided it was time to shut my mouth. I got on my stomach and tugged her down. She joined me on the ground.

"It smells," she complained.

"Of course it smells, Frankie. It's mud. Come on. Breathe through your mouth and let's do it."

As quickly as we dared, we crawled through the mud. Frankie was hyperventilating the entire time. I was scared she would pass out. Everyone was cheering us on, and somehow that helped. At last, we made it to the other side without setting off the alarm.

Jax helped her up and slapped her on the back a couple of times, causing mud to fly and hit Mike in the nose. Mike wiped it off with a good-natured grin.

Frankie was so happy she'd made it, her eyes filled with tears. "I did it. Oh, thank you, Angel."

"You did all the work. I was just moral support." Although, even as I said it, I marveled that I'd done it. I'd never been anyone's moral support before.

Bo waited until we finished, but he started the second we were through. He was almost done when his large form set off the alarm. "Crap." He scooted out sideways and jogged back to the beginning.

"You've got too many muscles," Wally called out, and we all laughed.

Finally Bo made it across. A quick glance at the time indicated another nineteen minutes had passed. We were exhausted and muddy and smelled rank, but we had to hurry.

We ran to the next obstacle, and when we got there, we stopped in amazement. A single beam had been stretched across another mud pit.

"This shouldn't be too hard," Kira said.

"What?" Frankie said in astonishment. "We're completely covered in mud and slippery. How is that not hard?"

"If we take off our shoes, our bare feet will give us better grip." Hala started untying her shoes.

"She's right," Bo said. "Everyone get barefoot."

We started taking off our shoes and socks. Mike finished first, so he started across with Kira following close behind. They were both acing these challenges. They would have left all of us in the dust if it hadn't been a group effort.

"When you're ready, go," Bo instructed the rest of us as he pushed his shoes aside. "Don't wait."

I was ready, so I went after Kira. Hala came behind me, but she yelped and slipped off about the halfway point, falling into the mud pit with a thump. It startled me so much, I almost slipped off with her. Somehow I managed to straighten myself and continue. Hala stood up in the mud pit, furious with herself.

"I just took a wrong step," she yelled. "And I've done the balance beam a million times without slipping. This is so frustrating!"

I made it across, and Mike stretched out a hand to help me off the beam. "Thank God," I said as my feet hit the ground. I'd actually completed a challenge on my own.

"Wally, go," Bo yelled as he reached down to pull Hala out of the pit. Wally still stood on one end of the beam, looking at it.

"Okay. Sure. I'm on it."

Wally climbed up and started his way across, but he was unsteady. He was moving so slowly, at the rate he was going, it was going to take him an hour to cross. There was also a ninety-nine-percent chance he was going to fall simply from shaking so much.

"Wally, you can do it," I shouted. "Imagine you're crossing the Imogen Bridge in *Hidden Realm*. You've done it a hundred times. Just keep moving. Step by step."

Bo told Frankie to go next. She climbed up on the beam and started walking. She was surprisingly sure-footed and caught up to Wally before he knew it.

She held out a hand, and he used it to steady himself. "You've got this," she said matter-of-factly. "I'm right behind you. If you fall, I'll jump in after you."

Whether he was bolstered by her presence, terrified she'd knock him off the beam, or afraid she really would jump in after him, he started moving faster. Soon, they were both across. I hugged him, Frankie slapped him on the back, and Wally collapsed to the ground, kissing it.

Hala got up on the beam to cross again, but this time she did it much more carefully. Bo and Jax crossed without a problem, making it look so easy we all frowned at them.

"We've got sixty-two minutes left, people," Jax said.

"Move it," Bo urged us as he jogged past toward the next obstacle. Mike offered a hand and helped Wally off the ground, and we followed, running to catch up.

The next obstacle was a curved cement wall about twelve feet high. According to the instructions, we were supposed to get up to the top ledge and slide down the other side.

"Oh, crap," Wally said, looking up it. "I'll never get up that."

"I don't suppose there's a rope ladder hanging around somewhere," Mike said.

Kira walked around to the other side and then came back. "Nothing."

We were silent staring at the wall.

"It's pretty obvious we'll never get up that without a ladder or a rope to help us," Kira finally said.

"We have to," I said. "Every problem has a solution. We just have to think of it."

We looked at each other, our brains working furiously, but nothing leaped to mind.

I turned hopefully to Jax. "Can you snap your fingers and a rope will magically appear?"

My words must have triggered a thought, because he suddenly smiled. "Not exactly. Take off your shirt, Red."

CHAPTER THIRTY-SIX

Angel Sinclair

"Excuse me?" I looked at him incredulously.

Jax spread his hands to include the entire group. "*Everyone* take off your shirt and give it to me. We don't have a rope, but we can *make* a rope out of our shirts. I'll get up there first. If Bo gives me a boost, I should be able to pull myself up. Throw me the rope made of our shirts and I'll be the anchor at the top. Among us, we should be able to get everyone up."

All of the girls had sports bras on, so it was kind of like wearing a crop top, not that I'd ever worn a crop top in my life. Regardless, all the essentials were covered, and there was no time for modesty.

"I'm an Eagle Scout," Wally offered. "I'll tie the knots."

"Hurry," Kira said.

Bo was already standing at the wall. He bent down and Jax climbed on his shoulders, steadying himself against the wall. He was still shy of reaching the ledge, so he warned Bo he would have to jump to make it. Bo nodded and braced himself with one hand against the wall. Several of us stood behind Bo, bracing him from the back.

We held one collective breath as Jax bent and jumped up, his fingers barely gripping the edge. With a grunt, he pulled himself up onto the wall and rested. We cheered as Bo rotated his shoulders.

"Throw me the shirt rope," Jax shouted.

Wally was frantically tying the last of the knots, and Kira had been helping by handing him the shirts. When Wally was done, Kira threw it up to Jax. It took four tries, but Jax finally caught it.

Kira went first, bracing against the wall and using the shirt rope to pull herself up. Once she was up, the two of them helped the rest of us get up. We slid down the other side, pumping a fist when we finished.

"Keep going," Bo said as soon as Jax met us at the bottom. He slapped Jax on the back. "Good thinking."

We followed him, but the truth was we were beyond exhausted, and we had no idea how many more obstacles we had. We left our T-shirts behind, as it would take too much time to untie them, and ran to the next obstacle. We had to go around the KIT building before we came to an area with a flagpole about twenty feet high, surrounded by air-filled, bouncy exercise mats.

"What's this?" Hala said in astonishment.

We all exchanged puzzled glances with each other.

Bo picked up the instruction card. "It's the final obstacle." He glanced at his watch. "We have thirty-four minutes to complete it. The goal is to get whatever is at the top of the pole. The only thing we get to help us is, apparently, this coil of rope and those bouncy mats, presumably in case we fall off while trying."

"Where was the rope when we needed it for the last obstacle?" Mike grumbled.

"Let's go," Wally said, clapping his hands. "Let's

shimmy up the pole and get the thing. It looks like an oversize hockey puck."

Jax grinned at him. "Slow down, cowboy. Let's see if we can knock it off first."

"Oh." Wally paused. "That's a good idea."

"Everyone find a rock and try to dislodge it," Jax said. "The instructions didn't say *how* we had to get it, just that we get it."

"What if it's something dangerous inside like a bomb or something?" Frankie asked.

"I would think the instructions would have told us to be careful with it."

We glanced over at Mr. Donovan who stood in the shade, watching us.

"I'm with Jax," I finally said. "Let's see if we can knock it off."

We scattered, looking for some rocks. I carried back several, as did everyone else. We all stood to one side and threw the rocks at the object, hoping to dislodge it.

Jax was the first to make a direct hit. It didn't budge. "It must be attached."

"Attached?" Kira said. "How?"

"I don't know." Bo shrugged.

"So, we have to climb to get it?" Kira looked agitated.

"No, not climb." Mike now stood next to the pole examining it. "It's too big around for one person to shimmy. Even if it wasn't, it's greased."

"Greased? Ah, come on." Jax blew out a frustrated breath and walked next to Mike, rubbing his fingers on the pole. "Mike's right. We'd slide like a greased pig trying to shimmy this thing."

"Even with the rope?" I asked.

"Even with the rope," Jax confirmed. "It'll slide, just like my feet would if I tried to climb by bracing my feet against the pole."

Bo was silent as he circled the pole, considering.

"Maybe we could wipe the grease off," Frankie offered.

"No time or materials to do that," Bo said. "We're going to have to stack."

"Stack?" I repeated.

"Climb on each other's shoulders until we reach the top," Jax explained. "I bet that's what the mats are for."

"What?" Frankie said in horror. "Stand on each other's shoulders?"

"Yes. Bo and I will anchor at the bottom, standing side by side in order to better distribute the weight. There will two people on top of us and then two more on top of them. Then one person will stand single and the lightest person will stand on that person's shoulders to reach the object at the top. We can do this." He turned to me. "Red, can you calculate our heights against the length of the pole? Are we tall enough together to reach it if we do it that way?"

I looked up at the pole and then asked everyone for their heights, reminding them not to lie. "It'll be close," I said when I finished the calculations in my head. "I could be off by a foot, and that would be a problem. It's all estimation at this point."

"We don't have another choice," said Bo. He looked between Hala and me. "Between the two of you, who weighs less?"

I gave my specs first followed by Hala. She outweighed me by a measly two pounds.

"Angel is on top, then," Bo said. "Wally and Mike, you stand on top of Jax and me. Frankie and Kira, you're to stand on them."

"I'm not sure this is a good idea," Frankie said.

"It's the *only* idea, and we're short on time," Bo countered. "Hala, you stand single on Kira's shoulders. Angel, it's up to you to climb onto Hala's shoulders and retrieve whatever's at the top. You'll have to climb over most of us to get up there."

"Right." I gulped. "No pressure."

"Take the rope in case you need it," Bo said, tossing the rope to me. "Just don't drop it."

I caught it and wound it around my neck and shoulders. "Okay, but before we stack, I would suggest asking Mr. Donovan the one question we've been permitted."

For a moment, everyone just stared at me. I guess between exhaustion and stress, the question thing had slipped their minds.

"What do you have in mind, Red?" Jax said.

"We need to know how whatever is up there is attached. If I'm tasked with getting it off, I need to know exactly what I need to do to remove it. I don't want to be standing precariously on all of your shoulders trying to figure it out."

"Good thinking," Wally said. "She's right."

I glanced at Bo and he looked at the group. "Are we in agreement that Angel should ask the question?"

Everyone nodded, so he swept out his hand toward Mr. Donovan. "Ask away."

I walked over to Mr. Donovan, who was watching us from the shade of a tree, his arms crossed against his chest.

"Mr. Donovan?" I said. "We have our one question ready."

"Go ahead, Ms. Sinclair."

"How is the object we're supposed to retrieve from atop the pole attached?"

Mr. Donovan smiled. "It's snapped in and rotated once."

"Okay, thank you."

"Satisfied?" Bo asked me.

"Yeah, let's do it."

One by one, we climbed up on top of each other, a human pyramid of sorts. Those of us who were climbing last helped get everyone below us in place. Climbing last had its advantages, as I could watch how everyone else did it before me. When it was my turn, it wasn't as hard as I thought it would be. Still, I watched where I stepped and didn't look down even once.

Climbing up Hala was the hardest, because she was so small. She crouched the best she could, and I carefully put each of my feet on her shoulders. She steadied my ankles with her hands as I stretched myself up. I was trembling. My fingers nearly touched the top, but I was still a few inches too short.

"I'm just shy of reaching it," I announced.

A collective groan came from below me. I inadvertently glanced down and saw a crew had blown up and arranged the mats closer around us, presumably to protect us if we fell. I looked straight ahead as my stomach flipped in anxiety.

I leaned slightly against the pole to steady myself, but it was greased, even up this high up. I had to be careful not to put too much of my weight against the pole for fear of slipping off.

"Don't worry. I have an idea." I carefully removed the rope from my shoulder and began forming a knot. "I'm going to tie a noose with the rope and slip it over the object. I'm close enough to do that. I think. Then I'll tighten it and pull. Hopefully, it will pop off."

"Hurry up," Mike called up. "We have eleven minutes."

I fought the urge to rush. Rushing meant mistakes, and we didn't have time for even one. I drew in slow, careful breaths as I tied the knot, eyeballing the opening to ensure it was smaller than the pole so it wouldn't slide down.

"Okay, knot is tied," I yelled. "Stand by."

I reached up, carefully pushing the noose up to the top of the pole. Using my arm to toss or throw it was out of the question, as the movement could topple me off. I'd have to use my wrist to flick it as hard as I could over the object.

When I had gone as far as I could reach, I flicked my wrist and gently pulled. The noose came right back to me, landing on my back. It hadn't gone over the object.

I tried twice more, but no success. Sweat dripped down my temples and blurred my vision. My shoulders and back were screaming from the strain. I could hear whimpers from Hala below and knew my weight had to be digging into her shoulders.

I closed my eyes, took a breath.

"How's it going, Angel?" Bo shouted up.

"Stand by," I answered, reaching up and giving the noose another wrist flick. This time when I pulled, the noose didn't come back. I carefully tightened it. I pulled as hard as I could, but I wasn't at the right angle to twist it.

"Guys, I've got good news and bad news. The good news is I've got the noose around the object. I've pulled, but from my vantage point, I can't rotate it enough to pop it off."

More groans came from below.

"We've got only one option," Bo called up. "We're going to have to move."

CHAPTER THIRTY-SEVEN

Angel Sinclair

"Whoa, what?" Wally said.

"We're going to have to shuffle as a group with Angel as she pulls on the rope at the same time," Bo repeated.

"Well, whatever we're going to do, we'd better do it fast," said Mike. "We've only got six minutes left."

I gulped, then shouted, "I'm ready, let's just do it."

"Angel, which way do we go?" shouted Bo.

I froze. Good question. Why hadn't I thought to add that to the one question I asked Mr. Donovan?

"I don't know," I said honestly. "I'm going with clockwise. It's the most logical."

"Maybe that's exactly why we should go counterclockwise," Wally shouted back.

"Just decide and do it quickly," Jax yelled. His voice sounded strained. The collective weight of all of us on his and Bo's shoulders had to be killing them.

"Clockwise," I said decisively.

"Clockwise, it is," Bo shouted. "On my mark, I want everyone to gently shift their weight with me to the right. I'm going to shuffle about an inch, and then I'll call a stop. Just try to stay with me. Then we'll go another inch, and so on, until that baby pops off."

I pressed my lips together and tightened my hands on the rope. They were slick with sweat. The odds were high our stack would collapse when we moved.

"Now," he shouted and I could feel the group move slightly to the left. For a second we swayed precariously and then straightened out. I pulled on the rope, but nothing. What if Wally was right and it was counter-clockwise? I would have ruined it for everyone.

Focus, Sinclair. Second-guessing at this stage of the game isn't helpful.

"Again," I yelled.

"Now," Bo called out. He shuffled, the rest of us coming along. This time we swayed even more. There were a lot of groans and some muffled cussing. I wasn't sure we could take one more movement.

"Come on," Jax shouted. "You can do it, Angel."

I pulled as hard as I dared, but nothing happened. In sheer desperation, I lifted myself slightly off Hala's shoulders, putting all my weight on the rope. I felt the object turn, and then with a pop, it flew off the pole and headed toward the mats below.

I almost went with it.

"It worked!" I shouted. I landed back on Hala's shoulders a bit harder than I intended, but she steadied my ankles with her hands. For a moment afterward, our balance was precarious. Miraculously, we all managed to lean into the pole and stay up. We let out a collective sigh of relief.

After that there was a lot of cheering until I heard Frankie speak. "While that's all great and wonderful, guys, the clock is still ticking. How the heck do we get down from here?"

I looked over at Mr. Donovan and noticed he was

clapping his hands. "Jump," he shouted at us. "It's safe. You'll bounce on the mats."

Since I was on top, I had to go first and have faith he was right. Closing my eyes, I pushed away from the pole and jumped. I landed on the mat and bounced around a bit, but eventually rolled off.

"It works," I shouted. "Jump!"

One by one, everyone unstacked and collapsed in exhaustion.

Bo again kept us on track. "We have one minute and seventeen seconds left. Who goes across first?"

"I vote for Bo," I said. "He was our commander today, and we wouldn't have made it without him."

"I agree," said Wally. "Without him, we'd all be toast. Especially me."

One by one, we nodded our consent.

Bo shook his head. "I don't feel right about this. This was a group effort."

"We were only a group because *you* held us together." Jax slapped Bo on the back. "The vote is a done deal, bro, so don't bother protesting. Walk across the finish line so we can follow you and get cleaned up, okay?"

Bo finally nodded. "Thanks, everyone, for the vote of confidence."

The moment he crossed the finish line, we rushed him in a happy surge. I'd never been so exhausted in my life, but the fact that I'd finished what I'd considered an insurmountable part of my training made me hope that maybe I *could* do this after all. Another trial down, and I was still standing.

Only one question remained. How much more could I stand?

CHAPTER THIRTY-EIGHT

Angel Sinclair

The next morning, every muscle in my body hurt. Arms, shoulders, back, butt, thighs, you name it. I could barely walk, even after taking ibuprofen. Regardless, there was no way I was missing the regular Saturday trip into town. I needed to buy some supplies and wanted to do some reading.

Neither Frankie nor Wally made it into town, as they'd both elected to sleep in. I didn't see Kira, either, as she'd already been gone when I awoke. The rest of us sat on the bus quietly, staring out the window, sore from the difficult physical challenges of the trial.

The bus dropped us off, and we all went our separate ways. I headed straightaway for the main square, where I could make some calls. I talked with my mom for about twenty minutes, and then Gwen for another fifteen. I kept my comments to glowing endorsements of the curriculum and staff and mentioned zip about the physical pain and emotional roller coaster I was riding. After I hung up, I headed to the small bookstore café, which had become a favorite, to do some private research on my dad.

The café was nearly empty except for two girls sitting at a table and looking at their phones and the old guy who'd paid for my hot chocolate the last time I'd been in here.

He looked up from his newspaper. "Well, hello again. You've got money today?"

I held up my wallet. "I'm happy to pay you back."

"You will not. It's not every day an old man like me gets to buy a young lady a hot chocolate and croissant."

"Thank you very much. It's much appreciated."

"My pleasure."

He went back to reading his paper as I got in line to buy a hot chocolate. I added a cinnamon roll to my order, because it smelled heavenly.

I picked the same table I usually had so I could angle my laptop to the wall and no one could see what I was doing. It was just a precaution, but after the email warning me to beware of possible criminal elements in the NSA who might be monitoring me, I had become exceptionally careful about what I did online. I ate half of my cinnamon roll before I started reading information on Joseph Lando. When my hot chocolate cooled, I drank it, enjoying the rich flavor.

The bell on the café door rang, and I looked up as Jax strolled in. He spotted me, and I swear his eyes lit up. He made a beeline for my table, so I quickly closed my laptop, resting my elbows on top of it. This was turning into a regular meeting place for us, but oddly, I'd started to look forward to it. "Hey, Jax."

"Hey, Red. How's the hot chocolate today?"

"Excellent as always, and I actually paid for it by myself."

He slid into the chair opposite me and looked over his shoulder. "Even though your boyfriend is here?"

"Very funny. He's really nice. I offered to pay him back, but he wouldn't take my money." The teenage girls looked at Jax and giggled. I tipped my head toward them. "Those girls like you."

"What girls?" He didn't take his eyes off me.

"The girls at the table over there. You passed them on your way in."

"They're not my type."

"Oh, you have a type?"

"I do." He grinned and leaned forward, lowering his voice. "I'm partial to redheads."

Even though I thought he was just teasing me, my cheeks heated anyway. "You're impossible, you know." He seemed amused by my blush, so I decided to change the subject. "How are you feeling after yesterday's trial?"

He leaned back, shrugged his shoulders a couple of times. "My shoulders and arms are killing me, but personally, I think the obstacle course was way too easy. Something's off. I have a feeling they're preparing to spring something big on us. Something to shake things up."

"What are you talking about?" I looked at him incredulously. "The trial yesterday was *not* easy. Every part of my body hurts and might possibly hurt for the rest of my life."

"It was easy," he insisted. "They're priming us for something else. A shock, an unexpected twist. They think we're complacent, so they're going to make us change the way we're doing things."

"Complacent? Are you serious?"

"Completely."

I cocked my head, studying him. "And you know this…how, exactly?"

"Instinct." He lifted his hands. "I told you I'm good at reading people and situations. It's a gut feeling, but it's a strong one."

I didn't know what to make of his so-called gut feeling, but I figured I'd find out soon enough. "Fine.

Go get your coffee and tell me more about this gut feeling of yours."

He raised a dark eyebrow. "Are you inviting me to coffee, Red?"

"Only if you bring me back another cinnamon roll."

He laughed and stood. "Ah, now that's a deal I can get behind."

CHAPTER THIRTY-NINE

Isaac Remington

"D id she finally wash out?" Isaac sat in his car at the parking lot of his favorite French restaurant, L'auberge, speaking to Sampson on the burner phone.

"Strangely, she did not. In fact, not one of the kids has washed out yet. It's crazy. I think the entire class is going into the final trial together."

"Impossible. What's going on over there?" Isaac swore under his breath.

"I don't know, but she was at the bookstore café again working on her computer—on what, we don't know. She's still being extraordinary careful behind the keyboard. She called her mother and sister from the cell."

Isaac drummed his fingers on the steering wheel. Who would have guessed that the girl would hang in there for so long at the trials? One of his first duties as the new NSA director would be to overhaul the UTOP program, ensuring the standards remained high.

"So, what happened during your meeting with the director?" Sampson asked.

Isaac watched a couple walk into the restaurant. The man was in a suit and the woman in towering heels, clutching onto his arm for support. Two ordinary citizens who had no idea the lengths to which their government went to keep them safe. "He's on the fence. While he's concerned about the terrorist information not panning out the way he thought it would, he wants to wait until the next contact with Sinclair to make a final decision."

"That could be dangerous. Sinclair is getting desperate."

"Exactly, which is why we need to make sure the next contact never happens. Let's put the play for the daughter into place. Finalize the arrangements, and for God's sake, be discreet. Make sure there is no trail."

There was a pause, but Sampson came through. "Done. Next Saturday?"

"Next Saturday," Isaac confirmed.

"The UTOP trials will be finished by then. What if she makes it?"

"She won't. But even if she does, I have it on good authority they won't announce who's going through until the evening. Snatch her that morning while she's in town talking on the phone. You said she's usually alone then."

"That's correct."

"Do it then. If that doesn't work, improvise. Just see that she doesn't return to the UTOP campus. We need the leverage."

"Understood, sir. I'll let you know when it's done."

CHAPTER FORTY

Angel Sinclair

Monday morning we were instructed via loudspeaker to report to Room 101 after breakfast instead of reporting to our first class.

As we ate, I couldn't help thinking about what Jax had told me—how they were going to shake things up. He was noticeably absent from breakfast, as was Kira. What was *with* those two? They always seemed to be missing at the same time.

I choked down some cereal and followed Frankie and Wally to Room 101. Frankie chatted cheerfully the entire way, but Wally sensed my apprehension and shot me several questioning glances during our walk to the classroom. When we got there, we slid into our seats and waited quietly. Jax and Kira were the last to arrive and came in together. Kira sat near the front of the room, while Jax sat in his usual spot two desks behind me.

Mr. Donovan shut the door. "Students, we wanted to let you know we were quite pleased with your performance on Friday. It was nice work from all of you. Excellent teamwork, strategic thinking, and a good utilization of your strengths."

He leaned forward, bracing his hands on the teacher's desk. "However, I do have a couple of important announcements before you begin your week's activities. First, while I know it is disconcerting not to know your exact standing in the class, rest assured we're looking at *all* aspects of your character. This includes capability, mental toughness, stamina, physical fitness, intelligence, special skills, flexibility, and adaptability. We're conducting a complex and thorough evaluation. So if you feel as if you aren't doing well, I'm here to assure you, you are."

We all looked at each other, but none of us said anything. What could we say? He'd told us exactly nothing.

"So, after considerable debate and conversation, we've decided to make something about the competition known to you," he continued. "Although each of you has admirable and excellent skills, we've decided we're only going to choose two of you to proceed to the UTOP Academy to further your studies as an operative."

The room was so silent, you could hear the birds chirping outside the window. I stared at him, speechless.

What. The. Heck?

Only two of us?

"Two?" Wally finally spluttered. "Why only two?"

Mr. Donovan crossed his arms. "Because, Mr. Harris, that's the number of students we want. Now, if any of you feel this is unfair, or would like to drop out of contention, please say so now. If not, you may leave and continue with your day's schedule."

We remained silent, so he smiled. "So be it. That concludes my announcement for the day. Please head to your next class."

Jax was the first to rise and leave the room. As he passed by, he glanced at me. His expression clearly said, *I told you so.*

"They're going to do something to shake things up."

Holy crap. He'd been right. They'd done *exactly* that.

One by one, the rest of us filed out without a word. However, as soon as we got in the hallway, Wally pulled Frankie and me aside.

"Did you hear that?" he whispered heatedly. "They're only going to take two of us. It's not fair. We haven't even finished the trials yet."

Frankie's expression looked heartbroken, which now that I thought about it, was the first time I'd ever seen that look on her. That worried me far more than what Mr. Donovan had said. "What's wrong, Frankie?"

Sadness shimmered in her eyes. "Only two of us are going forward. At best, at least one of us will get left behind."

I felt sick at the possibility. Break up the White Knights after we'd been through so much? Worse, what if both of them were selected and I got left behind? Or I got selected and they got left behind. Or any variation thereof.

None of those options were acceptable.

"Maybe it's just another test." I knew I was grasping at straws, but there had to be some way to make this work. "You know, to see how far we're willing to go— to step on each other—to make one of the two slots."

"I'm not going step on either one of you," Frankie said.

"Me neither," Wally agreed.

"Well, I'm not, either," I said. "But I don't think the others will share our sentiment. Kira will be the first to step on all three of us."

"She won't," Wally said, crossing his arms against his chest. "You've got her all wrong, Angel."

"I don't have it wrong, Wally," I said irritably. "She's out for herself and no one else."

"You're not giving her the credit she's due," he insisted. "Jax is the one we should be worried about. I think he'd undercut us in a fast minute."

"Don't try to deflect this from Kira," I said hotly. "You're thinking with your hormones instead of your brain when it comes to her."

"Stop it, both of you." Frankie put a hand on each of our shoulders. "What are we going to do?"

"I don't know." I shook my head. "I guess we proceed and see how it shakes out. We've got to go. We can talk about more later."

We split up, heading for our respective classes. My emotions were swirling when I walked into group session. Bo, Jax, and Mr. Kingston were already there. Bo sat silently, his hands folded on the table, while Jax sprawled in his chair, scowling. I took my place between them and swallowed hard.

"Good morning, Ms. Sinclair," Mr. Kingston said. "Today for our session, I'd like us to do something a little different. I want to hear your impressions of how the competition is going so far."

He looked between us, but no one said anything.

Mr. Kingston raised an eyebrow. "No one has any comments?"

"Fine," Bo said, his voice so sharp I jumped. "You want me to comment? Okay, I'll comment. You spend the past several weeks dissecting us, making us confess our darkest secrets, then forcing us into teamwork. Now that we've started to work together and build trust, you're splitting us up, presumably to see how we'll act now that there are only two slots available."

Mr. Kingston didn't seem disturbed in the least at Bo's accusations. "That's an interesting assessment, Mr.

Coleman. So, you didn't see this as a competition from the beginning?"

"No, I did not. I thought we were being judged on our individual capabilities."

I nodded in agreement. "I'm with Bo. I thought we all had an equal chance to make it."

"But you *do* all have an equal chance to make it," Mr. Kingston said.

"But you're only selecting two of us," I countered. "That changes things. If that was always going to be the case, why didn't you say that at the beginning? Why all the secrecy?"

"Because they're manipulating us," Jax offered. "They're keeping us on our toes, mixing things up to gauge our emotional flexibility and adaptability."

"That's a fascinating perspective, Mr. Drummond," Mr. Kingston said, shifting in his seat to face Jax. "Do you think this will change anything in your behavior?"

"Not a thing."

"I didn't think so. What about you, Ms. Sinclair?"

"Me? I don't know." I answered honestly. "I need more time to think about it."

"Mr. Coleman, would you like to add anything?"

Bo remained silent, but I could tell he was really upset. His jaw clenched, and his hands curled into fists on his lap. I was getting to know everyone's moods a lot better the more time we spent together.

Mr. Kingston threaded his fingers together, his elbows resting on the table. "I don't typically do this, but let me venture a guess for you, Mr. Coleman. You feel as though you're the de facto leader of this group. I think that's a fair assumption given your performance on Friday's trial. You helped your teammates succeed, but, at the same time, you couldn't have succeeded without them. They chose you to take the extra points for your leadership. Now, if you take one of the two slots, you'll leave six of your teammates behind. Is that what a true leader would do?"

Blowing out a frustrated breath, Bo shoved his chair back from the table and left the room without a word.

Jax laughed and started clapping. "Bravo. Test that boundary of honor. See how far it will stretch."

"Jax," I hissed. "Knock it off."

Mr. Kingston seemed amused as he regarded Jax. "You think you have all the answers, don't you, Mr. Drummond?"

"Not all of them." Jax shrugged, then smiled. "But trust me, I know enough."

CHAPTER FORTY-ONE

Angel Sinclair

Everything is so weird now," Wally said as we headed down to the gym. "It's like walking on eggshells with the other kids. Crazy strange."

I agreed. Jax had been right. They'd done something to shake us up, and now we weren't sure how to act around each other. It changed *everything*. Even Frankie was unusually reserved, which freaked me out more than I cared to admit.

Tonight, I'd finished my homework early, but I had a lot of nervous energy. Frankie didn't want to go to the gym, Hala wanted to talk to her parents, and Kira was missing, probably already at the gym. I decided to swim to work off some of my restlessness. I talked Wally into coming with me—probably because he hoped Kira was there—so we headed into the gym together.

Mike was on the rowing machine, his eyes closed, headphones in his ears. Kira was doing an impressive number of chin-ups, her blonde hair in a ponytail, her face scarlet from exertion. Jax was on a corner of a mat doing sit-ups.

Wally went off to walk on the treadmill while I dived in the pool and swam lap after lap. When I finally got out, I toweled off and looked around. It was just Wally, Kira, and me left in the gym. Jax and Mike had left at some point.

I went into the girls' locker room to change, and while I was blow-drying my hair, Kira walked in.

I ignored her, but she walked right up to me so I had to turn off the dryer and face her.

"What do you want?" I asked, narrowing my eyes.

"Can I talk to you for a minute?" she said. "Please?"

I was so surprised by the politeness of her request, I nearly dropped the dryer. "You want to talk to me?"

"Yes. I'd appreciate it." She pointed to the bench.

After a moment, I put down the dryer and sat, wondering what she wanted. She joined me on the bench, twisting her pale hands together in her lap.

"Look, this is hard for me to say, but I'm sorry for acting like such a jerk. To you, to Frankie, to everyone."

I stiffened. "I thought you made up with Frankie."

"I did. Didn't she tell you what we talked about?"

"No. Should she have?"

"Well, I asked her not to tell anyone."

"And she didn't." I let out a breath of exasperation. "Frankie is good like that. Keeping confidences, I mean. Honestly, I don't care what you told her. Your business is your business. You made it clear you weren't interested in getting to know any of us." The frustration and anger I'd been feeling towards her slipped out.

"It's not that simple, Angel. This opportunity is important to me. I really want to make it."

"We *all* want to make it, Kira." Irritation rose inside me. Why were we even having this discussion? We weren't friends or confidants. What did she want from me? Maybe this was just a ploy on her part now that the competition had started stacking up.

"No, it's not like that. You see, my father was a spy for the US during the Cold War. He was recruited by the KGB and became a double agent for America. He was very successful. After the collapse of the Soviet Union, he was brought here to US. He met my mother, several years his junior, in California. She is Ukrainian American, but she's never lived in the Ukraine. My father's dream was for his son, my twin brother, Anatoly, to go to UTOP." It had all come out in a fast rush, but now she paused to let the words sink in, or perhaps to gather the courage to continue. "But, you see, I wanted it, too. Badly. Anatoly is smart and capable, but his ability comes easy. I worked harder, so when the time came for the invitation, I asked for a chance to be included, too. My father agreed, I think, because he never believed a female would make it. And even if I did, he didn't believe I would pose a threat to my perfect brother. But when the invitation came, it was for me. Not Anatoly."

She fell silent. The entire time she'd been talking, she'd been looking at the ground. But now she looked directly at me, her expression miserable, obviously waiting for a response.

I had no idea what she expected me to say. "Well, good for you, Kira. You earned your slot here." It sounded harsher than I intended, but subtly in conversation was not my forte.

"That's what I thought," she said quietly. "Still, I needed to prove myself, to my family, but especially to my father, that I deserved to be here. But now...it's clear I don't have what it takes. My father was right all along about me." She looked at the ground again.

What was she trying to say—that she was giving up? My pent-up anger started to melt, and I started feeling guilty she was even confessing this to me.

"Why do you think your father was right, Kira?

You've done great in the trials so far. You're in amazing physical shape. You didn't need help on a single obstacle except for the wall, and we all needed help on that. You were an excellent diplomat in our role-playing game, which means you're clearly intelligent and capable. If I'm honest, you're also probably the most beautiful girl I've ever seen outside of Hollywood. None of the guys can keep their eyes off you, especially Wally. You've got everything going for you." I stopped myself, not sure why I'd said any of that. Why had I brought Wally into this? Why was I playing therapist? But more importantly, had I just been *nice* to her?

She twisted her hands together. "I screwed everything up. This is all my fault. I wanted to put distance between everyone and me, especially the girls, because I was afraid if I liked you, I would hesitate to do what it took to beat you. I could not afford to risk that. But then I fell to Frankie. She saved me, even when I was terrible to her. She's impossible to resist."

"That's true," I agreed grudgingly. "She did the same to me, and I still don't know how."

Kira gave a wry smile. "As the competition went on, I realized that while I was competent and able, I don't stand out like the rest of you. I'm smart, but I struggle with advanced math concepts. It's my weakness. Jax has been really good about helping me. He's spending a lot of his spare time tutoring me in calculus—for free! I offered to pay him, but he wouldn't take the money."

Surprised, I stared at her for a long moment. That would explain why he and Kira were often missing at the same time—Jax was helping her with math. My estimation of him jumped a notch. "That's nice of him," I admitted. "Especially the free part."

"It is, but regardless, it's clear I'm not going to be one of the two people selected for UTOP. Anatoly would have had a better shot at it, but I took that from him, too."

I fell silent for a moment and then asked, "What's your special class, Kira? You know, the one you take alone with no one else."

She pushed back the hair on her shoulders. "Biology. I wanted to be a doctor before the UTOP training. I thought maybe I could be both, but perhaps it was foolish to think there'd be a place for a doctor who is also an operative."

I stared at her. "Are you kidding me? You want to be a medical doctor? That would be an incredibly useful skill to have as an operative."

She looked at me hesitantly. "You think so?"

"I think so. I really do."

Color crossed her cheeks. "They're also testing me for fluency in Russian, Ukrainian, Belarusian, Polish, Serbian, Croatian, Czech, and French. I hope maybe that will help my scores some."

"You *hope*? You speak all of those languages?" I suddenly felt very outclassed. What did I even do with my time?

"Mostly. French and Czech are my weakest, but I'm completely conversational in all of them."

"What, no Spanish?" I joked weakly.

"Oh, no, Mike has that covered," she answered. "What's your special class, Angel?"

I hated even answering, given that she'd just majorly shown me up. "Cryptology."

She sighed. "You're very smart in math and computers."

"Well, I certainly can't speak ten languages and cut someone open on the operating table. The sight of blood makes me gag."

"It's only nine languages, counting English, and I could help you with the gagging thing."

236

That made me smile. It was a little smile, but nonetheless, there'd been a connection. I wasn't sure how to feel about that because now everything seemed more complicated. Why did she want to have this talk with me in the first place? Were we now supposed to be friends, frenemies, or polite acquaintances? How the heck was I supposed to know?

I sighed. "I guess the bottom line is that none of us know *who* they're going to pick or *how* they'll decide. It could be any one of us. Don't give up now. You've got a good shot at this. In fact, after hearing what you just said, maybe a better shot than most of us. We have one more trial coming up this week. So, get out there and do your best." It was cheesy, but I said it anyway. "Show them girls can kick butt, too."

She smiled and nodded. "Fair enough. Only if you do the same." She held out a hand. "Truce?"

I took her hand and shook it. "Truce. Now, go and make your dad proud."

CHAPTER FORTY-TWO

Angel Sinclair

The rest of the week continued as usual but with the extra layer of mind games we were playing among ourselves. More classes, more psychological testing, and more anxiety as we got ready to face our final trial.

On Tuesday evening when I was reading in the library, Mike came in and asked if I wanted to play chess. We set up the board and played seven straight games. He crushed me in all seven.

"Wow, you're really good," I said, pushing back from the table. "I thought I was a decent player, but you killed it. That's pretty impressive."

He smiled and thumped his chest. "Captain of the chess team."

"I can see why. I'm going to have to up my game before playing you again. By the way, I hear you speak Spanish."

"Yep. My mom's from Mexico. *Tienes bonitos ojos azules.*"

"What does that mean?" I asked.

"You can google it later," he said, chuckling. He punched me lightly on the arm before packing up the board.

As I walked back to my room, I realized I could be friends with him...with *everyone* at the trials. It was a startling thought for someone like me, who had made her first two friends just over a month ago. Somewhere along the line, I had started to know and like the other candidates, and now we were going to be torn apart.

It totally sucked.

I had a huge math test on Wednesday, which I was pretty sure I aced even though I barely studied. Psychological testing was the strangest. As soon as I came into the room, Mrs. Thompson told me this would be a short session.

"Okay," I said, cheering up. Any shortening of a class I despised was a plus in my book. "What are we doing?"

"I have just one question to ask you and, unlike our previous sessions, you have permission to think about your answer. I request only that you answer from the heart. Don't say what you think I want you to say. I want to hear the truth. Then you're free to go for the rest of the session."

"Really? One question." How hard could that be?

Ms. Thompson placed her hands on the table and leaned forward. "I want to know why you want to become an operative. It's a dangerous, complicated job that requires a lot of work and secrecy. It's difficult and, at times, terrifying. Why do you want to do this kind of work instead of something else?"

It was an intriguing question. Had she asked me this at the beginning of the trials, I might have had a different answer. So, why had I accepted the nomination? Was it because my friends were here? Or had I been enticed by the free education and promise of a steady job after graduation? Maybe it was the lure of excitement and adventure—the challenge it presented.

Or perhaps was it something else entirely.

Given my skills behind the keyboard, the future was mine to command. I could work almost anywhere I wanted, request a salary that would leave me quite comfortable in life, and do all the things I loved to do. So, why was I stressing out about a government job that probably wouldn't pay half of what I'd be worth in the commercial sector and be dangerous to boot?

I considered my thoughts, and when I had my answer ready, I spoke from the heart. "It's pretty simple, Ms. Thompson. I want my work to matter to the world, even if no one else knows what I'm doing. That's a really powerful thing."

She smiled and stood. "It is, indeed. Thank you, Angel. You're free to go."

By Thursday night, my anxiety was sky-high. I went to the gaming room to blow off some steam. It was empty, thankfully, as I felt like being alone for a bit. I loaded up a game, cleared my head, and started playing. I'd been at it for about an hour when the door opened and Jax strolled in.

"Hey, Angel. Mind if I join you?"

My mood had improved, so I didn't mind. "Sure."

"What are you playing?" He plopped down on the couch next to me, stretching his long legs out in front of him.

"*Black Salt Kingdom.* It's a fantasy role-playing game not unlike the one we played for the trial. I'm playing the computer."

"You need some help?"

I glanced sideways at him, my fingers still moving rapidly. "You've played this before?"

"Not this game, but close enough."

Remembering his performance when Mike, Wally,

and I had all played *Quaver*, I looked back at the game and tried to think of something he could do that wouldn't ruin my score too badly. Then I saw him reviewing the general's actions and sighed inwardly.

"Want to be my general?" There it was—my kind act for the day.

His eyes lit up. "I'd love to."

We were immersed for another hour and a half when Jax starting killing it with a bunch of brilliant military maneuvers. After we handily won the kingdom, I put the controller down and leaned back on the cushions.

"You're good," I said. "Really good."

"I can rise to the occasion when required." He gave me a high five. "Way to go, Your Majesty."

I wasn't going to let him off the hook that easy. "You downplayed your ability when you played with me before. Why?"

"I wasn't playing with just you." He tossed his controller on the table and didn't offer any more of an explanation.

It took me a second to process that. "So, why do you do that? Keep so much about yourself hidden?"

"Do I?"

"You do."

"I'm not hiding the fact I like you." He scooted closer and wound a strand of my hair around his finger. When he let go, he pulled a small piece of wrapped chocolate from the strands and presented it to me.

I took it and shook my head in disbelief. "How do you do that? I was looking at you the whole time and I didn't see you reaching into your pocket."

"I told you, it's magic."

"Intellectually, I know it's just an illusion, but I'm still impressed. It's a real talent. How did you learn that?"

"I had lots of time to practice. Mostly when I was hiding in the closet from my dad."

That made me stop, consider my next words carefully. "You had to hide in the closet from your dad? Was it hard growing up with him?"

"Hard?" He laughed, seeming to be genuinely amused by my question. "I wish it had been hard. It wasn't hard. It was brutal. You asked me the other day at the gym why I touch the wall when I swim. It's because of him."

"What do you mean?"

"I can swim just fine, but I need to be near a wall so I can grab it if I start to feel panicked. That's why you always see me swimming on one of the side lanes."

"Why would you panic? You're a good swimmer, Jax."

"Yeah, well, anyone can master a technique. I'm not afraid of swimming."

"Then what *are* you afraid of?"

"Drowning." He leaned forward, not looking at me and pressing his elbows on his thighs. "My old man was a drunk. When he wasn't beating my mom or me, he was torturing us. When I was four, he threw me in the deep end of our apartment pool for wetting the bed. My mom tried to jump in after me, but he held her back. I could hear her screams as I kept going under. I would have drowned if it hadn't been for some guy walking past the pool to get to his room. He jumped in and saved me. No one said anything, no charges were pressed, and it was back to life in hell, as usual. Sometimes when I'm in the water, I have unexpected flashbacks. There are fewer and fewer as the years pass by, but the wall steadies me, reminds me I'm in control."

I had no idea what to say. "I'm so sorry, Jax," I finally choked out. "I had no idea. Your mom...she stayed with him?"

"Yeah. She stayed with him." He looked at the screen, where our game was frozen with our winning score. "I think she was planning to leave, but she never got the chance. One day, she was slow in bringing him a beer. He knocked her down hard. She hit her head on the bricks when she went down. Died instantly. I was six and witnessed the entire thing. My old man told the police she slipped, and they bought it. Then, when she was gone, he only had one target left."

I was so revolted, I pressed my hand against my mouth. I finally managed to locate my voice. "Is your father still alive?"

"No. He died."

"How?"

"I killed him."

"You did…*what?*" My eyes widened in horror.

"He came home late one night, drunker than I've ever seen him. He hauled me out of bed and started beating me without even uttering a word. Smashed my nose, my eye, broke a rib and my arm, and almost choked me to death. He would have succeeded, but he was too drunk to hold on, and I wasn't a little kid anymore. I got away, but I had limited vision because it was dark and the eye he'd hit had swollen shut. I slipped on the stairs and fell. I hurt my ankle and couldn't walk, so I crawled through the living room, trying to get out the back door. He caught me at the fireplace, same place as Mom. As his fists came down, I pulled the poker from the fireplace stand and used it to protect myself."

"Oh, no." My voice was hardly a whisper. "How old were you?"

"Twelve."

"What happened after that?"

"No charges were pressed against me. I'd been beaten within an inch of my life. Every cop in the room knew what had happened. I had no other family, so I was placed in a state-run group home. This year, at seventeen, I was able to declare myself independent and support myself on various odd jobs while I finished up school. Then came the UTOP offer, and here I am."

"You live on your own?"

"I did until now."

My mind whirled from his revelations, remembering he tutored kids after school and worked odd jobs. He was alone and supporting himself at seventeen. It was staggering to imagine how hard that must be for him.

"Your father's death—it wasn't your fault," I finally said.

He shrugged. "No one else held that poker."

"You were protecting yourself. It was self-defense."

"True, but it doesn't change what happened."

I tried to compose myself, but my emotions were running high. "Does Mr. Donovan know?"

"Of course he knows. They all know."

"Well, they haven't held it against you," I said. "You wouldn't have gotten invited here if that was the case."

"Perhaps. I like to tell myself I'm here because I'm intelligent, I take tests well, and I can think on my feet. Or even maybe it's because I have some skills that could be useful for an operative, like a hypersensitivity to people's behaviors and body language. It's a skill I learned from an early age when trying to judge my father's moods. Occasionally, I entertain the idea that they're impressed by my sleight of hand. But do you want to know what I really think is the reason I got invited to UTOP?"

I was almost afraid to respond. "Yes," I finally whispered.

"I'm pretty sure I'm the only one among us who's killed someone. I bet they figure if I did it once, I could do it again." He pushed off the couch. "So, now you know my secrets, Red. Good night, and good luck on the trial tomorrow."

Without another word, he walked out of the gaming

room, closing the door behind him. I sat there in silence, shamed I had pushed him to reveal such a hidden part of himself.

Pressing my hands over my face, I wondered what dark secrets the rest of us were hiding.

CHAPTER FORTY-THREE

Angel Sinclair

"Angel, are you asleep?"

I rolled over in the bed and peered down at Frankie on the bottom bunk. She was sitting up in the bed.

"No. I'm awake."

"Can I come up?" she whispered.

"Sure." I sat up and crossed my legs to make room for her to sit.

Frankie carefully climbed up the bunk ladder and sat at the foot of my bed, her feet hanging off the bed. "I can't fall asleep."

"Me neither."

"Are you worried about the trials?" she asked.

"No." I sighed. "Yes."

I'd been thinking about Jax all night, wondering what would happen to him if he didn't make UTOP. What would his future hold? How would he manage without the support and love of a family?

Then I thought about Kira. Would her father permit her to be a doctor if she didn't make the cut? What would happen to Mike, Bo, and Hala if none of them made it, too?

I blew out a breath, deciding to be honest with Frankie. "I'm worried about everyone. I'm also worried about us, the White Knights. The only way this plays out well is if none of us make it."

Frankie was silent for a moment. "Do you want to go on to UTOP, Angel?"

"Yes." I lifted my hands, miserable. "I wasn't even sure I wanted to do this in the first place. But now that I'm here, a part of me *really* wants to win one of those two slots. This is just a little taste of what we would get at UTOP, and if I'm honest, I like it. I haven't been this challenged in my entire life—intellectually or emotionally. It's...exhilarating. But I don't want to get a slot at the expense of yours or Wally's friendship. The others have a lot to lose, too, if they don't make it."

She put a hand on my shoulder. "Angel, you aren't going to lose my friendship, or Wally's, either, if you get chosen and we don't, or vice versa. Real friendships don't just disappear. The others will find their own paths, as well. You heard Mr. Donovan. Candidates are just encouraged to show their skills in different ways within the intelligence agency."

"Do you want to make it, Frankie?" I asked. "You know, live the life of an operative?"

"Of course I do. That's why I'm here. But regardless of what happens, it's all part of my journey to becoming a better person, a productive person."

"How do you do it?" I twisted my sheet between my fingers. "You seem to go through life without anxiety. But think about it. If one of us went on to UTOP and the rest of us didn't, things would change, and I was just getting used to having you guys around. I like having friends, Frankie."

"And your friends like having you." She hugged her

knees to her chest, resting her chin on her kneecaps. "But friendships change regardless. It's called growth. If you went to UTOP without us, it wouldn't change that."

I loved her, I really did. But I didn't believe her. "It might, Frankie. Seriously, it really might. That's the part that has me worried the most—although I don't know why I'm stressing so much. I'm not getting one of those two slots. I've outright failed two of the trials and sucked at most of the rest other than the gaming challenge."

"That's so not true. You don't have anything to worry about. You're always coming up with original ideas."

"Yeah, well, executing those ideas is the problem."

She patted my knee. "Do you know what Charles told me?"

"Charles?" I searched my brain in confusion but came up empty. "Who's Charles?"

"Charles Mayford, the personal trainer/lifeguard guy with the dark curly hair and pretty blue eyes? For heaven's sake, Angel, you've seen him a dozen times at the gym. He's really sweet and engaged to be married this summer. His fiancée, Renee, is a homicide detective. Imagine that."

I searched my memory and came up with a dark-haired guy that I barely remembered. I shook my head. "Is there *anyone* you don't know, Frankie?"

"Of course. There are dozens of people here I haven't met. Yet." She rolled her neck. "Anyway, Charles gave me an excellent piece of advice. He told me that 'continuous improvement is better than delayed perfection.' He's right. This is a *school*, Angel. Even if it's a spy school, no one expects us to be perfect right out of the gate. What they're looking for is potential. And of all of us, *you* have the most of that."

I lifted my hands in astonishment. "You *really* believe that about me?"

"I *really* do."

I couldn't wrap my head around it. There was a serious probability that she might be the most intuitive person on the entire planet. She'd said exactly what I needed to hear at this moment—that I had potential, and an honest shot at one of the slots.

"Thank you, Frankie."

She chuckled and crawled across the bed to give me a hug. "No, thank you, Angel, for the talk. I feel sleepy now. I'll see you in the morning."

After she climbed back down and settled into bed, I lay awake staring at the ceiling. How did she do that? She'd somehow turned around the conversation to make it seem like I was helping her when, in reality, she'd *known* I needed this talk to get my head straight. That girl had mad people skills I couldn't even begin to fathom.

I was dang lucky she was my friend.

CHAPTER FORTY-FOUR

Angel Sinclair

"**P**lease report to the front of the building after breakfast at oh seven forty-five and wait for further instruction."

It was Friday morning, and all eight of us were eating breakfast in the cafeteria. I'd tried to make eye contact with Jax, but he had headphones in and was sitting with his back to us. I wasn't sure how to handle what he'd told me last night, but it made me see him in a new and different light.

When the announcement to go out front came over the loudspeaker, I dropped what was left of a bagel on my plate and exchanged a worried glance with Wally.

He looked at me, scared. "Why are we going to the front of the building? Are they going to take us somewhere?"

"Probably."

He nervously wiped his hands on a napkin. "I just hope that whatever we do today, it's not physically demanding. I think my body has reached final capacity on that front. Everything hurts."

I hurt, too, but the truth was, we were all looking leaner and stronger. I kind of liked the way it made me feel—a bit more confident and sure on my feet. Unfortunately, the exercise hadn't seemed to improve my awkwardness or social skills. Guess that was going to take a different kind of training. Still, I agreed with Wally's sentiment. The last thing I felt like doing was grappling with another round of push-ups, pull-ups, and chin-ups that I couldn't manage. Not that I had any control over what we'd do next.

A little before seven forty-five, we all filed out of the front of the building. A bus was idling, waiting for us to get on. My heart started pounding in my chest, and every cell in my body wished it were twenty-four hours from now.

Wally leaned over and whispered in my ear. "Oh, boy. Here we go."

"Good luck," I whispered back. "You've got this." I tried for an optimistic inflection in my voice, but it sounded fake and stilted. Wally was too nervous to notice.

Once we were loaded, including Mr. Donovan, the bus drove past the UTOP campus. We looked at the buildings with undisguised curiosity, particularly because it was forbidden to us. I assumed the students were in class, because there were just a few kids walking around. The campus was prettier than the KIT compound, with strategically placed redbrick colonial buildings, pretty courtyards, and well-kept flower beds. We passed the campus and kept driving on a paved road into the woods. It made me wonder how many square miles the entire area encompassed.

The bus stopped in a small lot, where a couple other cars were parked. We got off the bus and waited for further instructions. Mr. Donovan slid on his sunglasses and waved a hand at us. "Students, please follow me."

We walked up a tree-lined path toward a rectangular building sitting at the top of a small hill. I couldn't get a clear view of the building, because it was obstructed by a screen of large bushes. When we stood in front of the bushes, Mr. Donovan held up a hand, stopping us.

"Your trial will take place here. There are several stations you must successfully navigate. After the first station, you may proceed individually or as a group. Unlike previous challenges, not everyone is required to finish together in order for you to complete the course."

I glanced at Frankie, who shielded her eyes with a hand pressed against her forehead as she listened to Mr. Donovan speak. She seemed remarkably calm, which in turn relaxed me. If Frankie wasn't afraid, I shouldn't be, either. She was right—we should do our best and let the chips fall as they may. The best two people would be selected, and that was how it should be. I felt the band of anxiety gripping my stomach ease.

"There are five stations in the final trial, with a two-and-a-half-hour time limit to complete all the stations," he continued. "To get started, an individual will be randomly selected to be the 'eyes' for the first station. After that, you can decide for yourselves how you intend to address each challenge."

I felt someone looking at me, and when I turned, I saw Jax's eyes on me. I gave him a tenuous smile, and he nodded briefly but said nothing.

"Throughout the trial, there will be multiple obstacles or objects that are painted red or lit with red lights." Mr. Donovan spread his arms. "These objects may not be touched by any student, nor may any object be used by a student to touch a red area. For example, a student may not walk across a red-painted moat, nor may you lay a board on the moat to walk across it. If any competitor touches a red area, or an item they're controlling touches a red area, it will result in a five-minute penalty for that individual and they must return to where they were before they touched the red area along with any items. Progress will be monitored and penalties assessed by video monitoring."

That sounded ominous. Wally exchanged a worried glance with me.

"If you incur too many penalties and run out of time, you'll fail the challenge. Please be reminded that only two competitors will be selected. There are a lot of points up for grabs in this final challenge, so good luck to each of you. Are there any questions?"

We stared at each other, but no one spoke. I had a hundred questions, but without having seen the challenges, it was difficult to articulate them. Instead, I wrapped my arms around my waist and kept quiet. Everyone else must have been in the same boat, because no one else spoke up.

"Fine. I'll move on." Mr. Donovan unsnapped his briefcase and pulled out a flattened brown paper bag. He opened it and stuck his hand inside. "For the first challenge, there are no red zones, which is good because most of you won't be able to see. I'm going to draw a name out of this paper bag. That person will be referred to as Eyes. The rest of you will don swim goggles that have been painted black so you cannot see. We will then proceed around those bushes behind me. You'll be required to assemble the object on the far side. I will show Eyes a picture of what you're to assemble. Once you begin, Eyes will not be able to touch anything to help you with the assembly nor can they tell you what it is you're assembling. However, Eyes *will* be able to provide you with directions to assemble the item. Once you hear a bell, you'll know that the item is satisfactorily assembled. You may then remove your goggles and proceed to the next station. I will leave as soon as we proceed around the bushes, after I show

Eyes the picture. I will give Eyes up to two minutes to survey the station and develop a plan. The timing for the overall challenge begins at the end of two minutes or when Eyes gives the first instruction. You'll have to figure out where to go and how to pass each subsequent station on your own. You will not see me again until after you have completed the trial or the time limit is up. There will be timers along the way to show you how much time is left. Pay close attention to them. Every minute matters. Are you ready?"

He studied us one by one, waiting for us to nod. Was it my imagination or did his look linger a little longer on me?

He reached into the brown bag and pulled out a piece of paper. He lowered his sunglasses and said, "Angel Sinclair."

I blew out a breath, and everyone stared at me. Anxiety flooded my veins. If I failed in my duty, I would sink everyone. Holy crap. No pressure.

Mr. Donovan remained staring at me, waiting for an acknowledgment, agreement, or something. I straightened my shoulders and gave him a curt nod.

I could do this.

Satisfied, he put the bag away and pulled out a handful of swim goggles that had blackened eyepieces. He handed them out to everyone but me and instructed the students to put them on. Once they were on, he checked each student for tightness and fit to make sure no gaps were visible.

"Just a reminder, we will be monitoring each of you by video and will issue severe penalties for anyone caught cheating."

Once we were duly warned, he arranged everyone behind me in a straight line, each person holding on to the shoulders of the person in front of them. I walked slowly as everyone shuffled awkwardly behind me.

We came out into a grassy clearing near the side entrance of the large white building we'd seen on our trek up. I could see a closed door with a large number two over it. I assumed that would be where we'd go if we completed the first obstacle.

Mr. Donovan moved toward me holding a card. "Ms. Sinclair, please remember you may not tell your fellow students what they're assembling. If you do, you will fail the obstacle. Do you understand?"

I nodded. "I understand."

He handed me the card. It had a picture of a large four-pole awning, the kind that people raised at the beach and soccer games to stay out of the sun. The card also contained a one-sentence instruction that read: *Raise the awning.*

My eyes widened. Raise an awning? I'd never even put up a tent in my life.

A closer look at the grassy area indicated there were some indistinguishable items located there. I started to hyperventilate. Why the heck had he pulled my name out of the paper bag? Why couldn't it have been Bo or Mike who could have easily explained to us how to assemble something like this?

I had the worst luck!

Mr. Donovan clapped me on the shoulder. "Okay, students, I'm going to leave now. You're on your own. We will be watching carefully. Good luck to all." He turned and disappeared back down to the parking lot.

For a moment, I stared at him, wishing I could shout at him to come back and take this responsibility from me. But the rest of the kids were standing there blindly with blacked-out goggles, waiting for me to lead them.

I breathed deeply and stared at the photo of the large tent-style awning, trying to decide what the right order of tasks would need to be performed. Time was going to be of the essence.

"Stand by," I said to the others. "I've got two minutes to figure how to best do this."

I dashed out into the clearing and saw at once what my problem would be. The items for the awning were in different piles and not centrally located. The awning fabric was rolled up on one part of the clearing and appeared to have some kind of tie around it. Farther away on the same side, I could see some long poles. About fifteen yards from the poles was a pile of ropes. I dashed to the opposite side of the clearing and found a small canvas bag with a hammer lying in the grass. I couldn't see what was in the bag, but my best guess was they were the stakes that would hold the awning up once it was raised. My eyes lingered on the hammer. Trying to hammer stakes in the ground without being able to see was going to be extremely difficult, not to mention downright dangerous.

How in the heck was I going to walk them through that? I forced myself to calm down. We'd just have to cross that bridge when we got to it.

"Red?" I heard Jax call out. "What's going on?"

I jogged back to the group. "Okay, this is what we're going to do. I want Bo, Mike, Jax, and Kira to hold on to each other's shoulders and take ten large steps to your direct right and wait for me. Frankie and Wally, you go straight ahead fifteen steps. Hala, turn left and take ten large steps."

The group starting bumping into each other and cursing, tripping over each other. It might have been a funny situation, except we didn't have time for my incompetent direction.

"Stop," I shouted.

Everyone froze.

What was I doing? I had to guide them *every* step of the way. I was the only eyes of this operation. Success would hinge upon me using the limitations given and a lot of creative thinking.

Think outside the box.

I ran over to the awning fabric. "Bo, Wally, Mike, and Kira, walk toward the sound of my voice." I kept shouting and encouraging them until all four stood next to the fabric. I quickly did the same for the others until I had those I wanted at each pile.

"Bo, kneel and reach out in front of you." When he did what I asked, I explained further. "You'll find a large canvas tied with some kind of rope. It looks like it's tied in a bow. Undo the tie and unroll it. It's large, so Kira, when Bo tells you he has freed it, get down on your hands and knees and help him smooth it out. Jax, you and Mike take three steps to your left and then ten steps forward. You'll find four large poles at your feet. One end is sharp, so be careful. Pick them up and stand by to bring them back to Bo and Kira on my command. I'll be right back."

I ran over to Frankie and Wally, who stood patiently waiting for me. "Guys, there are four coils of rope in front of you. Each of you pick up two and then wait for my next instruction."

I dashed over to Hala, who stood near the bag with what I assumed were stakes and hammer. Upon closer inspection I saw the bag had a knot in it.

"Hala, sit down and grab the soft cloth bag that is front of you. It's next to a hammer. Forget the hammer for now. Focus on the bag. It's tied with a knot. I need you to untie it so we can get what's inside."

"Okay," she said and promptly sat down. I guided her to the bag and she pulled it in her lap and started working on the knot.

"I'll return in a minute," I told her and ran back to Frankie and Wally. They had successfully gathered all of the ropes.

"Good job, guys. Follow my voice this way."

I led them over to where Bo and the rest of his group were trying to unroll the fabric. It wasn't going well. The fabric was only half unrolled, and they were arguing. Kira was sitting on half of it, Jax had his knees on another part, and it was crooked. They were completely clueless as to what to do, and that was my fault.

Despair shot through me. Time was ticking. We'd never be able to complete this station and move on if they didn't know what they were doing.

I replayed Mr. Donovan's instructions word by word in my head, looking for a loophole. Then, I suddenly had it. He'd told me I couldn't tell them *what* they were assembling, but he never said I couldn't describe the *effect* it would provide.

I clapped my hands so everyone stopped talking and listened. "Guys, we're already down at least fifteen minutes," I said. "We need to focus so we can get this task done. Trust me, it will be nice to have a little shade when you're done. I don't think it will take us longer than ten minutes, although I haven't done anything like this since my last Girl Scout campout."

Bo stilled, and then a smile crossed his face. One by one, I saw the understanding dawn on their faces. Bo felt the fabric and then told Kira what to do. Jax and Mike bent down to help. Suddenly everything started falling into place. Now that they understood what they had to do, they could coordinate their own efforts. Relieved, I dashed off to see how Hala was doing with the knot. She was still struggling.

"Angel, I can't get it," she said in frustration. "I can't see what I'm doing."

"I know it's hard, but you've got small hands like me. You're the best person for this job. Just keep it at. You can do it." I instructed her to turn over the knot a couple of times, but without being able to see, she wasn't making any progress. Encouraging her to keep trying, I ran back to the other group.

They had already spread out the awning and positioned the poles so the ends with the metal spikes were all aligned and pointed down. Those spikes would go into the ground and the other side would slide through the grommet hole at the top of each corner of the awning. Once those top poles were through, the ropes would loop over the metal top where it came through the fabric and be tied to a stake and pulled taut. Now that everyone knew what we were doing, the process would be a lot faster, since they would understand the mechanics.

"Great job!" I shouted enthusiastically. "I need one pole and one coil of rope at each corner. Remember, sharp point of the pole pointing down. Slide the other end of the pole through the grommet, then loop the rope in, too. I'll be back in a minute."

I rushed back to where Hala was swearing in what I assumed was Arabic. "I take it that means you're not making progress."

"It's not working, Angel." She threw the bag to the ground. "I can't undo the knot."

I knelt down to inspect it closely. The cord was extremely thin, which made the knot small and difficult for her to feel with just her fingertips. She picked it up again, and I tried to direct her, but it just wasn't happening.

I glanced over at the others. Time was slipping away at an alarming rate, but they'd assembled the tent and gotten the poles and the ropes looped through the grommets. Now they were standing there waiting for one thing to secure it. The stakes. But once we got the stakes, how in the world would they hammer them blindly?

Hala had started making small, panicked noises as she struggled with the knot. What in the world were they thinking when they presented us with an impossible task?

I froze for a moment considering that.

Impossible.

Maybe it *was* an impossible task.

Perhaps they never intended for us to get the bag open. It could be that recognizing that was part of the test. I pulled the card out of my pocket and read the instructions again.

Raise the awning.

They didn't say anything about securing it. We just had to raise it and we could move on, or at least that would be a literal interpretation. But given the way things were going, it was worth a try.

Hoping I was right, I straightened.

"Drop the bag and leave the hammer," I said to Hala. "We're not going to use them."

"What?" Hala looked up with blacked-out goggles. "Why not?"

"Let me worry about that. Just come on, okay?"

She stood, and we dashed back to the others. Bo, Jax, Kira, and Mike already stood at the corners, awaiting my orders.

"Red, what's next?" Jax said calmly.

I took a calming breath. "Okay, I want each of you at the four corners to grab the rope connected to your pole. Jax, call out to Frankie. Frankie, go to him, and when you get there, steady his pole. Hala, you do the same with Bo, and Wally, you assist Kira. Mike, I want you to just stand by, okay? Hold your rope and the pole, but don't move yet. We're going to raise your side last."

Soon as everyone was in place. One person held a rope and one person steadied the pole, except for Mike, who continued to hold both.

"Now, on the count of three, I want everyone except Mike to step back two paces holding the rope taut and the pole steady," I said. "One. Two. Three."

Everyone except Mike stepped back in near perfect sync. Three sides of the awning went up perfectly. I almost cheered, but we weren't done yet. I gave a few additional adjusting commands and then had Frankie move to where Mike held the remaining rope and pole. His side was still partially collapsed, but Frankie grasped the pole and Mike held the rope.

"On my command, Frankie, you and Mike take two steps back and hold on tight," I instructed. "The rest of you stay where you are and hold your sides tightly."

Two steps later, the last side of the awning was raised. It looked perfect, even if it wasn't nailed to the ground with stakes.

Heart pounding, I spread my arms and turned in a slow circle. I had no idea where the monitoring cameras were located, but I swept my hand toward the awning and hoped with all my heart I had done the right thing.

"Task completed," I shouted. "It's officially raised."

CHAPTER FORTY-FIVE

Angel Sinclair

My proclamation was met by dead silence. My heart sank.

I'd been wrong, and now I'd wasted valuable time. Goodbye at any chance of making UTOP.

Just as I was turning around to instruct someone to fetch the bag with the stakes, the clear peal of a bell sounded through the clearing.

"Yes!" I screamed, jumping up and pumping my fists in the air.

Everyone dropped the awning in a jumble of poles and ropes, stripped off their goggles, and swarmed me. We allowed ourselves a few seconds of congratulations before I detached myself and pointed at the building. A large timer hung over the entrance. It had counted down to 116. I assumed it indicated the minutes we had remaining to finish the rest of the tasks.

"No time to waste," I said. "On to the next task."

Kira reached the door first and flung it open. We crowded around the entrance, jostling to see what was inside. At first glance it looked like the building was a large warehouse with high ceilings. The room had a narrow walkway painted white on the floor—about two people wide—while the rest was painted red, stretching out all the way to the walls on each side. The white path ended about twenty feet from the door at a slightly raised platform.

Bo stepped back and looked at me. "Do we go in?"

I wasn't sure why he was deferring to me, but I answered anyway. "Yes." Taking a breath, I stepped into the building, careful to stay on the white path. "Don't touch the red floor," I warned. "Proceed carefully."

I made my way carefully to the foot of the platform and stopped. Kira was directly behind me, and others followed. Kira lifted her leg to step up onto the platform, but I held out an arm, stopping her.

"Wait. Let's think about this first, okay?" I said.

She nodded and stayed where she was. We all surveyed our surroundings. On the opposite wall of the door and above another closed door hung a huge digital timer that was counting down. It showed 112.

"That's all the time we have left to finish," I said.

"What's that?" Hala asked. She pointed beneath the timer where several medieval characters had been painted on the wall, seemingly moving in procession toward the door. It looked like a king and queen, a couple of princes and princesses, a few lords, and some knights on horses.

"What the heck?" Jax muttered.

"We'll figure it out," I said, stepping up onto the platform. Kira joined me on a horizontal white-painted area just big enough to fit eight of us if we stood side by side. The others came up slowly and took their places.

When everyone was up, we studied the platform's surface. It was comprised of rows of large square blocks arranged in columns and rows that went to the very edge of the platform. Each block had letters and a red-lighted line around it. Some of the letters were Greek, and others were English. Some blocks had only one letter, but most appeared to have two. The platform wasn't rectangular, as its last three rows were missing some cells in the middle, but it ran all the way up to the door surrounded by the painted medieval figures. Above the door was the countdown timer.

"What in the heck?" Mike knelt to get a better look at one of the blocks. "Are we supposed to step on them to get to the door?"

"I don't see any other way, do you?" Kira asked.

"I don't."

"Okay, so we're in agreement that the challenge is to step on the blocks to get across the platform to the next door," Jax said. "It can't be as simple as running across."

Bo leaned over and examined a block. "The blocks look slightly raised. I think if we step on them, they will sink and something will happen."

"Probably turn red and the person standing on it would get a penalty," Hala offered. "Remember Mr. Donovan said whoever steps on something red is clocked five minutes of time and has to go back to where they were before they touched it."

Frankie giggled and we all turned to look at her. "What's so funny?" I asked.

"I'm thinking this looks a lot like the Indiana Jones movie where if you step on the wrong square you get shot with a poison arrow, your head is sliced off, or you fall into a snake pit below."

We stared at her in astonishment before Wally said, "She's right. We have to figure out which blocks we can safely step on or suffer consequence."

"Well, we'd better hurry," Kira said. "Time is ticking."

She was right. We'd already wasted five minutes just

talking about it. In fact, a part of me couldn't help but wonder how much of our tasks were designed to make us waste time so we couldn't finish. My eyes met Jax's, and it was like he knew exactly what I was thinking.

"We have to rule out that this isn't just a puzzle designed to mess with our heads." Jax said. "We need to test the hypothesis that we can't just walk across."

"Dude, they aren't going to all this trouble just to mess with our minds," Mike said and then looked doubtful. "Right?"

"I think we should be cautious," Bo said. "Try to figure it out first."

"No, Jax is right," I said quietly. "Time is our enemy. We have to eliminate that possibility."

"But which one of us would risk it?" Kira asked. "What if we're disqualified?"

"No one will be disqualified," I said. "Mr. Donovan specifically mentioned a five-minute penalty, but not a disqualification. It's a legitimate move."

Wally looked around. "So, who among us would volunteer for a possible five-minute penalty?"

I stepped forward. "I will."

"Too late, Red." Jax stepped onto a block in the first row with the Greek letter kappa on it.

While we watched, the cell sank slightly and started flashing red. Jax jumped back off as a voice came over a loudspeaker.

"Five-minute penalty to Mr. Drummond."

"Why did you do that?" I asked Jax. "I was going to do it."

"My idea. My risk." He swept out a hand. "I just confirmed our hypothesis that we must deduce a pattern to cross."

"There has to be a clue in those letters on the squares," Hala said. "Why are some in English and some in Greek?"

"They look really familiar," Wally mused. He stood

at the edge, his hand on his chin, staring at the letters as if they would magically speak.

"The only thing I know from Greek is *The Iliad* or *The Odyssey*," Hala offered. "But I barely remember what happened."

"There was Euripides," Kira suggested. "Didn't he write several significant plays in Greek?"

"Guys, you're overthinking," Wally said. "These are just letters. Symbols." He turned to me suddenly and snapped his fingers. "Symbols! That's it. It's the periodic table of elements."

"What? The periodic table?" I repeated confused, staring at the blocks. "The last time I checked, there were no Greek letters in the periodic table."

"Regardless, that's what this is, Angel." Wally's voice was excited. "Look at the pattern of the blocks. They match exactly to that of the periodic table of elements...except they're messed up."

"Really messed up," I agreed.

"No, Wally's right," Mike said. "Those letters on the cells could be the two-letter element designations."

"But what's with the Greek letters?" I asked in exasperation.

Wally looked at me, his eyes distant, which meant he was in deep thinking mode. "Well, there's a Greek equivalent to the English alphabet, you know. Maybe the Greek letter is being substituted for the English one, just to make this more challenging. In fact, that makes sense if you look at that top left block. It says *H* and the Greek letter epsilon."

"Um, what's an epsilon?" Frankie asked. "Chemistry isn't my thing."

Wally pointed toward a funny-looking E. "Essentially it's the Greek equivalent to an *E*. It's the fifth letter of the Greek alphabet. In this case, if you translate, HE, it equals helium."

I could feel my own excitement growing, but something still wasn't right. "That works, but it's in the wrong place on the periodic table, guys. Helium should be in the top right, and it's in the top left on this one."

Wally nodded. "I know. Somehow the table is jumbled. Maybe that means we have to jump across the blocks in order to match the periodic table."

"That would be impossible," Mike argued. "Those blocks are way too far apart. I mean, if we were to go in order, helium and hydrogen would be the two elements we'd have to jump on first, and they're the farthest away from us. None of us could jump that far."

"He's right," I said.

"Well, maybe we need to do it backward," Kira offered. "You know, start with the last element and get off at the first, which would be hydrogen."

"Still won't work," I said. "The door we need to go through is in front of helium, not hydrogen."

Frustrated, we stared at the blocks. I couldn't even bear to look at the timer as valuable time slipped away. It felt like the answer was staring us in the face, but none of us could see it.

"Wait," Wally finally said. "We agree the elements are mixed up, but take a closer look. At least the elements are still in the same rows they're supposed to be in. That has to mean something."

"True," Mike said. "They *are* in the correct rows. Way to be observant, Wally."

"Thanks. But what does it mean?"

I wished I could contribute something, but I was coming up blank. My anxiety heightened.

"Not to be the bearer of bad news, but tick tock, everyone," Jax said.

I tried not to be annoyed at him and everyone else that the pressure was just on Mike, Wally, and me to figure it out. I guess since we were the experts in chemistry, it was only fair, but still.

"Okay," I finally said, thinking aloud. "Let's look at what we know. We think this is the periodic table of elements. The elements are mixed up but are in the correct rows. We know we have to cross the blocks using some kind of pattern that has to do with the elements. Jax tried it randomly, and it didn't work. They can't expect us to pull a pattern out of thin air. So that means there *has* to be a clue somewhere in this room to help us determine that pattern."

Frankie raised her hand, pointing it at the wall. "My bet is the clue has to do with the royalty painted on the wall. Other than the Greek designations on the blocks, that seems to be the only other obvious sign."

My focus snapped back to the wall with the paintings. Frankie was right. The clue had to be on the wall.

"So what does that painting signify?" I mused aloud. "Kings, queens, knights? Where's the clue in that?"

We all studied the mural as if the answer would magically come to us.

It didn't.

"I don't know," Mike finally said, throwing his hands up in frustration. "What in the heck do a bunch of kings and queens have to do with chemistry?"

"Well, there are also knights and horses, which indicates medieval times," Hala pointed out. "Maybe it's highlighting an important discovery in chemistry that happened in that time frame?"

"But what?" Wally said. "Nothing leaps to mind. You got something, Angel?"

I shook my head. "I've got nothing."

"Okay, what if we come at it from an entirely different angle?" Frankie said. "What do all those nobles have in common other than the fact that they're really rich?"

As soon as the words were out of her mouth, Wally, Mike, and I looked at each other in stunned shock. "Noble!" we shouted at her in unison.

We gave each other high fives until we realized the rest of the group was looking at us as if we'd lost our minds.

"The noble gases," Wally explained. "Frankie, you're a genius. Noble gases are the only nonmetal elements in the periodic table. There should be enough of them to get us across the platform. And, by the way, helium is a noble gas, and it's at the front of the door. So that theory works."

I nodded excitedly. "Exactly. All we have to do is decode the gases from the Greek and we'll know which block to step on." I threw a worried glance at Mike and Wally. "Except I don't know what order the noble gases go in. Do you, either of you?"

Mike shook his head, but Wally grinned and tapped his head. "I got it right up here, baby." He started walking along the first row, sliding into his commanding general role. "Okay, I see it now. That's why they mixed up the rows—to make it harder for us."

"That wasn't hard enough?" Hala said.

I walked over beside Wally, looking at the blocks in a new light. "What are you looking for?"

"We have to go from the bottom up like Kira suggested, since helium is in front of the door. So if we start with the last of the noble gases, that would make it oganesson or Og." He stopped in front of a block that had the Greek letters omega and gamma. "This is it. Here I go."

Blowing out a nervous breath, he stepped onto the block. It sank, but stayed white. No voice came over the loudspeaker indicating a penalty.

We all cheered.

"Way to go Wally!" I said.

"Okay, I'm going to make my way across slowly," he said jumping on the next blocks. "Radon, Rn, xenon, Xe, krypton, Kr, argon, Ar, neon, Ne, and helium, He." He paused on the last block and raised his hands in the air. "Just like that, I'm safely at the door. It worked! But now what do I do?"

"Can you open the door?" Bo called.

"Not from up here on the block. It's a short jump down, and it looks like there is a white area where I can safely land."

"Well, do it!" Jax shouted.

Wally jumped down, and the door slid open. "It worked," he yelled. "The door is now open."

"I'll go next," Kira said.

Wally stayed at the foot of the platform telling her which block to jump on until she made it across. She jumped down next to him, and suddenly the door slid shut.

"What the heck?" Wally said. "The door just closed." Kira banged on the door, but it wouldn't open.

"What happened?" Bo asked. "Why did it close?"

"I don't know," Kira said. "When I jumped down next to Wally, it closed."

"Jax, go next," I said. "See if you can figure out what happened to the door."

He crossed the blocks, and when he jumped down next to Kira and Wally, the door slid open.

"What in the world?" Wally said.

Jax stepped through the door. "I'm going in to investigate."

"I'll go with you," Kira said, following him. They both disappeared from view.

"Everyone else, hurry up and cross," Wally shouted. "I'll walk you through it."

Hala crossed next, and when she jumped down next to Wally the door slid shut, trapping Kira and Jax on the other side.

Pounding came from the other side of the door. "Open up!" Kira shouted. "We can't see a thing in here."

"Can you open the door from your side?" Wally asked.

"No," Jax yelled back. "There's no handle or release for the door on this side, at least not that we can feel. We can't see a thing with the door shut. We're in a narrow corridor in pitch-black. There's no light switch, at least not that we can find."

"I'll see if I can help them," Mike said as he quickly leaped across the squares on the platform. When he jumped off the block to the white space below, the door slid open. Jax and Kira spilled out.

"Well, that was interesting," Jax said. "It's pitch-dark when you move away from the door. There were no evident light switches, either, and we felt along the walls. We were afraid we might step on a red floor, but we couldn't see anything."

"They can't penalize us for stepping on something we can't see," Kira objected.

"Guys, hate to break it up, but we have a problem out here," I said from the other side. "The door appears to open when every other person jumps to the platform. There's eight of us. The last person to cross the platform won't make it through the door. As soon as they leap to the floor, the door will close and they'll be stuck on this side. Unless we can find a mechanism on the inside of the door to open it again. If not, one of us will have to be eliminated."

For a moment, we all just stared at one another, absorbing the impact of my declaration.

"Why can't one of us who has already crossed just climb back up to helium and jump down and open the door again?" Hala suggested.

"Good idea, but I don't think we should risk it," Jax said. "What if the door is programmed to open only seven times?"

None of us had an answer to that.

"No one stays behind, and no one takes another risk," Bo said. "It's simple. The last person to go across doesn't jump to the floor."

"Well, how are they going to get through the door?" Mike asked.

"They jump from the platform through the door."

"Are you nuts?" Wally said. "The jump is like fourteen feet."

"I can't jump that far," I said, shaking my head.

"Me neither," Frankie agreed.

"I can," Bo said grimly. "You girls go across and the rest of you go through the door while it's open. Just get the heck out of my way, because when I come through in a full jump, if someone is in the way, I won't be taking any prisoners."

"The corridor is really narrow," Jax said. "Make that jump count."

"Bo, are you sure about this?" I asked uncertainly.

"I'm positive. We don't have time to debate this. Just trust me. Everyone else go through the door. Frankie, it will close when you jump down. Wait for Angel, and then when it opens, go through and get the heck out of my way."

"Okay." I turned to Frankie. "You first."

As she crossed, I called out the blocks for her. Before she jumped down to the white-painted area, everyone else went through the door and disappeared. When she hopped down, the door slid shut. I crossed the blocks and then, with a look over my shoulder, leaped down to the white area. The door slid open.

"Okay, Frankie and Angel, go through the door," Bo shouted at us. "And get out of the way."

Frankie grabbed my hand. We stumbled across the threshold and were immediately swallowed by utter blackness.

CHAPTER FORTY-SIX

Angel Sinclair

Someone grabbed the front of my shirt, yanking me forward. I clutched Frankie's hand so tightly, I brought her with me. We were pressed back against a wall when I heard Jax's voice.

"Everybody, stay where you are. We have to give Bo the room he needs to make the jump."

Seconds later I heard a thump, swearing, and a crash.

"Bo?" I called out into the darkness. "Are you okay?"

"Mission complete," he said. "I made it and the door stayed open. Although I think I took someone down with me."

"That would be me," Wally said, his voice shaky. "I'm okay, though. Just a little roughed up."

"I took a glance at the timer before I went through, and we have eighty-three minutes and an unknown number of challenges left," Bo informed us. "Let's go."

I felt around, my fingers touching a fabric-covered wall. "Where are we?"

"In a dark corridor," Jax said. "Follow the sound of my voice and let's go deeper. Maybe a light source is ahead of us."

We mostly felt and bumped our way along the corridor as it snaked back and forth several times. At some point, it ended and we staggered into an open room. We paused inside, hoping for some relief from the dark, but it was still pitch-black.

No one spoke as we contemplated what to do next.

"We have to have light," Hala said, stating the obvious. "That has to be our number one priority."

"But what if we step on a red section in the dark?" Frankie asked.

"Well, if we can't see it to avoid it, they can't see us to know that we did it," Kira offered. "Right?"

"Yeah, because three US intelligence agencies don't use infrared cameras…said no one ever," Mike retorted.

"Stop arguing," Bo said curtly. "We have to feel our way along the wall. Head toward the walls and find a light source as soon as possible."

We took his advice and moved ahead, waving our hands in front of us blindly. I crashed into Hala.

"Ouch," I said, rubbing my forehead.

"Sorry," Hala whispered back.

"Marco," someone else called out jokingly, and someone else answered, "Polo."

"Knock it off, guys," Bo said. "We need to concentrate."

My hands finally hit a wall. As I felt along, I hit something hard. "Hey, there's something on the wall. A painting or something in a large frame."

"Yes, I have the same thing on my side, too," Kira called out. "There's more than one painting or framed photograph over here. I've felt at least three."

I continued along the wall until I bumped into another frame. "I found more, too," I said. "What does it mean?"

"Nothing, unless we find a light switch," Jax said. He was somewhere behind me, to the left.

Suddenly a loud crash sounded. "What was that?" Bo said.

"It was me," Mike answered. "I tripped over something on the floor. A box."

"Is there a flashlight in the box?" Bo asked hopefully.

"I don't know. Give a minute." I heard more noises, presumably Mike rummaging through the box. "I didn't find a flashlight, but I did find something that feels like a battery. AA size, to be exact. I think there may be some small LED bulbs in the box as well."

"Sounds like someone wants us to build our own flashlight," Jax offered. "Apparently in the dark."

"Hey, there's furniture in here, too," Kira suddenly said. "There's a chair and desk."

"Any chance there's a lamp on that desk?" Hala asked.

"Not that I can feel," Kira replied. "Nothing is on the desk that I can tell."

"Well, keep looking for a light source," Bo said. "Mike, can you build a flashlight in the dark?"

"Not without more stuff. It's hard to see what's in this box in the dark, but at the very least, I'd need electrical tape and wires."

"Hey, I think I found a door," Wally said.

"Where are you?" Jax said.

"Over here," he said.

Jax must have made his way over because he said, "Confirmed Wally found the exit. There's something on the door in place of a handle, but I'm afraid to touch it without being able to see it."

"Oopmph," Hala said, followed by a loud thump and what I guessed was swearing in Arabic. "I just tripped over another box."

"Are you okay?" Bo asked.

"I'm fine."

"What's in the box?" Mike asked excitedly. "Can you check it out?"

There was a rustling noise, and then Hala answered. "It feels like wires and switches."

"Perfect!" We could hear the excitement in Mike's voice. "Can you push that box toward the sound of my voice?"

While Hala was doing that, the rest of us kept searching fruitlessly for a light switch. Bo, Kira, and I made a couple of passes along the walls, running into Jax, who was standing guard at the door. We found plenty of paintings or photographs or whatever the heck was hanging on the wall, but no light switches. Frankie told us she was moving around the room waving her arms, hoping that maybe a chain or a string would be hanging from a light in the ceiling, but she didn't have any luck, either.

"It looks like we're supposed to build a flashlight in the dark," Jax said.

"I don't think I can do that," Mike said. "I need to see the wires."

"Why don't you just take the boxes back through the corridor to the door entrance where there is light?" Frankie suggested. "We left the door open, right? As long as you don't step on the white platform and close the door, you should be able to build it there."

There was complete silence, then someone—it might have been me—did a head slap.

"Frankie, that's the smartest thing anyone has said all day," Mike said. "She's right. Someone needs to help Hala and me take these boxes back to the opening."

"I'll help," Jax said. "I can put together a flashlight, too."

"Me, too," I added.

"Okay, the rest of us will keep looking for clues or hopefully a hidden light source," Bo said. "Just whatever you have to do, make it fast."

"We're on it," Jax said confidently.

I managed to find Hala in the dark and fumbled around until I had one side of her box. We made our way back to the entrance and put the boxes close enough the door so we could see, but not too close to the white platform. Mike knelt in the middle of the narrow corridor and began to examine the contents in the boxes, making a small pile of things he could use.

"See if you can find me more batteries," Mike instructed the rest of us.

Hala and I sorted through the items, looking for batteries, while Jax used his teeth to strip a couple of wires. It took us only minutes to discover there was only one battery, but I found a roll of black electrical tape. I tossed it to him, and he added it to the pile.

After a moment, Mike and Jax started putting together a flashlight. Electronics wasn't my specialty, but I knew the mechanics of what they needed to get things working. So, I squeezed in next to Mike, offering suggestions and handing over wires and tape. In fairly short order, the four of us constructed a workable LED flashlight. Unfortunately, when Mike attached it to the battery, it flickered, indicating that there wasn't much juice left.

"Well, that stinks," Hala said. "We're going to have to be quick to figure out how to get out of the room."

Mike stood, helping Hala to her feet, while Jax pulled me up.

"Let's go," Jax said. "We can't waste any more time."

We made our way back to the room, not using the flashlight. When we entered the room, Jax led us to the door, while explaining our situation to the rest of the crew. "We've got a flashlight, but it doesn't have much power or life. We need lots of eyes on the door to figure out what to do next. Is everyone ready?"

There was a chorus of yes, so Jax told Mike to connect the wires to the battery. Suddenly the room was lit by a flickering light. Several heads swiveled to whatever was on the door. I backed away and instead glanced around the room. I saw the empty chair and desk Kira had told us about, as well as several strange paintings hanging on the wall. Frankie was still looking for a light switch. She reached out to examine a painting when the flashlight flickered wildly and died.

Once again we were plunged into darkness.

CHAPTER FORTY-SEVEN

Angel Sinclair

"Not again," Wally shouted. "Turn the light back on."

"I can't," Mike said, cursing. "It's out of power."

"What kind of challenge gives you a dead battery?" Kira asked in frustration.

"Well, one thing is for sure," Wally said. "We aren't getting through that door if we don't have any light."

Someone slammed a fist against the wall, while others started grumbling.

"Wally, what did you see on the door before the light went out?" I called out.

"Some kind of colored wires," Wally said. "I think we're supposed to connect them."

Jax told Mike to hand over the flashlight. He also tried to get it working, mostly by banging it, but repeated attempts failed to make it come back to life. Someone moaned the challenge was unfair. I was working my way toward Wally and the door when the light in the room came on, effectively blinding us.

"What the heck?" Mike exclaimed in astonishment.

I shielded my eyes with my hands, blinking rapidly, trying to get accustomed to the brightness.

"Who turned on the light?" Bo asked, squinting at me.

"Me." When my eyes adjusted, I saw Frankie standing next to a light switch hidden behind a large hinged painting. She'd apparently swung it open to reveal the switch.

"Guess what I found, guys?" she said, grinning.

After a moment of shock, we jumped on Frankie, hugging and congratulating her. However, our excitement was short-lived when a voice came over the intercom.

"Once the timer expires, the door will remained locked for two hours," the voice said.

We whirled around. Above the door, a new countdown timer, apparently just for this task, had illuminated. It showed 4:35 and was ticking down, indicating it must have activated when the light switch was thrown.

As a group, we rushed to the door, examining the wired panel. Like Wally said, instead of a door handle, there were two horizontal rows of ten colored wires coming out of the panel. The bottom row had the same colored wires as the top row.

I stared at it totally uncomprehending. "What are we supposed to do with *that?*"

Mike, who had knelt in front of the panel, looked at me over his shoulder. "I think we need to match the right combination of top wires to the bottom wires to unlock the door."

"That's an impossible task given the time constraints and the fact that there are way too many possibilities to try in that short of a time," I said.

"You can figure it out, Angel," Frankie said.

A combination. There had to be an answer.

I pressed my hand to my forehead, trying to think. "Okay, they know we can't try them all randomly, so there *must* be a color-related clue in this room. We have a little less than four minutes to find it. Everyone get to work. In the meantime, Mike, start trying as many combinations as you can."

"What if I get penalized?" he asked.

"Then we'll each try a combination. Just try something."

He turned back to the panel and started randomly connecting wires.

"I'll go recheck the boxes of electronics to see if there is something in there that could give us a clue," Jax said.

"I'll help you," Hala said, and they dashed down the corridor to retrieve the boxes.

We started looking at the paintings, the desk, the chair, *everything*, while the timer counted down. We found nothing.

Mike tried several combinations without penalty. It emboldened him, because he was working at a blindingly fast speed. Jax and Hala came skidding back in with the boxes.

"We've got nothing," Jax said, dropping the box on the floor and rummaging through it. "No notes, no wires tied together, no clue that we could see."

At least no one was panicking. Outwardly everyone remained calm. I was just glad no one could tell my heart was thumping wildly.

I moved closer to watch Mike, who was trying different combinations of the wires. He was incredibly nimble with his hands, but nothing was working and we were out of time. The timer started its countdown from under a minute.

Just as the timer hit thirty seconds, Kira suddenly pushed her way forward.

"I think I have this," she said. "But I need some help. Quickly, help me unfasten any wires that are connected and let's start fresh."

Wally and I leaned forward to help, and in seconds we had all the wires all free.

"Okay, match the red, violet, blue, and green wires together," she said. "Nothing else."

I glanced up at the timer. Eleven seconds. I leaned over Mike's shoulder and connected the blue wires while he worked on the green ones. Kira matched the violet, while Wally twisted the red ones together.

The timer froze on three seconds.

A loud click sounded, and the door slid open.

For a moment, we stared in disbelief until Wally shouted, "Yes!" and gave Kira a huge hug.

"Did we make it in time?" Frankie asked, looking around in bewilderment.

"We did," Mike said. "By the skin of our freaking teeth."

Shouting, cheering, and smacking each other on the back, we spilled across the doorway and into the next room.

"So, how did you figure it out?" Wally asked Kira.

"It was on the painting where Frankie found the hidden light switch," she explained. "When she swung open the painting, the picture turned to face the wall, so none of us saw it. I just happened to swing it shut, and when I did, I saw there was a girl sitting there, holding a scroll. There was a poem written on the scroll. It said, *'Roses are red/Violets are blue/Throw in a green and you'll find your way through.'* I wasn't sure if violet counted as a color or not, but when I got close enough to see the purple, I just went with it. It was risky, but it was our last chance."

I stepped forward and put my hand on her shoulder. "Excellent work, Kira. You kept your cool, and you figured it out. You and Frankie really saved us on that challenge."

"I was just doing my part," she said modestly. But her cheeks flushed happily, and I knew she was proud of what she'd done.

"Come on," Jax said, urging us forward. "We've got more challenges to face and not much time left to finish them.

As we surveyed the environment of our new challenge, it seemed simple. We were in a small indoor basketball court with a door at the far end. A timer hung over the door and read 52. Fifty-two minutes. It was all the time we had left for whatever challenges still awaited us.

The light in the gym was dim, with the only illumination coming in from a single window high on the wall to the left of us. Old gym equipment decorated the gym, including basketballs, barbells, and climbing ropes that reached the ceiling.

Leaning against the right wall was a tall ladder. I did a full rotation, noting the wall next to the door we'd just gone through had a series of vertical mirrors and a ballet barre.

We walked easily to the far end of the gym to the door.

"Careful," Jax called out as we got closer. "Watch where you step."

On the floor across the room in front of the door was a horizontal, six-foot-deep red-painted strip that prevented them from gaining access to the door. Centered in front of the door almost ten feet away was another small red square that was about two by two feet wide. The door appeared to have a locking mechanism, but it was too far away to get a good look at it.

Bo stood next to the small red square and studied the door. "Why would a small red square be painted here in the middle of the floor?"

Mike walked up to the edge of the six-foot-thick red

strip in front of the door, trying to determine what he could about the mechanism on the door.

"My guess is the challenge is twofold," Wally said. "Get across the red zone and unlock the door."

"Well, how are we going to unlock the door if we can't stand close enough to unlock it?" Kira asked.

"There's not enough light in here to be able to make out any details," Mike said. "I can't even see what kind of lock it is. It's hidden in the shadows."

"Okay, apparently we have multiple challenges," I said. "Let's identify everything we need to do so we can break up the challenges and figure out solutions. First we have to figure out how to reach the door and the lock without touching the red-painted area. Then we figure out what we need to unlock the door. I bet that's what the ladder is for."

As I was speaking, Jax and Bo were retrieving the ladder and carrying it back. Just from eyeballing it, I estimated it as sixteen feet. Interestingly, it didn't appear to be adjustable. I wondered how that played into the challenge.

Bo and Jax maneuvered the ladder toward me when Bo almost stepped on the small red square. Wally grabbed his arm at the last second, saving him from stepping on it.

"Thanks, Wally," Bo said, safely stepping over it and standing the ladder upright. He held it tightly to prevent it from toppling into the red-painted area.

"Okay, guys, ideas on how to best do this?" I asked.

Jax spoke. "It makes sense for us to place the ladder here and lean it up against the wall. Someone climbs up the ladder and takes a look at the lock on the door."

He tried to position the ladder to reach the door at a lower angle, but the red square was precisely where he would need to set the ladder down so it could reach the door.

"Well, we now know the purpose of this small red square precisely in this spot," he said in frustration. "It keeps us from putting the ladder's base in the right spot so that we can easily access the lock. We have to put the ladder high on the wall or not use it at all.

"What if someone climbs the ladder and hangs upside down from the rungs?" Kira asked. "Could they reach?"

I shook my head. "Not from that angle. None of us is tall enough, not even Bo. Besides, even if we get the door open, how would the person hanging upside down on the ladder rung get through?"

"Maybe someone could swing on the climbing rope and fly in through the door?" Frankie suggested.

"First of all, we'd have to have the door open first," I said. "But even if we get it open, the rope is too far away for us to swing through or get close enough to swing and jump, even if we were pushed."

Jax stared intently at the ladder. "What if we had a rope?" he suggested. "We could lower someone down after they climbed on the ladder."

"They'd have to hang upside down by their feet to reach the door," Mike said. "That's just crazy."

"Actually it's not *that* crazy," I said. "A rope would work because we could pull the person back up and bring the ladder back to us as needed. But where would we get a rope?"

We all turned to look at the climbing ropes, but Bo shook his head. "They're attached at the ceiling, and even if we could figure a way to detach them, it would be a long fall to the floor. Not a smart move."

"What if some of us hold the ladder and someone else climbs up and cuts it down?" Frankie suggested.

We looked around the gym, but there were no tools that would permit us to cut the rope. Besides, this rope was too thick. I wasn't sure we could tie it around someone's ankles even if we wanted to.

"Wait. I have an idea," Hala said, snapping her fingers.

To our astonishment, she raced back through the door from where we'd just come and disappeared.

"Where's she going?" Mike asked.

"I don't know," I answered. "But we can't waste any more time. I suggest we get some light on the locking mechanism so, at the very least, we can see what we need to do to get the lock open."

"How are we going to do that?" Bo asked. "There's only one small window up there." He pointed up at the window in the corner of the gym where a sliver of light was shining through and hitting the gym floor. "There's no other light in here."

"Not again." Frankie sighed dramatically. "What's with the no-light, dim-light thing?"

"It's like they're purposefully making it hard for us to see the lock," Kira said. "Why?"

I watched Jax turn around in a slow circle, surveying everything in the gym. Suddenly, he ran over to one of the ballet mirrors and ripped one of them off the wall.

"What are you doing?" Frankie cried aghast.

As soon as I saw him coming back with the mirror, I knew *exactly* what he had in mind. I ran to meet him where the sunbeam struck the floor.

"Over here," I said.

"This should get us some light," Jax said setting the mirror on the floor.

Together we positioned the mirror and, with some adjustments, cast a direct reflection of light onto the door mechanism.

"Okay, that's just smart thinking, dude," Mike said as he got as close to the red strip as possible, peering at the door to see if they could make out what was on it.

"It's a numerical keypad with digits ranging from zero to nine," Kira reported excitedly. "Looks like a punch-in combination."

I looked up at the timer, which read 40.

"Okay. We're running out of time," I said. "We need to find the numerical clue. It has to be here somewhere. Spread out and look around."

Everyone started lugging various gym equipment near the red zone in front of the door, examining it for numbers, as we tried to brainstorm a solution. Suddenly Hala appeared with several ropes wrapped around her body.

We stared at her.

"Where did you get those?" Bo finally asked.

She smiled. "The tents."

"You ran all the way back to the first challenge to get those?" Jax said.

"I'm a fast runner," she said, taking off the ropes and dropping them at her feet.

"But what about the periodic table challenge?" Wally asked. "How did you get from the platform through the door?"

"I remembered the pattern," she said. "Plus, you forget, I've been doing gymnastics for years. If Bo could make the jump, I knew I could do it, too. And I did. Anyway, here's my idea. We tie one of the ropes to the top of the ladder so we can lower it slowly to the wall and then pull it back afterward as desired. I will climb up the ladder and tie one of the other ropes around my ankles, so I can hang upside down from the ladder. Someone on this side can lower me to the lock so I can see what's there. Just don't drop me on my head. I'm used to hanging upside down. Plus, I'm light, which will make it easier for you guys to raise and lower me."

"That could work," Mike said thoughtfully. "But not unless we find the combination for the door lock."

288

"There's a combination lock on the door?" Hala asked.

"A punch-in-number lock," Bo explained. "The problem is, however, even if we do get the door unlocked, how would we get everyone through after we pull you and the ladder back up?"

"That's easy," Hala said, looking around as if she couldn't understand why we were clueless. "Once I unlock the door and open it, you pull me up and I'll untie the rope from my ankles and climb back down the ladder on this side. I'm going to jump across the red zone, and Bo, you're going to have to help me. You stand as close as possible to the red zone with your hands cupped. I'll take a running start and jump into your hands with one foot. All I need from you is a giant push to get to the other side. After the platform jump, this one will be a breeze. When I get there, throw some weights through the door after I get out of the way. Then slide the ladder down to me and I'll prop my side up with the weights. You do the same on this side and we'll use it to walk across the zone. Nothing touches the red zone. Simple, right?"

It was far from simple, but it was a pretty ingenious, as well as ambitious, plan. But it would be all for nothing if we couldn't find the combination to the door lock.

"Let's do it," I said with resolve. "But first, everyone look for a series of numbers that could be the combination."

Wally, Mike, and Kira were already examining the gym equipment for strings of numbers or some kind of code. Jax, Frankie, and I walked around the gym looking for some clue to jump out at us, while Bo and Hala worked out their part of the plan.

Once again, it was Frankie who saved us.

"Hey, what's that up there?" she said squinting at something high on the wall to the left of the door.

I followed her gaze. It was a dark shape sticking out from the wall. It was barely visible at that height and in that dark corner. Jax joined me, and we strained our eyes to see what it was. I decided to put some light on it, so on my instruction, Jax and Wally reoriented the mirror toward that corner. The light revealed a thin black metal shape of unknown significance that didn't appear to yield any clues. Disappointed, I was just about to tell Jax to put down the mirror when Frankie shouted at me.

"Angel, wait. Look at the shadow the shape casts."

Frowning, my gaze moved from the shape itself to its shadow. I saw at once why she was so excited. The shadow clearly resembled the Greek letter pi.

And just like that, we had the combination.

CHAPTER FORTY-EIGHT

Angel Sinclair

Hala tied one of the ropes to the top rung of the ladder and connected two more together to make a long enough rope to lower her down by her ankles so she could reach the door. Bo and Jax carefully positioned the ladder between the moat and the small red square and lowered the ladder against the wall. Propping their feet against the ladder feet to keep it from slipping, they grabbed the other ends of the ropes.

Hala started to climb, stopping just short of the wall.

I watched her, not realizing I was holding my breath until I suddenly gasped for air. My nerves were at a breaking point. The timer showed 27. I wasn't sure that would be enough time to execute the plan.

Showing remarkable calm and poise, Hala tied the ropes around her ankles and then carefully slipped through the rungs until she was hanging underneath the ladder.

"Hold on tight, guys," she warned as she arched her back and let go.

Bo and Jax grimaced when the rope swung and ladder slid slightly under her weight.

"Whoa," Mike shouted as they almost lost control of the ladder. The rest of us tried to help Bo and Jax by steadying the ladder the best we could on either side, but Hala swung back and forth wildly, banging into the wall.

"You okay there, Hala?" Jax called. I could see the strain on his face from holding the rope and keeping the ladder in place with his feet. Bo said nothing, but his face was red, and his biceps bulged from the effort.

"I'm okay," she called back. "Just lower me a little bit more."

Slowly, they lowered her until she could reach the door.

"I can reach it," she called out. "Give me the numbers."

Just as I started to give her the digits of pi, Bo sneezed and his grip on the rope slipped. Hala started to fall and instinctively shot out her hand to protect her head, her fingers lightly touching the floor in the red zone.

The voice over the intercom boomed, "Miss Youseff, you have incurred a five-minute penalty."

Everyone automatically looked at the timer. 22.

"Dang it. I'm sorry, Hala," Bo said. I could tell he was really upset with himself, but Jax kept him and us focused.

"Shake it off, Bo," he said. "Keep your heads in the game, everyone. Pull her up and let's start over."

Working together, we pulled Hala back up to the door while I recited the numbers of pi for her. "Three, one, four, one, five, nine, two, six."

As she punched in the number six, the door abruptly swung open to sunlight.

We cheered, but it was half-hearted. The challenge was far from over.

Jax and Bo quickly pulled Hala up, and she removed the ropes from her ankles, adeptly scrambling down the ladder.

"Okay, Bo, we need to get me across first," Hala said. "After that, throw the weights over as soon as I get out of the way."

Nodding, Bo positioned himself at the edge of the red zone in front of the now open door and bent down, interlacing his fingers. "I'm not going to fail you this time, Hala," he said grimly.

She smiled at him. "You didn't fail me, Bo. Don't worry, we're going to finish this."

She backed up to get a running start and raced forward, stepping precisely into his hands. Bo straightened and boosted her over. She flew through the door but landed awkwardly on the other side. She was slow to get up and limped a little.

"Hala, tell me you're okay," Bo called out.

"I'm fine. Send over those weights now. I'm getting out of the way."

Bo waited until she disappeared before heaving a weight across the red zone. Jax threw one, and Bo hurled one more. Thankfully none of them landed in the red zone, incurring any more penalties.

"Perfect," Frankie said, clapping her hands.

"That should do it," Hala cried, coming back into view.

While we raised the ladder again, Hala arranged the weights by the door. On her command, we slid the ladder carefully down the wall. She caught her end and helped guide it onto the weights.

Kira, Mike, Frankie, and Wally helped slide the weights under the ladder on our side, and voilà, we had a ladder bridge right across the red zone with nothing touching. Exactly as Hala had envisioned.

"Who wants to be first?" Jax asked.

"I'll do it," Kira volunteered.

She walked carefully across the ladder, making it easily to the other side. "Come on," she shouted. "It's easy."

One by one everyone followed, except for Bo and me.

"You go next, Bo," I said. "You're heavier and I can hold it steady on this side for you."

Nodding, he crossed and I followed. I was almost across when one of the weights slid a little. Panicked, I jumped the rest of the way, ducking through the door just as the timer above my head flipped to thirteen minutes.

CHAPTER FORTY-NINE

Angel Sinclair

We dashed into an outdoor, walled courtyard with a white wall about ten feet high.

I did a 360-degree turn, examining the layout. In front of the wall were eight giant 3-D wooden puzzle pieces. The pieces were made out of square wooden blocks with some of the pieces two and three blocks long. I got closer to one of the pieces, I saw the puzzle piece was painted red with only one visible white side. Each piece appeared to have two indented white areas with small metal bars that were obviously designed so the blocks could be picked up and moved. I was still figuring out what we needed to do with the puzzle pieces when Mike spoke up.

He was way ahead of me.

"We have to assemble the puzzle and use it to climb over the wall," he said, walking around the pieces. "We can't touch the red sides, but each piece has at least one white side and two handles. It shouldn't be too hard to drag and lift them into the position we want. I assume all the white sides all go on the same side so we can climb on the white side and have a white top to stand on to get over. Come on, everyone help me assemble them."

Everyone started pulling pieces together when Hala collapsed on the ground. "My ankle," she said ruefully. "I injured it when I jumped."

I expected an evaluator to swoop in and get her, but Kira knelt next to Hala, whipping off her shirt. She'd worn an extra tank underneath, which was brilliant since the last time the girls had to give up our shirts, we had only sports bras underneath. "I'll stabilize it," she said. "Don't worry. Hala. We'll get you over that wall. Everyone is going to finish this."

"Don't bother," Hala said. "It's too late for me anyway. I'll never make it over in time."

"Yes, you will," Kira said, carefully removing Hala's shoe and expertly wrapping her shirt around her ankle. "We're all going to finish this."

"We need to figure out where to assemble that puzzle," Bo called out. "There has to be something on the other side of that wall. Kira, you're tall. Come over here. While the rest of the team assembles the puzzle, let's take a look at the other side, so we know what's there and if we need to get the puzzle situated in a particular place."

Kira firmly tied the final knot around Hala's ankle and stood. "She's good to go, and so am I."

Bo held out his hands and crouched down. With surprising ease, Kira took his hands and stepped on his shoulders, bracing herself against the wall. With impressive chin-up, she pulled herself up onto the wall until she could flip a leg over the ledge.

She lay there, looking over the other side. "Guys, there's a giant inflatable slide on the other side, this way." She started crawling along the top of the wall, then stopped. "Line up the puzzle up right here. When you get to the top, you can just slide down. It looks like the finish line is just beyond that. All we have to do is slide down and cross the finish line. Woo-hoo!"

She suddenly disappeared, presumably down the slide. "Kira?" Wally shouted, but was met by silence. He tried again. "Kira!"

"Give it up," I said to Wally. "She's already down the slide and across the finish line by now. Good for her. Come on, let's finish getting this puzzle assembled so the rest of us can get over."

A loud voice boomed over the loudspeaker. "Mr. Drummond and Miss Youseff, your time has expired. However, participants may continue to the finish line if they're able and so desire. Individuals who elect to complete the course may receive some small extra credit over those who don't finish at all. Anyone who wishes to leave the competition at this point needs only to let us know.

For a minute, we paused, staring stricken at each other. We looked at Hala, who lifted her chin. "I want to finish it."

Jax nodded in agreement. "Me, too. Like Kira said, let's *all* finish this."

We madly pulled the puzzle pieces into place. When we were done, Bo lifted Frankie up to the top of the puzzle. She heaved herself onto the top of the wall and, with a cheerful wave, disappeared down the slide. Bo lifted me next to the top of the puzzle. However, instead of going over the wall, I reached down stretched out a hand to help Mike up.

"Red, what are you doing?" Jax demanded.

"It'll go faster with someone up here helping," I said. "Just send everyone up quickly."

Mike grabbed my hand, and I pulled him up the last little bit, shoving him toward the wall. "Go, go, go," I yelled.

297

He disappeared over the wall as Wally came next. I pushed him toward the wall, too.

"No, you go next, Angel," Wally said puffing.

"I'll follow in a second. Just go." He looked indecisive but teetered for a moment atop the wall ledge and then disappeared with an oomph.

"Red, get out of here," Jax shouted at me.

He and Bo were holding Hala between them, carrying her toward the puzzle. My heart, already a wreck with the adrenaline, stumbled in my chest. Bo wouldn't finish on time if he stayed behind to help Hala.

"Bo, you're running out of time," I warned.

"So are you. Go on, Angel. We'll help Hala. It's all right."

I understood now. He didn't intend to finish on time. Apparently, he'd made his peace with that. He was sacrificing his time to ensure they all finished. Unfortunately, I didn't see how that would happen. Getting Hala on top of the puzzle without banging her ankle, and possibly injuring it worse, would be difficult without one more person to help them out.

Me.

A sense of calm descended. It suddenly didn't matter if I finished or not. Sometimes, there were more important things in life than a test.

"Hand her up to me," I said. Hala glanced up in surprise, pain and anxiety etched on her face.

"Are you crazy, Red?" Jax said, his face flushed from exertion. "Get out of here."

"I'm not going anywhere," I said firmly. "Everyone here is taking one for the team. Why should I be the exception? Stop arguing and hand her up to me."

Perhaps realizing he wasn't going to change my mind, Jax finally nodded. Bo helped him get halfway up the puzzle, and Jax clung to the side of a block with one hand, while the other stayed under Hala's injured ankle, protecting it, as Bo lifted her. I grabbed Hala by both hands when she held them up, pulling her onto the top of the puzzle just as a klaxon split the air, indicating the trial had come to an end.

We'd run out of time.

"Candidates, the time limit for this trial has been reached," said the voice from the loudspeaker. "I will repeat that participants may continue to the finish line if they desire. If you complete the course, you'll receive extra credit over those who don't finish at all."

Jax climbed the rest of the way up and joined us atop the puzzle piece. We looked down at Bo. With no one to help him, Bo decided to tackle the wall instead. He jogged backward and then took a running jump at the wall. He leaped high, his fingers curling over the side of the wall. He pulled himself up to the ledge and swung a leg over it.

"What?" he said in alarm when he saw us staring at him.

"Are you kidding me?" I said. "You could have done that at any time. The second we left the gym and you saw the wall, you could have jumped over it and finished the trial. You could have been in first place. Bo, why didn't you go for it?"

He shifted his weight on the ledge. "For the same reason you stayed and helped the others over the wall, Jax stepped on that block to give us the information we needed to solve the puzzle, and Hala hung upside down by her ankles on a rope to open a door for the rest of us. It's what was needed. Now, shall we finish?"

We nodded at him. I'd never been so honored to be a part of the team.

"Good." He adjusted his position on the wall so his knees were on the ledge. "I'll slide down first. Hala, if you're okay with it, Jax will go down with you so he can protect your ankle from any further bumps."

"I'm okay with it," Hala said.

"Perfect. I'll be there waiting at the bottom to catch you guys. See you in minute." He crawled along the ledge until he was above the slide, saluted us, and slid down.

Jax settled himself on the ledge, his feet propped up by the inflatable slide. I helped Hala get situated onto his lap, her injured ankle resting atop his leg.

"We're going to slide down together as carefully as possible," Jax assured her. "Bo will be at the bottom to slow us. We've got this."

"Okay. Thanks, Jax." She looked back over her shoulder at me. "And thank you, Angel, for staying behind to help me. You didn't have to do it, but I'm grateful you did."

"You didn't have to risk yourself for us hanging upside down on the ladder to punch the code in or leap across a gym, but you did," I answered. "Bo is right. This was a group effort."

Jax smiled at me before he pushed off, holding Hala securely in his lap.

After another minute or so, I figured it was safe enough for me to go down. I hopped up on the edge of the wall and slid down the long, inflatable slide. When I got to the bottom, Jax and Bo were there waiting. They each grabbed a hand, pulling me onto my feet before my bottom had even left the slide.

As I straightened, I looked around, my mouth falling open in astonishment. Everyone stood there waiting for me, including Kira.

What the heck was going on?

"Why is everyone here?" I said in disbelief. "Why didn't anyone cross the finish line?"

Kira stepped forward. "We started this trial as a team. We're going to finish as a team. Together."

Smiling, she held out an elbow. Wally linked his with her, Mike with him, and Frankie slid her arm inside Mike's. Bo and Jax lifted Hala between them, her arms stretched across their shoulders to relieve any weight from her ankle. Jax held out his elbow to me.

"You ready, Red?" he asked.

Swallowing the lump of emotion in my throat, I nodded and slid my arm into his. "I'm ready."

Arm in arm, the eight of us crossed the finish line as one.

CHAPTER FIFTY

Angel Sinclair

Saturday morning we were invited to attend a special evening ceremony to learn the results of our UTOP candidacy. The ceremony would take place in the gym at 7:00 p.m. sharp. While I seriously doubted I would be one of the two candidates passing through to UTOP, I was at peace with myself and my actions. The trials had been an amazing experience and had taught me a lot about myself. I didn't regret one minute of it.

"So, who's going into town?" I asked as I pulled a dark-blue sweater over my head. "It's Saturday, after all."

"Me," Frankie said cheerfully.

"Me, too," Kira said.

"Me and my boot," Hala said, lifting her leg. She'd suffered a mild sprain in her ankle after her leap across the gym. Last night she'd been fitted with an ankle boot and would have to wear it for a couple of weeks. At least she could walk on her own without crutches. We were all grateful she was going to be okay.

302

We gave each other a high five and smiled. How things had changed in just four weeks.

Not surprisingly, I was the first to be ready. While the others were getting dressed, I announced I'd wait out front for them. I was the only one there until Mr. Donovan walked up, apparently heading inside.

"Good morning, Mr. Donovan," I said.

"Good morning, Ms. Sinclair. You look in remarkably good spirits this morning."

"I am." The stress and anxiety of the last few days had evaporated, leaving me strangely giddy. I guess there was some relief in knowing that nothing else we did at this point could help or hurt us in terms of our candidacy to UTOP.

"Are you feeling okay after the trials yesterday?"

"I'm good, thank you."

"How is Ms. Youseff feeling?"

"She's fine. The boot is helpful, and I think she's glad she doesn't have to hobble around on crutches."

"I'm glad to hear that." He crossed his arms and regarded me. "Would you mind if I asked you what the hardest part of the trial was for you yesterday?"

"The hardest part...for me?"

He nodded. "Yes, for you."

The entire challenge had been hard, but when I thought about it, one part stood out as particularly difficult. "I guess I'd have to say the hardest part for me was guiding seven blind people in separate tasks to do their individual jobs and then get them to work all together to finish it off, all while being extremely pressured in terms of time. It was crazy complicated. I mean, how unlucky did I have to be to get my name drawn for that task?"

Mr. Donovan smiled. "There's no luck involved when your name is the only one in the hat." He patted me on the shoulder and walked away, leaving me standing there with my mouth open.

What did that even mean? They'd intended for me to be the Eyes all along? Why?

I barely had time to think about it as Kira, Hala, and Frankie joined me, jostling and laughing. I considered telling them what Mr. Donovan had said but didn't see why it would matter at this point.

All the boys showed for the trip into town, as well. Wally looked happy, too. He was laughing and clowning around with the other guys. For once, he was clearly comfortable, looking like he belonged. How would we deal with that loss if we had to return to Excalibur? It hit me hard that I was really going to miss the camaraderie I'd formed with this group.

We climbed onto the bus. Today everyone wanted to stick together instead of going off to do their own thing. It was like we knew the end was coming soon for all but two of us, so we wanted to spend as much time as we could together. I'd planned to call my mom as usual, but opted to postpone since we'd decided to go to the café for hot chocolate and snacks as a group.

We piled into the bookstore, chatting as we got in line to get our snacks. I looked around the bookstore café, but didn't see the elderly gentleman who'd bought me the hot chocolate. His chair was empty. This could be the last time I was in this café, and I hadn't had a chance to say goodbye to him.

Hala sat down while Jax and Frankie pushed a couple of tables together. The rest of us brought the food and drink over and sat down. As we nibbled on éclairs, scones, and other pastries and drank our hot beverages, we began to discuss what we'd tell our families if we were sent home.

"I guess I'd just tell my parents I didn't like it," Mike said. "I mean, what else could I say?"

"You could tell them the food was gross," Frankie said. "My parents would believe that one from me."

We laughed, but the mood was turning somber as reality sank in. Six of us would be going home tomorrow. Wally starting talking about what he would say to his folks when my phone vibrated in my lap. I held it up, expecting it to be my mother wondering why I hadn't called, but I didn't recognize the number. I almost put the phone back in my pocket, but I suddenly got this feeling like I *had* to answer it.

I angled my chair away from the table and accepted the call. "Hello?"

A strange male voice said, "Angel?"

For a moment, I wondered if it were my dad. Maybe he was trying to reach me and would confirm he was still alive. "Who's this?" I asked, my voice shaking.

"Angel?" A burst of static sounded through my phone and the signal dropped to one bar. I stood and moved around to try and get a better spot for reception, but it didn't work.

"Angel, is everything okay?" Frankie stood and came to stand beside me, apparently concerned by the look on my face.

I plastered a smile on my face. "Sure. I'm just going to step outside for a minute and take this."

I brushed past her and left the café, the phone still spitting static. "Hold on," I said to whoever was on the phone.

I got another bar once outside the cafe, and the farther I moved away, the more bars I got. "Are you still there?" I asked.

I didn't have a chance to hear an answer, because a black sedan screeched to a halt in front of me. A man jumped out the back seat of the car and grabbed me, trying to drag me inside.

I dropped my phone and screamed, kicking and scratching. But he was huge and easily hauled me under his arm like a sack of potatoes, pulling me toward the car. I managed to grab the door rim, slowing our progress, and held on for life. He cursed and starting prying at my fingers. Out of the corner of my eye, I saw Kira throw open the café door and hurtle toward us with Mike close behind her. But at this point, we were mostly in the car, and it had started to pull away.

They were going to be too late.

Boom!

The grind and screech of bending metal rent the air as another car plowed into the back of us. The collision threw me halfway out of the car. Screaming, I tried get away, but the guy who'd grabbed me was leaning out of the car, still clutching the back of my sweater.

I looked up just as Kira executed a perfect kick over my head and directly onto the guy's wrist where he held my sweater. He howled in pain, releasing me. I scrambled away, but he got out of the car to come after me.

To my surprise, Mike blocked his way, coming between us. Apparently thinking Mike couldn't stop him, the guy lifted his hand to knock him aside. Instead, Mike adeptly jumped toward the car, using the vehicle as a platform to leap through the air. He twisted his body around while his legs whirled and scissored through the air. One of his feet hit my attacker squarely in the jaw, the force of Mike's body slamming his head backward into the car. While the guy was reeling, Kira spun around, delivering a final, brutal kick to his temple. He grunted once as his eyes rolled back in his head before sliding down the car and onto the sidewalk in a crumpled heap. Jax and Bo jumped him, making sure he stayed down. The driver of the damaged getaway car floored it, leaving his conspirator behind in a squeal of tires.

"I've got the license plate," Frankie shouted into her cell, and I hoped she was talking to the police.

Hala hobbled out in her boot. "What happened? Are you okay, Angel?"

"I'm fine." I looked in disbelief between Kira and Mike. "How did you guys know how to do all that self-defense stuff?"

Mike dusted off his jeans with his hands and straightened. "I'm into parkour." He grinned and pointed both thumbs at himself. "I told my parents it would come in handy someday."

"What's parkour?" I asked.

"Free jumping, flipping, climbing, running, and balancing. Wicked crazy stuff. There are tons of competitions for it around the world and even on television. I do it for fun, but it started as a special kind of training for the French special forces."

"Wow." I glanced at Kira. "You know parkour, too?"

"Oh, no. I'm a third-degree black belt in taekwondo and the female East Coast national champion in sparring for ages sixteen and seventeen," she said. "I'll have to defend my title this spring to stay that way, though."

"And you just happened to forget that when you told me about your special talents?" I said.

"Sorry," she said sheepishly.

"Wow, well, whatever you guys did, it was totally incredible," I said. "Thanks for having my back. I really appreciate it."

Wally and Frankie rushed me, asking if I were okay. Hala handed me my phone, and I saw the corner had been cracked when I dropped it. At least it still worked. I stuck it back in my pocket and glanced over my shoulder as the elderly man from the café exited his car and walked toward me unsteadily on his cane.

OMG! He was the one to ram the other car?

I quickly disengaged myself from the others and walked quickly to intercept him. "Are you okay?" I asked, putting a hand under his elbow. "You just saved my life."

"I'm fine. Have you been harmed?" he asked.

"No, I'm okay, thanks to you. Just a few bumps and bruises."

"I'm glad to hear that. It was lucky I was just driving by and saw what happened."

"I don't know how to thank you. First you buy me hot chocolate and then you save my life. You're a true hero. My hero." Impulsively, I threw my arms around him and gave him a big hug. "Thank you so much."

He hugged me back. "It's been a long time since anyone called me a hero."

I stepped away and looked ruefully at his car. "I'm sorry, though. Your car is ruined."

"Don't be sorry. It was worth it. Besides, it was time for me to stop driving anyway." There was a twinkle in his eye, and I couldn't help but smile despite the circumstances.

Before we could say anything else, several police cars with sirens screaming and an ambulance screeched to a halt in front of the café. In moments, we were swarmed by officers, who relieved Bo and Jax of the bad guy and began taking statements from everyone.

I was telling an officer my story, including how Kira had knocked out the guy after the elderly gentleman from the café had rammed into the getaway car, when a guy in a red baseball cap walked up and angrily interrupted us.

"Hey, that's my car," he said to the policeman. "Someone stole it. I just reported it, but now it's wrecked."

I frowned. "Excuse me, but you must be mistaken. That's not your car. It's his car." I turned around to where my friend had been standing, but he was gone. I scanned the area but didn't see him.

"Who's he?" the policeman asked me.

"The gentleman who saved me...he rammed his car into the sedan."

"Where is he now?"

"He was right there a minute ago." I pointed to the last spot I'd seen him. "I don't know where he went. I don't even know his name."

"That's *my* car," the guy in the ball cap insisted. "The registration is in the glove compartment. Come on, I'll show you."

The policeman went off with him to check, while a medic examined me and another officer finished taking my statement.

"So, you have no idea who would want to kidnap you?" she asked me.

"No. No idea." It wasn't exactly the truth, but how could I explain everything that was going on with my search for my father, especially when the police had never believed there was anything suspicious in regards to his disappearance? Plus, I didn't want to have to explain any of the hacking I'd done to get the information.

Another thought occurred to me. What if this attempted kidnapping attempt didn't have anything to do with my father? Maybe it was just a random snatch or another test to see how we handled ourselves under attack. That wasn't the vibe I got, especially because the police were involved and people had been hurt. I didn't think Mr. Donovan or UTOP would go that far. But how could I know for sure?

"We haven't found the car or the accomplice yet, but

we'll question this guy," the officer told me. "Hopefully, we'll have them all behind bars soon."

"I hope so," I said with feeling.

The officer sighed and put away her tablet. "We may have to question you and your friends again, but we have enough for now," she said. "The medic has cleared you, and we've contacted your boarding school. They'll get in touch with your parents. They've sent a bus for the lot of you, so you're free to go. Just be careful, okay?"

Everyone asked me a million times if I was okay. I was. I just wanted to get back to my room and far away from what had just happened.

When the bus arrived, we piled on. Frankie took a seat next to me, breathlessly recounting every detail of the incident. I hardly heard her. I kept looking out the window, hoping to catch a glimpse of the elderly man who had saved me.

Where had he gone? Was he okay?

I shifted on the seat. "Frankie, you saw the old guy, right? The one who rammed his car into the back of the sedan."

"Yes, of course I saw him. He saved you. Your own personal superhero."

Relief flooded me. I hadn't imagined him, and my mind hadn't played any tricks as a result of the trauma. Thank God. "Did you see happen to see where he went?"

"No. I guess he went home."

I looked out the window again, thinking. Finally Frankie fell silent, as did the rest of the group. We'd just arrived at the KIT compound and were getting off the bus when my phone vibrated in my pocket again.

I pulled it out, noting I had a text from an unknown number. I swiped to read it.

I warned you to be careful and that criminal elements were watching you. Stop looking for me. I'm fine. I want you to be careful. I may not be there every time to help. Good luck at UTOP. I'm proud of you.

I reread the message, my heart pounding. "Dad?" I whispered.

CHAPTER FIFTY-ONE

Isaac Remington

Isaac snatched his burner phone the second it rang. "Is it done?"

"We've got a problem. The engagement failed. Walter was detained."

"What?" He closed his eyes at the incompetence of it. How hard could it be to snatch a sixteen-year-old girl? "How did they bungle this?"

"Judson got rear-ended by some geezer as Walter was getting her into the car. Her friends stormed the car, getting her out and bringing Walter down. Judson got away, ditched the car, and got rid of the plates."

"Tell him to lie low for a while."

"I will. No worries. Walter knows nothing. He's hired muscle and disposable."

"He better be." Isaac hung up the phone and tossed it in the trash.

Damage control was in full effect. At this point, all he could do was play it by ear and hope Sinclair made a mistake. From this point on, the girl and her family would be further protected, making it even harder for him to get at them.

Still, not all was lost. While it was a setback, he'd survive. The core would survive. Then, when he was calling the shots as director, it would be easier to deal with minor annoyances like this. After all, at this point, things had gone about as badly as they could, and he was still firmly in control.

He stood and went to look out the living room window of the mansion where he lived alone. Not really alone, as he was watched 24-7 by the Secret Service. Protected by the government, as were all high-ranking CIA, NSA, and government officials. He could see the agents sitting in the white sedan, parked next to the curb on his street. In many ways, they were just hired muscle, too.

His personal cell phone dinged, and he went to the kitchen to retrieve it. He picked it up and read the text.

You've lost control. You're going down.

Frowning, he checked the number the text had come from. It read 666-666-6666. He clenched his fist around the phone, not amused. He didn't care what he had to do.

There was only one person going down, and it was Ethan Sinclair.

CHAPTER FIFTY-TWO

Angel Sinclair

Unfortunately, after we got back, I wasn't allowed to go hide in my room. None of us were. It hadn't been a test. Someone had tried to kidnap me.

We were exhaustively interviewed by Mr. Donovan and a few agents I'd never met before. When I was certain I couldn't handle another question, Mr. Donovan called an end to the questioning. He wanted to call my mom immediately, but I begged him to wait until tomorrow, after we'd learned the results of the trials. He reluctantly agreed.

I took a shower and changed my clothes, but my head was spinning during dinner and I didn't have much appetite. Guess I was more shaken by the incident than I had thought. The text from my father kept also playing on repeat in my head. He said he was fine and I should stop looking for him.

If he was fine, why didn't he tell me he was my father? Why did someone want to kidnap me? Why was he in disguise at the café, and how mortified should I be that he wore makeup better than I did?

There were no answers, only more questions.

At 7:00 p.m. sharp, we filed into the gym. The mood was somber. Jax caught my eye, looking worried. I tried to shoot him back an encouraging look but was pretty sure I failed. Wally and Frankie flanked me on each side.

White Knights until the end.

All of our teachers and trainers were already in the gym, sitting side by side on a raised platform. They smiled at us, but their mood was reserved, too. Several of them stared curiously at me. I'm sure they were wondering why I'd been the target, or whether it had just been random.

After we were seated, Mr. Donovan stood behind the podium and cleared his throat. "Well, it's certainly been a long, eventful four weeks for everyone. I want you to know that while it has happened a few times before, rarely does an entire class finish without anyone leaving. You all should be extremely proud of yourselves. You performed admirably and deserve our congratulations."

The teachers and trainers clapped for us, and I exchanged a glance with Frankie and Wally. Frankie was smiling, but Wally looked like he was going to throw up. I just hoped that if he blew, he didn't dump it in my lap.

"There are also other things you should be proud of," Mr. Donovan continued. "You should know that no one has ever completed the final trial within the time limit, including adults. In fact, in the six years we've used this course for evaluation, not one team has even *gotten* to the fifth station, let alone gone over the wall. Several of you could have finished within the time provided yesterday, but chose not to, which presents, in itself, an interesting development. What stood out, to me and all of the evaluators, is that you worked together better than most, if not all, of the adult teams. Congratulations."

The teachers clapped, while we looked at each other and smiled.

Pride, satisfaction, and contentment swept through me. The trials had been hard. Harder than anything I'd ever done in my life. Slash had said they'd test me to my limits and beyond, and he hadn't been exaggerating. But I'd risen to the occasion when I needed to, and while I hadn't succeeded at everything, I'd given it my best. I'd made choices that were hard, complex, and emotionally draining. But they were my choices, and no matter what happened, I *was* proud of what I'd accomplished—what we'd *all* accomplished.

Mr. Donovan adjusted the microphone and regarded us. "So, now comes the time to announce who is moving on to UTOP. First I want you to know how we evaluated you. While all of the candidates invited to try out for UTOP are exceptionally gifted in many areas, not everyone is suited to the life of an operative. It requires sharp intellect, creative thinking, courage, excellent observation skills, willingness to work hard, and persistence in the face of danger. That's because an operative must spend hours of extremely difficult and complex preparation before even going on a mission, followed by a short periods of extreme, adrenaline-pumping action during the mission. That, students, is the real life of an operative."

We were silent. The trials had taught us how frustrating and difficult it could be to figure things out and improvise while under a strict timeline. Yet we'd done well, especially now that we knew we were the only group to ever finish the course, even if it were past the time deadline.

Mr. Donovan took a minute to look purposefully at each one of us. Was I imagining it or did his gaze linger a bit longer on me? "Please remember, it doesn't mean that you can't work somewhere else in our intelligence agencies, if you so desire. Trust me, those doors will always be open to you."

Wally kept shifting uncomfortably in his seat, enough that it was distracting me. "Are you okay?" I whispered to him.

"I'm fine," he whispered. "Just nervous."

"It's okay," I whispered back. "White Knights forever, remember?"

He blew out a breath and nodded. "I remember."

Mr. Donovan was still speaking. "Although an operative often works alone, he or she is also an important member of a larger team. So, during your four weeks, we also looked carefully at the dynamics of your interpersonal relationships with each other and your individual personalities. How do you think? How do you process information? How quickly can you think on your feet and execute a task using only the resources you have at hand? How accurately do you grasp the complexity of a situation, and what kind of innovation do you use to get the required results? We're not looking for students who already have all the answers or are experts in any one field…yet. Skills can be cultivated. We're looking for potential. Basically, it came down to three things. Can we train you? Can we trust you? And can you excel in this kind of environment?"

I dared a glance at Bo and Jax, who were seated next to each other. They were staring at Mr. Donovan, completely fixated on his words. I was certain we were all playing back every single thing we'd done and said since we arrived, wondering how it would hold up in terms of the evaluation.

We were about to find out.

I gripped my hands together so hard on my lap, my knuckles turned white. Frankie reached over to hold my hand, and after a moment, Wally took the other one. Linked together, we waited to hear our fate.

"Students, I have one final question before I announce who's going through," Mr. Donovan said. "Who can remind me the primary objective of an operative?"

Jax raised his hand. "Intelligence gathering."

"Exactly, Mr. Drummond." He looked pleased Jax had answered so quickly. "Not high-tech gadgets, fast cars, and gambling in a tuxedo, although there may be times this kind of thing is called for. Intelligence gathering is always key. Now, who can tell me which person at the KIT compound is getting married in a few months?"

For a second we all stared at him in confusion before Frankie shot her hand in the air, waving it around wildly. "Oh, oh. I know."

"Yes, Ms. Chang."

"That would be Charles Mayford. He works in the gym. His fiancée, Renee, is a homicide detective. Isn't that so cool? Kind of like the movies." She pointed to Charles on the stage, who smiled and waved at her.

"That is correct, Ms. Chang," he said. "Now, which of you knows Suzanne Robinson?"

Frankie's hand shot up again. Mr. Donovan looked around at the rest of us, but none of us moved. "Okay, Miss Chang. Who is Ms. Robinson?"

"She works for us in the cafeteria," Frankie offered cheerfully. "She made cupcakes for Angel's birthday. She's really nice."

"Do you happen to know what Ms. Robinson does other than work in the cafeteria?" he asked.

"She's studying forensic anthropology at the University of Maryland. She has a boyfriend she's been dating for two months named Johnny, a dog named Rex, and she also has juvenile diabetes. She's allergic to shellfish and loves Zumba. Is that enough?"

"That's enough. Thank you, Miss Chang."

I stared at Frankie in astonishment, the realization of what was happening finally hitting me. How could I have been so stupid? While the rest of us were focused on passing the trials and making ourselves look good to the evaluators, it'd been Frankie who'd completed the actual mission. She was the one whom everyone trusted, even the other candidates. She was so nonthreatening and kind, everyone talked to her. *Everyone.* She'd gathered intelligence on each person throughout the entire KIT compound. I was certain not one of us had realized it—perhaps not even Frankie herself, who was just being who she was. But she'd been the real operative. She was a natural for the job.

An operative's primary objective is gathering intelligence. How had we lost sight of that?

He let that sink in for a moment before speaking again. "While we graded you on many factors, intelligence gathering was by far the most important one. That grade, combined with scores in several other critical areas, elevated one person to the top of your class. I'd like you to all congratulate your valedictorian, Frances Chang. Congratulations, Frances. You're the first in the class to pass into UTOP."

CHAPTER FIFTY-THREE

Angel Sinclair

Frankie gasped in shock and clapped her hands over her mouth. I leaped from my chair, pulling her to her feet and hugging her excitedly. "OMG! You made it, Frankie. You did it!"

"I did?" She looked completely stunned.

Seconds later, she was mobbed by Wally and everyone in the group. There was so much excitement that the gym filled with noise, even though there were only eight of us. As strange as it seemed, everyone was genuinely happy for Frankie. How couldn't we be? Everyone liked Frankie. She'd be the perfect spy someday. No one would ever suspect her.

After a few minutes, we returned to our seats. Frankie still looked dazed that she'd been selected, while Wally clutched my hand as we waited to hear the final announcement.

"Now, for the next person going through, we'd like to say it was exceptionally close. In fact, the scores were so close, they were almost indistinguishable. It's never happened before in the history of UTOP. It was difficult for the evaluators to determine the next candidate to go through, so…" He paused, looking among us.

For an agonizing moment, all eight of us held our collective breath.

"So…we decided to pass *all* of you," he finished.

Frankie screamed so loudly I was momentarily deaf before she pounced on me, nearly collapsing my chair. I was unable to speak. Wally slipped to the gym floor on his knees, chanting, "Oh, thank God. Oh, thank God."

A moment later it was sheer pandemonium in the gym with everyone shouting, high-fiving, and hugging each other. The instructors and evaluators came over to congratulate us, beaming and laughing. I felt wetness on my face and I wasn't sure if it was from my tears or someone else's. I kept getting hugged so hard I couldn't breathe, and yet I didn't mind in the slightest. It was a blur of sheer happiness and excitement. I knew, one day, I'd look back on my life and count this as one of my finest moments.

As soon as we finished celebrating in the gym, we headed back to the cafeteria together for a special spread of desserts. Laughing, we continued to congratulate each other, each of us humbled and grateful for our success. We were eight people who were as diverse and different as we were alike. Now we were bonded and entering into a new phase of our lives together.

It didn't matter that I had no idea how I'd perform at UTOP or what my future held. I didn't know if I'd ever see my dad again, learn what had happened to him, or discover why he'd left us. I didn't know if my mom would even let me come back when she found out about the attempting kidnapping.

But at least I knew I had the potential to be a good spy, and I'd do everything I could to capitalize on that. I also knew who'd have my back while I was doing it.

In a way, the White Knights had just expanded, and one thing I'd learned was that sometimes, good friends were all you needed to succeed.

*Thank you for taking the time to read **Knight Moves**. If you enjoyed this story, the greatest way to say thank you to an author and encourage them to write more in the series is to tell your friends and consider writing a review at any one of the major retailers. It's greatly appreciated!*

More from Julie Moffett

The White Knights series continues with **One-Knight Stand**. Check Julie's website at www.juliemoffett.com for more information or send her an email via the contact page on her website. If you haven't read Book #1 in the series, **White Knights**, you can find it at all major online retailers!

Julie Moffett   Julie Moffett

Check out the
Lexi Carmichael Mystery Series!
Get Your Geek On!

Julie's Bio

JULIE MOFFETT is the best-selling author of the long-running Lexi Carmichael Mystery Series and the young adult, spy/mystery, spin-off series, White Knights, featuring really cool geek girls. She's been publishing books for 25 years, but writing for a lot longer. She's published in the genres of mystery, young adult, historical romance and paranormal romance.

She's won numerous awards, including the Mystery & Mayhem Award for Best YA/New Adult Mystery, the HOLT Award for Best Novel with Romantic Elements, a HOLT Merit Award for Best Novel by a Virginia Author (twice!), and many others.

Julie is a military brat (Air Force) and has traveled extensively. Her more exciting exploits include attending high school in Okinawa, Japan; backpacking around Europe and Scandinavia for several months; a year-long college graduate study in Warsaw, Poland; and a wonderful trip to Scotland and Ireland where she fell in love with castles, kilts and brogues. She almost joined the CIA, but decided on a career in international journalism instead.

Julie has a B.A. in Political Science and Russian Language from Colorado College, a M.A. in International Affairs from The George Washington University in Washington, D.C. and an M.Ed from Liberty University. She has worked as a proposal writer, journalist, teacher, librarian and researcher. Julie speaks Russian and Polish and has two amazing sons.

Sign up at www.juliemoffett.com for Julie's occasional newsletter (if you haven't done it already) and automatically be entered to win prizes like Kindles, free books, and geeky swag.

Watch Julie's Lexi Carmichael Mystery Series book trailer on YouTube: http://bit.ly/2jFBsiq

Follow Julie on BookBub and be the first to know about her discounted and free books:
https://www.bookbub.com/authors/julie-moffett

FIND JULIE ALL OVER SOCIAL MEDIA!

Facebook: JulieMoffettAuthor

Twitter: @JMoffettAuthor

Instagram: julie_moffett

Julie's Facebook Readers' Group (run by fans):
http://bit.ly/1NNBTuq

Made in the USA
Las Vegas, NV
18 July 2022

51820734R00198